DWELLING

DWELLING

LAURIE FREEDMAN

WINNIPEG

Dwelling

Design and layout by Matt Stevens and M. C. Joudrey

Published by At Bay Press October 2023.

Library and Archives Canada cataloguing in publication is available upon request.

ISBN 978-1-998779-03-1

Printed and bound in Canada.

This book is printed on acid free paper that is 100% recycled ancient forest friendly (100% post-consumer recycled).

First Edition

10 9 8 7 6 5 4 3 2 1

atbaypress.com

For my daughter and her daughter

And for my mother

Blood pools slower than milk.
She follows the growing red stain on the floor.
What a shame. It will be difficult to clean.

1

Pay attention to the roses.

She pulled out dead stems from a vase on the mantel and feigned interest while police in her front hallway discussed the matter in low tones, stepping around the mess. After they closed the van doors and disappeared with Carter down the hedge-lined drive, she read the appointment card they'd given her. A few more questions tomorrow at four o'clock. Strictly routine. She took what she had set aside earlier, walked out of the house and through the town and didn't stop until she boarded the train.

She inched down the narrow aisle between the rows looking for an empty seat, ideally with no side companion to pester her with conversation. The car filled up, but there was a two-seater and both seats were unoccupied. One seat was covered with newspapers and magazines, and the other had a damp-looking spill on the cushion. She shoved the paper over the wet spot and sat down next to the window.

She'd taken nothing with her. Just the clothes she wore and her coat. Grabbed an old wallet and her least favourite purse because it was not stylish anymore and therefore inconspicuous. She felt the lightness of the purse in her lap without the house keys and car fob. A light new life. She'd even picked a new name: Nora Davis.

Luck had graced her so far. There was the nice surprise when she purchased the ticket and discovered the midweek fare was half-price. Handy, because she'd stuffed the old wallet with only one credit card in Carter's name and the small wad of emergency cash from her dresser drawer. She'd have to be careful with the credit card—every purchase would leave a trail of breadcrumbs straight to her. But only if someone were looking.

Nora picked up a magazine from the collection on the seat. *The Economist.* Must have been left by an early morning money manager on the way downtown from the suburbs. She couldn't imagine any reading more boring than world financial news, but she'd leaf through it and keep her head down. She undid her coat in the warm coach and pushed up the sleeves of her turtle-neck sweater. Three spots of blood stained her wrist. Had she cut herself in the rush? She rubbed at the red marks until they were gone. It was *his* blood.

If only the train would go faster. There were a few more stops along the way, and at each of them, she feared they might be on the platform looking for her. She was almost there. The city. Free to disappear in the crowds and wait until it all blew over.

"Ingersoll Station. Tickets, please." The conductor announced the next stop, and she dug in her purse for the ticket to prove she'd paid all the way to Toronto.

"Making good time today," she said, smiling as the man punched a hole in her ticket and handed it back to her. Though she had no idea whether they were or not. She'd taken many trains before, but never this one, never this route. She couldn't look at the dull magazine any longer and put it down to watch the people. More passengers got on at the next stop, private school kids in an unruly group knocked against seatbacks as they came pushing down the aisle. And then, from the other direction, squeezing through the pack of kids, an older woman, wiry and energetic despite the grey hair, and making a beeline straight for Nora.

She knew this kind of person; her town was full of them. An overly familiar, talkative woman who would ask Nora a million questions about her day, where was she off to, and—

Turn away, look out the window, there, wasn't that a beautiful view of the woods and—

"Hello, dear," the woman said. She had already picked up the pile of newspapers and thrust them towards Nora. "Do you mind if I take this seat? There's nothing else left."

Nora put the papers on her lap and her purse on top of the pile. She would stare out the window. It was only another half-hour.

"My goodness," the woman said. "Such rain for November. Who would have thought? I expect more snow this time of year. I'm meeting my niece for a little shopping." The woman wasn't going to stop talking. Big purple earrings bobbed as she spoke. Nora tried to stare sideways and ignore her.

"Your coat doesn't look warm enough, dear." The woman examined Nora's beige trench. It wasn't a winter coat, true enough, but it was rainproof and the one thing she'd grabbed from the front closet. Why was this woman so nosy?

"I like a good double-breasted myself," the woman prattled on. "And did you know—"

Nora thought of escaping into the washroom; there was one between cars, locking herself in and hunkering down in the tiny cubicle until the train got to Toronto. But the thought of trapping herself deliberately in the cramped bathroom was unbearable.

"Oakville." The blare of the loudspeaker.

"That's me," the old lady said. "Oh, and dear, excuse me for saying so, but there's a tiny stain on the hem." The woman pointed a bony finger at Nora's lap, to the edge of the fabric bunched at her knees, to a pinprick of red.

"Bye-bye then." The woman heaved herself up and left. Nora scratched at the insistent red dot. Could something so insignificant betray her?

2

The train rolled on. Trees, farm fields fallow and wet, homogenous subdivisions of squat brick houses on square lots, treeless and brown, a shimmer of lake.

And then they were parallel to the highway, tangled intersections and a dozen lanes of traffic. The conductor walked briskly through the car yelling, "Union Station!" and the train entered a tunnel. The interior went dark for a moment before the lights came on, and Nora stood up. She chose one of the newspapers to carry with her off the train. *The Globe and Mail*, because it appeared the most serious. She rolled it up, put her purse on one arm, and buttoned her coat. She looked like a businesswoman stepping off the train.

* * *

She hadn't been to Toronto since she was last here with her parents as a kid. Once, they'd driven the family car to the summer fairground on the lakeshore, where she screamed on an old wooden rollercoaster. The simple family vacation was all they could afford. There was a photo of that trip showing the three of them eating candy floss in different colours. Pink, yellow, green.

Her parents had said maybe you'll grow up and live here someday. Have a big city job. But she'd never wanted to live anywhere other than her small town. Until now.

* * *

Nora entered the cavernous great hall of Union Station, its four-story arched windows and marble colonnades towering over her. Light spilled through the windows onto shiny tiled floors; the shine gave way to puddles under wet boots as people rolled suitcases, pushed children in strollers. The din of human movement, echoes of voices calling in languages unknown to her.

She ordered a coffee at the bustling kiosk under the arrivals board. The menu in white chalk on the blackboard, the cups in brown unbleached paper. She asked for the first thing listed, espresso.

She drank the coffee. A flash of orange caught her attention. A man wearing a signboard advertising bus tours of the harbour, his sign the colour of a tangerine. She unrolled the newspaper and looked at the pages without interest. A skirmish on the Suez Canal, a global economic summit scheduled for Geneva, and on the back page, a small ad, the type she thought no one placed in a newspaper anymore:

> APARTMENT FOR RENT
> IN CHARMING VINTAGE
> BUILDING. SUITS ONE.
> $500 MONTHLY.

There was no email or phone number, no name listed. Only the address: 9 Farmdale Lane. She tore out the ad and left the newspaper on the counter. It might be the kind of place she needed. For now.

"Excuse me," she said to the coffee vendor. He looked up from the steam spigot he was wiping with a white cloth. Moisture glistened on his thick brows and handlebar moustache. "Sorry to bother you," she said. She showed him the ad. "Do you know where Farmdale Lane is?"

He put down the rag and took the paper in his wet hand. "No idea." He handed it back to her. Nora turned to leave.

"Wait," he said. He poked at his phone. "What was it again?"

She gave him the address, and he turned the screen to her, showing her a map. A grid of criss-crossed streets, dead-ends and train tracks. "Looks far," he said. "West end."

* * *

Outside Union Station, Nora walked between massive stone columns. The sky over the wide boulevard was woven with clouds, the horizon obscured by tall buildings. Which way was west?

She crossed the street amid a swell of tourists disgorged from the station and stood under the blue awnings of The Royal York Hotel. Red and gold flags fluttered in the wind; a liveried doorman saw her waiting and blew a whistle to hail a taxi. A yellow cab slammed to a halt at the curb, and the doorman opened the back door for her. She was only sheltering from the wind for a moment. The taxi would be warm, and she was tempted, but the little money she had couldn't be wasted. She asked the doorman if there was public transit going west.

He pointed out the stop on the corner. The bus came, and she boarded and sat on a bench facing sideways near the front. It began to rain and rivulets of water streaked down the windows as the city crawled by in tones of grey, grey concrete towers in the financial district and grey sky above.

The bus lumbered ahead and made frequent screeching stops. She followed the show of colours out the windows. A shock of red brake lights on wet pavement, the warning haze of flashing amber, green at traffic signals, all of it blurry in the rain, like dissolving chalk drawings on a sidewalk.

With every halting stop and lunge forward of the bus, Nora thought of getting off. Was she really going to live here now?

Skyscrapers gave way to strips of shops and restaurants and then row houses with shabby curtains. Then came blocks of gritty low buildings with broken windows. Gas stations with rusty pumps. The bus lurched along the pot-holed pavement. She looked at the address again on the torn paper; the street number now smudged from the coffee guy's damp hand. The stops grew farther apart as they moved west. She didn't know where she was going, but she felt purposeful. She was looking for a cheap and suitable place to live. No one on the bus cared who she was or what she had done. She watched the driver, intent on his task. The bus lurched and then slowed. The driver's strong arms gripped the horizontal controls, swerving the bus to avoid hitting a woman in a shabby red coat crossing the road in the rain.

3

She was the last remaining rider on the bus. A half hour, an hour. Farmdale was far away from Union Station and downtown. Far away from her life in her house and her town.

The rain let up, and the windshield wipers made a final pass over the front of the bus. A broken black umbrella lay like a dead spider on the sidewalk. Had she thought things through enough?

The bus rounded a curve and came to a dead end in front of a bar where a white neon sign flashed 'draft beer'. The bus braked to a final stop. The driver craned his neck to look at her as if he couldn't believe anyone would bother to come this far. He said he was going to the turnaround loop to head back downtown. He said Farmdale was a few blocks west. She got off.

She stepped over puddles in her suede ankle boots and tried not to splash water on herself. Her long dark hair was pulled back in a ponytail. She hoped it wouldn't go frizzy in the damp air. Her belted trench coat was too flimsy for November, and the thin fabric flapped open in the icy breeze. She used one hand to press it down at the thigh and the other hand to clutch tightly at the shoulder strap of her purse. She walked quickly, as if the wind could undo her.

She crossed paths with a guy in a hooded jacket, shoulders tight and hands stuffed deep in the pockets. He kept his head down, not even a glance her way. None of the casual friendliness she was used to on the sidewalks at home. But isn't that what she wanted, to disappear?

*　*　*

Farmdale Lane was a narrow street of small, crooked houses, dilapidated and jammed together, leaning to prop each other up like structures made of playing cards. Cold air blew through thin alleys between blocks and whipped at Nora's legs. Her skin chapped in the wind.

After the row houses, she passed a vacant lot penned in by construction hoardings, the wood boards tilted and plastered with ads for payday loans. The sidewalk was muddy under her boots. Finally, one building waited at the bottom of the street.

The building stood alone and loomed out of the wet, cold ground. At the sidewalk, a wooden sign was staked to the earth, red paint peeling off and black letters slick from rain: 'Farmdale Court Apartments,' a name too ostentatious for what it was.

The building was cheerless in the gloom, blackened in shadow as the sun set rapidly behind it. A mass of dirty yellow brick, chipped and marred by soot stains under the flat slate roof. Water dripped coldly from bent and broken eavestroughs, puddled under the first-floor windows like a shallow moat.

She shivered in the light coat.

The building hunched nervously around a central courtyard like a person hiding his last possession from thieves. Branches of gnarled oak trees drooped over a stone walkway to the front door. The windows were dark, expressionless, black-framed rectangles where cold air seeped through the glass to rooms inside.

A single light came on in an upper story as she approached the door.

She wasn't sure she should go in.

4

It will be warmer inside. She steeled herself, pulled off the pony-tail holder and fluffed out her hair. The mauve polish on her fingernails matched her glossy lipstick.

At the entrance, there was a directory of tenants. Attached to the wall with rusty nails in a dented metal frame, slips of paper slotted behind plastic shields. Mitchell, Quinto, Mergia. Some were blank, and the names in others were crossed out and scribbled over carelessly.

She pressed the buzzer marked 'landlord'.

"Hello," she said. She stepped close to the intercom. "Hello? I'm here to see the vacant apartment."

There was no answer, just a dull static and then pops of electrical cracking as the door lock released. She opened the glass-panelled front door and entered. The last ray of daylight came through the prism of leaded glass and broke into rainbow colours on the floor. The heavy door closed behind her with a thud. The lock clicked back into place.

She was alone in a small vestibule, her boots dripping onto

hexagonal black and white tiles. Plaster walls were uneven and bumpy with layers of repainting. The top colour of mustard yellow had mostly flaked and peeled away, revealing undercoats of rust-red and silt-green paint, streaked like scars. The damp floor smelled of mildew.

A steam radiator flanked one wall and a row of metal mail-boxes, some with broken locks, lined the other. Before her was a wooden staircase with treads worn down in the middle. There was no elevator.

She would wait a few more minutes and if nobody came to show her the apartment she would leave. She could go back to Union Station and stay in an inexpensive hotel room or even find a hostel if she had to. She could stay somewhere for one night, while she figured out where to go. She felt her own hot breath in the empty vestibule.

The building was silent. She brushed water off her hair. She could go back to the bus stop. Somewhere up above, a door opened and closed, softly, almost imperceptibly. Someone coughed. The echo of footsteps across a floor and then nothing.

"Hello?" she shouted, looking up through the small space etched out between the flights of stairs.

"Hi. Come on up. I have to keep the cat from running out."

A friendly voice, male.

She started to climb up the first flight, hoping the owner of the friendly voice would come down to meet her. She gripped the newel post for balance. It was topped with a wooden sphere, smooth and worn under her hand. At the second landing, two corridors branched off opposite each other. A window framed the final orange slash of the falling sun.

"I wasn't expecting anyone so soon." The voice was stronger now and carried down the stairs.

"Isn't there an elevator?" she said.

"Not in this old building. Come up to the top."

The top turned out to be the eighth story, where two doors faced each other across a small expanse of floor. Wooden doors divided into glass panels with crystal knobs on brass plates.

There was no one waiting for her. She was slightly out of breath from the climb. The door on her right was un-curtained, and she peered through it, unable to see much in the darkness beyond. The other door was protected by a red velvet drape. That door was slightly ajar. She knocked on it, rattling the glass.

A man immediately stepped out. "I like to keep her in," he said, and closed the door behind him.

She moved to make way for him on the narrow landing and stepped back close to the top of the stairs. He reached out and grabbed her arm, pulling her forward.

"You almost fell," he said. He was tall and blond, in his forties, with a handsome face. "I'm Henry," he said. "I look after this place." His voice was quieter now that she was only inches away.

A ginger and white cat appeared behind the door and poked its head under the velvet curtain in Henry's apartment. She was aware of herself as a woman alone with a strange man. But he had a cat. Men who liked cats, in Nora's opinion, were somehow less threatening. Cats were generally shy, so their owners had to be gentle.

"I'm Nora," she said. "I saw the ad for the apartment."

There was a greasy stain on the right leg of his jeans. He rubbed his palm over it. "Which one? I placed a few."

He seemed harmless. And besides, she could summon help easily enough by screaming, if she had to.

"I'm looking for a place to live that's affordable, but nice."

He was in stocking feet, and he smelled of cologne. "I see. Well, do you want to have a look?" A muscle pulsed at his jaw.

From behind the door, the cat whined. "That monster is Toffee," he said. "Belongs to my girlfriend."

His eyes were green.

"I'd like to see it. Yes."

He jangled a key-ring and opened the door across the landing. He let her enter ahead of him.

Inside, the apartment was dark and close, musty from being shut up too long, hazy in the sepia-toned dusk. Henry switched on the light and stood beneath the bare hanging bulb.

"There is only one room, I'm afraid." He stepped toward her. "I mean. There's a kitchen, obviously, but it's more of an alcove. Some tenants don't cook so it doesn't matter."

"I cook." She hadn't eaten since the morning, hours before they'd taken Carter away. She'd been too agitated to think of food while waiting for him to come home and there had been no time for it afterwards.

She was ravenous with hunger.

"I recently painted it all," he said. The walls were cloudy white.

"I like it," she said. "Is there a lease? Or can I go by the month? You see, I'm not sure—"

"There's a bathroom too, of course." He opened a door opposite the kitchen. She stuck her head through the opening, reluctant to enter the room, as if standing in the small bathroom with him was too intimate. There was an old-fashioned pedestal sink, a mirrored medicine cabinet above it, a toilet, and a small porcelain tub. The same hexagonal tiles as the main floor vestibule.

"They didn't have showers back then," he said. "But I could rig one up easily."

"Back when?"

"1918, when it was built. Charming, isn't it?"

He seemed oddly enamoured of the building's peculiarities.

"Does your girlfriend live here too?"

"Not anymore." A lock of hair fell across his forehead, and he brushed it back into place. There were darker roots under the blond. "Come see the best feature."

They crossed over the hardwood floor into the kitchen, his feet padding softly.

"It's been updated over the years." He stood aside to let her view it: a scene like a home-economics illustration from the nineteen-forties. A short, curved refrigerator, a stained white sink and an ancient stove with two gas rings on the cooktop. A tiny blue pilot light flickered under a burner. On the ridge of the stove back, a box of wooden matches and a clock. It was almost six.

"Look here," he said. "I want to show you this." As he spoke the cat rushed into the kitchen and jumped to the one small counter. He picked it up, tenderly scratched the animal's head. "How did you get out, you fiend?"

She said, "I don't have any pets."

He unlatched the window by the sink. It was sticky from the recent painting, and he yanked and pushed roughly until it opened. It was more a small door than a window and led to a fire escape about five feet across, connected to the unit next door.

"Voilà." He put a hand on her shoulder, prodding her forward. Cold air rushed at her from outside as a squirrel scrambled away. Over the railing, it scurried across black ironwork and open slats.

"You can use it like a balcony," he said from behind her. "Put out some folding chairs for hot summer nights, arrange flower boxes." He stood close to her. She felt the heat from his body on the back of her head. "Remember to prop the door open though," he said, "or it will close and lock you out." He gave her instructions to use a wedge in the opening if she went out there. The fire escape doors were designed to thwart thieves and burglars—he explained with some pride—and couldn't be opened from outside.

She tried to picture it. A clay pot of dead geraniums huddled against the cold wall. The fire escape looked dangerous: you could put a foot through the spaces between slats. And inhospitable, nothing but an iron ledge perched without cover on the side of the building, not an inviting spot to while away an evening in July.

She thought he was over-selling the vague appeal of the apartment. He likely made similar enticements to prior renters, and maybe he was persuasive with others. She wondered if past residents had felt at home in the place.

She looked at the fire escape where reflected light from the apartment stabbed at drops of water on the metal. Whoever had lived here before had abandoned the pot of geraniums, the stalks now black and frozen with neglect. Perhaps they had once made someone happy.

5

Knob and tube wiring. The pen darted up and down as the building inspector filled in the form.

"The most dangerous kind," the inspector said. "A fire hazard and contrary to the Building Code."

As if Henry was ignorant of the fact. "Hasn't been a problem," he said. He could read upside down and saw what the man marked off on the checklist. Hazardous. Insufficient insulation. His name there as authorized contact: Henry Weston. Dots of dandruff on the inspector's shoulders.

"Why now?" Henry said, meaning the inspection. The timing was bad for him.

He wanted to think about the woman. He'd initially regretted his decision to lease the apartment and hoped she would not come back. She was all wrong for the place. Her coat for starters, too expensive. The brown plaid lining showed when she walked, her thighs peeking through the slit. She'd not taken it off while viewing the unit, so he didn't get a complete look at her body. Enough to see she was slim, fit.

"I show up where they send me," the man said. He was looking under a sink now. "Sometimes we get a tip."

Henry had made recent repairs in this unit on the sixth floor, replaced a splintered floorboard, unclogged a drain. He'd left a bucket of black sludge sitting by the bathtub. If he'd noticed the bucket, the inspector hadn't commented on it.

"It's that builder across the street," Henry said. "Thinks he can lower the property value and buy me out." He eyed the bucket, wondered if he could pour it out quickly. "Did he call you?"

"You got some lead pipes," the inspector said. "That and the electric will have to be upgraded pronto." He scratched his head, releasing a shower of flaky skin.

* * *

After the inspection, Henry went back to tighten the trap under the chipped sink. He was a little surprised someone like Nora had answered the ad. She wasn't like the last one, a girl who was blind in one eye and worked mopping floors in a nursing home. Nora could probably afford to rent a coach house in leafy Rosedale or a Victorian semi near the university in the Annex. He thought she might leave after a month and stick him for the rent. And he'd have to search again.

He twisted the wrench until his wrist hurt. There was a vein of rust under the sink. He seethed over the building inspector's remarks. This was a forgotten neighbourhood of rooming houses, broken windows, and cracked pavement. He was shocked, in fact, that the city expected him to make improvements. Maybe he'd attracted attention and brought his own bad luck by putting the ad in the *Globe*, of all papers. The most pretentious one.

His lower back ached from stooping at the sink.

But the woman, Nora, was quite pretty. Clear, pampered

skin and shiny hair. And an intriguing challenge to have her right next door.

He had to empty the pail of thick gunk he'd taken from the drain. The city wanted him to comply with regulations? Maybe he would. Maybe he'd make them wait while he appealed their work orders. It would serve them right if he poured this bucket down the sewer grate in the street and gummed up the municipal system. He'd need to go upstairs to his own place to get his boots first before hauling the bucket downstairs and outside. The pail was heavy, and the liquid stank. He peered out the small bathroom window to the back alley. The old windows had no screens. He raised the sash and brought the bucket to the window, resting it on the window sill for a moment to ensure no one walked in the lane. He tipped the pail and dumped out the greasy water, let it splash against the bricks and spill onto the pavement.

* * *

In his apartment on the eighth floor, he changed out of the dirty cotton work pants and flannel shirt into soft faded jeans and a T-shirt. It was hot in his sitting room. The steam radiator behind the blue sofa generated too much heat, it gurgled like a strangled thing. He could swap the jeans for gym shorts to cool down, but what if she came back and knocked on his door for the key. He would look stupid wearing shorts in winter.

He smoothed down his hair with a drop of water. Still looked pretty damn good in the mirror. Handsome, and fit, still youthful. He deserved so much more than life had dealt him.

There was cold coffee in the pot from this morning, bitter and thick from sitting out, but he was running low on beans and should save them. Preservation was key. He'd make the woman a fresh cup when she arrived.

He picked up the metal carafe from the stovetop, the glass

lid dotted with condensation. The percolator was scavenged from another apartment. A benefit of access. He liked the old-fashioned way of making coffee, the burbling hot water, the pungent aroma. Reminded him of the cafeteria ladies at school who were always nice to him.

He warmed the dregs of the pot in the microwave and put cream in it, winced when the cream curdled on the surface. He fished the dodgy bits out with a spoon and drank it anyway, standing with the mug in front of the window. Wind rushed in the trees, tearing away the last autumn leaves. He was lucky to have so many windows. That's what he was told when they first hired him.

Lucky we're giving you this chance. Because you're family. Don't screw up again.

Initially, he felt shunted aside like a nuisance. Then he realized the advantages. A huge rent-free apartment. A small income in exchange for menial tasks. He sipped the coffee and paced. His was the only unit with windows looking to both the front courtyard and the back lane. A command post.

He'd done a fine job. They'd kept him on, and they'd been pleased with themselves for satisfying any familial obligation to him. He put the palm of his hand on the cold window glass. He'd had the last laugh, hadn't he? The uncles were all dead and gone now. The building was his.

6

The front walk was slick like a frozen pond from the rain and the night's plummeting temperatures. If Henry didn't want her to slip and injure herself, he had better throw enough salt down before she returned. He worked quickly, tossing handfuls of the clumped rock salt along the path and over the front stoop. Then he went in and bounded up two flights, two steps at a time. At the third floor, he slowed down, conserving energy.

He was relieved to fill the vacancy, but it would be an adjustment. The quiet he'd enjoyed on the eighth floor was about to end. The walls were paper-thin, you heard everything, and the previous tenant had been needy and demanding. A crier late at night, constantly on the phone wailing about her life. And not that interesting to listen to.

He swirled the coffee remaining at the bottom of the mug, thick and cold now, and drank it. He took his favourite spot on the brown couch, to work on his collection while he had time. She was moving in later today. He should go air out her unit, open the windows, sweep the floors. In a minute. He willed himself not to jump up from the couch. To stay focused.

He'd meant to catalogue new items, organize the collection. The building inspection had distracted him, and if experience was any indication, Nora would consume much of his time. He should take the opportunity now, while he had it. Scrapbooks and papers lay cluttered on the sofa.

He picked up the diary, the small clothbound book he considered the hallmark of the collection. He had found it wedged behind a broken radiator in an empty apartment. When he removed the rusted metal from the wall the book fell to the floor. Whether accidentally lost or deliberately hidden, the diary had been secreted away for decades. The pages were brittle and faded, and the stories they told were unknown.

> *Alice had no skates, so we borrowed from the boy downstairs. His mother was baking a pie, reminding me married women get better rations. When she inquired after my husband, I lied and said he was overseas with the war, and this satisfied her. The skates were too large for Alice, so I held tightly to her hand as she giggled and wobbled, delighted. Such a happy child! It was the first day Grenadier Pond was completely frozen over, and the ice was thin near the willow trees.*

Her name was written in curlicued longhand inside the diary's cover: Doris Carr. The date of the skating entry was December 20, 1917.

Henry heard a car honk, and he got up to investigate out the window. It wasn't her. A photograph fell from the diary.

The street was empty. No one buzzing for entry at the front door.

He used the photo as a bookmark, though it didn't belong in the diary, and had no connection to Doris Carr, as far as he knew. Workers outside a local garment factory in 1920, according to the date scratched on the border. Men, eyes humbly downcast, shoulders slumped wearily. The poor bastards looked positively miserable. People didn't smile for the camera back then.

Nora smiled while he showed her the apartment, in the manner of women who were eager to please. A tendency to be agreeable, as if offending him might be dangerous. Straight white teeth, meaning money spent on her appearance. Not at all what he had expected. And yet, hadn't he earned this? He'd struggled. After all his trouble and sacrifice, he deserved an exceptional tenant.

7

Self-inflicted wounds. The police officer had said so, standing there gazing down at Carter's body where it lay on the cool
terrazzo floor in Nora's hallway. A bullet to the head. And yes, she
wasn't going to disagree. Were there problems, the officers asked,
walking her through the immaculate living room, French doors
giving out to the garden. They'd touched the marble countertop on the kitchen island. Debt? Nora had nodded. Or an affair?
She'd turned her head, as if she herself was unsure.

Carter's body was strapped to the gurney and loaded into
the van. Black notebooks were tucked away in pockets. The one
officer half-smiled at her sympathetically. A widow now. Gave her
a card from the police service. Coroner will be in touch, he said,
after the examination, with an official cause of death. But Nora
knew what killed him.

Grief. Though not his own.

* * *

The apartment was small, she wouldn't need much furniture. A
simple bed and chair would do for now. But buying things for her

new life wasn't easy. Carter had drained the accounts, left her with nothing, and she was learning that credit was hard to come by.

At the bank this morning the teller was a young guy, fresh haircut like he was right out of school on his first job, a patch of pimples near his nose. "Welcome to Scotiabank," he said.

She'd only had the free coffee for breakfast at the hostel and her stomach rumbled. "Hi." She smiled at the guy and slid her application form across the counter. "I guess everyone wants additional credit this close to Christmas."

He seemed to take a long time to read it over. What was the problem? Her handwriting was totally legible.

"We can approve this right away," he said, "for the minimum level. If you want more it takes a few days for head office to—"

"Minimum's great." She thought of the bed she'd seen on a design store's website. Dark wood with a sleek headboard. A credit card in her new name was all she required to make the payment. And top it with a lovely down duvet.

"Just need some ID," the teller said. "Driver's licence, birth certificate or passport."

She stood there dumb and humiliated, feeling the red, oily face sneer at her, this punk who thought he was all that working as a teller. He pushed her application forward under the glass triumphantly, like he'd caught her trying to put something over on him. In her town, she and Carter had been prominent members of the community. There were funds available, lines of credit, no questions asked. My husband is a lawyer, she almost blurted.

* * *

She waited by the massive doors inside the second bank after she was refused there too, angry at herself for being so naïve. The landlord at Farmdale Court had been kind enough to waive the rent deposit, but she couldn't sleep on the floor. She shivered each time the doors of the bank swung open. She felt the eyes of the security guard bore into her back.

She checked her wallet as if hoping to find forgotten money. She took out the photo. Creased and bent to fit in the wallet, the beautiful face cut in half along the fold and faded from so much loving touch. There was Dylan in the highchair on her first birthday, balloons tied to the tray, her pudgy hands and cheeks smeared with chocolate cake.

She left the bank and crossed the busy main street to a public square where flashing billboards and neon signs reflected on the wet pavement. She walked by a hotdog cart and was hit by a waft of smoke. With a two-dollar coin she bought a bratwurst on a bun, and it was handed to her by a stout woman in a babushka. She covered it with ketchup and pickles and stood at the edge of the square to eat it.

Snow fell lightly. Students from the nearby polytechnic hung out between classes, laughing, jamming to music on headphones. Ragged men huddled under the electronic billboards, drinking and begging the students for handouts. A battered brown truck, a mud-spattered Ford pick-up, pulled up to the curb. The back cargo bed was overloaded with furniture, half covered by a dirty tarpaulin. The driver lowered a window and blew smoke from a face on which jowls sagged like poorly folded laundry. He dropped the cigarette butt to the gutter where a coatless man darted from a doorway and stooped to pick it up. The man sucked hard until it glowed again. The truck driver said, "Hey, you're welcome buddy."

She was cold in the thin coat as she watched the driver unload his cargo. He carried a chair inside a storefront and came back to the truck and hoisted out a bed. A yellow bed.

She followed him into the store. A narrow shop crammed full of junk. The man leaned the bed against a wall. A metal frame like an old-time hospital bed, austere and unadorned except for curved end pieces at the head and foot, supported by dented rods. The original metal—brass or iron—had been painted the colour of sunflowers and buttercups in a vain attempt to hide the scars and imperfections. The bed was small, barely wide enough for a single sleeper.

"Are you selling this?" she said. She put a hand on the yellow metal.

"Ready for bed?" he said.

Disgusting ugly man. "Kind of banged up," she said.

Another man, the junk dealer, leaned towards her. He hunched forward with scabrous elbows on the counter.

Guitars hung on the wall above the counter, and hockey sticks were crammed in the corner. The dealer bent over a cache of watches and bracelets. She wanted the yellow bed. It was compact and could double as a sofa. She'd never bought anything in a place like this before, but the bed compelled her.

"We buy and sell," the dealer said. A jeweller's loupe jutted from his forehead.

The bed was more expensive than she had thought.

"Could you lower the price?"

The driver hovered too close.

She pulled a few twenties out of her wallet. "Honestly, this is all I've got."

The dealer said she could pawn something. Explained what it meant, because she seemed dumb. But she knew, had heard of pawn shops from books and movies. "What about those earrings," he said.

Her hands went to her earlobes, felt the gold studs. If only she'd kept her wedding ring; it was worth a lot. The ring was in the back garden where she'd dug a hole and buried the diamond band. Where she'd never have to see it again. What a victory it would have been to trade it away in a pawn shop.

The gold earrings were a gift she'd given herself. Something to mark what would have been Dylan's second birthday.

The simple yellow bed was a sign, a promise of something she craved. She had to have it. And if she pawned the studs she could always buy them back later when she was settled.

*   *   *

For a few dollars more the driver took her and the bed across town to Farmdale Lane. He smelled like fried hamburger, and she stuck close to the end of the bench seat in the truck; no way was he getting close enough to put a hand on her thigh. He eyed her at every red light, and she edged closer to the passenger door, gripping the handle in case she had to jump out. Finally, they turned a corner to the oak trees and courtyard and the apartment building.

"You live in this dump?" the driver said. "Classy lady like you?" He heaved out the yellow bed, huffing and coughing. Left it in a sad heap on the sidewalk, like garbage.

He didn't offer to haul it inside for her, and she stood perplexed as the truck drove away. How to get it up eight flights of stairs? She looked at the bed and up at the dark empty windows lining the façade of the building. It was only a moment until Henry emerged from the front entrance, donning work gloves and grinning, as if he'd been waiting all along to help her.

8

She had a place to live, a home. She needed to get things for it. Nora took a bus to Walmart where she could afford to shop. The store was clean and nicer than any junk shop, with endless aisles of mesmerizing bright plastic. She'd been to Walmart in her town a few times. Even though her house had the finest of everything, acquired from exclusive sources, there was nothing wrong with a few cheap staples. This was a different life now, and she didn't have a big fancy house. Maybe in her new city life, Walmart would be the only choice.

Into the oversized shopping cart, she tossed a green and white striped towel and blue dotted oven mitts. Carter's credit card worked when she tapped it to pay. It hadn't been cancelled. She bought polyester sheets for the yellow bed. They'd be rough on her skin compared to the 500-thread count Egyptian cotton in the house. But at least she'd have the bed to herself, scratchy sheets or not.

Next errand: clothes for work. The plaza had a Value Village at the other end. If someone told her a week ago that she'd shop here, she would have scoffed. But so what? Did the new Nora need designer outfits?

She thumbed through second-hand blazers puffy with shoulder pads and pleated trousers; all of it was years out of style and reeked of mothballs. She couldn't bring herself to try anything on. Other shoppers pinched the cloth and yanked shirts off the rack. They tried on stretchy yoga pants other women no longer wanted and baggy tops previous owners had worn to hide fat bellies. There was a section of maternity wear, the fabric saggy and empty.

She still had on the black wool skirt and cashmere turtleneck sweater from the train, and her Burberry coat and suede ankle boots. She wasn't ready for cast-offs from the eighties. Stupid not to have taken more clothes when she left the house. But no matter. What she had was beautiful. She could simply keep wearing the same things. Her clothing would make an excellent impression at any job interview. She left the store.

* * *

In the apartment she hung her coat in the small shallow closet on a wire hanger she found there, her boots tucked in the back. A layer of dust covered the floor of the closet. Damn it, at Walmart she'd walked right by the brooms and hadn't thought to buy one. Dust blew from the arms of twisted hangers when she moved them on the short rod.

Henry said the building dated to 1918. People must not have owned much clothing back then if all they had for storage was one measly little closet.

She needed curtains for the window. Not like anyone could see her this high up, but naked windows felt so ... exposed. The apartment door was another thing. The glass panels on the front door gave her no privacy at all from the shared landing, leaving her visible to anyone who tried to—

How long had he been standing there watching her? Looking at her putting things away from her shopping, hanging up her coat. Staring at her from the landing. And she hadn't noticed, deep in her thoughts, busy. She hadn't heard a thing.

She saw him through the glass, lingering at the door, not peering in directly, not exactly, but looking. The tall male-form, half in the shadow. He smiled when she came to the door as if he were certain that she welcomed the intrusion. What did he want?

"Hello there," he said. "How are you getting along?"

He wore black jeans and a white T-shirt silk-screened with mountains and fir trees. His arms were muscular in the short sleeves. She should be nice to him since he'd helped her get the bed up the stairs.

"Oven working okay?" He stepped forward, his hip touching her body as he came through. She hadn't asked him in. She stayed at the door, one hand on the door frame and the other on the handle to keep it open. He looked around. "Nice. I knew the bed would fit under the window." He wore thick hiking socks, no shoes.

"It's a beginning," she said. "I need curtains and things, a rug." The room felt shabby with the dented iron bed and bare floors. "To warm it up."

"I wondered if you'd like to have a drink. A welcome to the building." He walked to the kitchen and his body took up all the space.

He wasn't awful. A bit odd, but attractive in his way. Yet she didn't want his attentions right now. She wanted to organize her space. She hadn't even bought groceries.

"Another time?"

"It's only next door," he said. "I've got everything." He

seemed harmless. A drink might be nice, and better a friendly landlord than the opposite.

"But you know what?" he said. "First come with me."

She was tired after the deflating shopping trip. It was easier simply to go along with him. And she was a little curious about what he wanted from her.

"Trust me," he said. "I think you'll like what you see."

She followed him down the stairs. He was quick, a little excited, and he hopped in his stocking feet as they moved. They passed a landing on every floor with a long hallway branching off. Each hall had many doors. She peered down the corridors and he told her their floor was the best one. Quiet because it was the only one with just two units, weren't they lucky?

She let him take her to the first floor and down to the end of the hall along a worn carpet, her curiosity compelling her to follow, even though she had other things to do.

"You'll like this," he said. He used a ring full of keys to unlock a door.

9

"I don't do this for all the tenants," Henry said.

She followed him through the door and into the room. It was too small to be an apartment, too large to be a storage closet. The room was stuffed with items, with no space to walk around between the things leaning against themselves. She breathed molecules of grime. Dressers, tables, chairs, and bicycles were piled against the walls and stacked on top of other things. The only window was obscured by a tufted mattress turned on its side.

"Think of it as a furniture showroom," he said.

Nora recalled the junk dealer and the array of sad items. This collection was sorrier still. Not possessions. *Dispossessions.*

Yet Henry seemed proud of the wretched mass. She didn't know what to say that wouldn't offend him. "Did you—was it you who collected this?"

"When people move out," he said. "They leave a lot behind." He ran his hand over the arm of a chair, making fingermark traces in the dust. "You'd be surprised."

She picked up a framed certificate. It was issued from the

University of Toronto, Faculty of Medicine, 1942. Someone must once have been so proud of this diploma, the years of dedicated study it represented, had probably displayed it on a wall above a massive oak desk in a doctor's consulting room. And here it was discarded with broken-down furniture. A crack in the frame.

"Makes you wonder," he said. "What people value."

People couldn't always take things with them, disappeared from their homes and all they contained. She imagined her house without her or Carter or Dylan inside it. Echoes in the hall. A clock ticking on a mantel. Perhaps estate agents had already combed over her things. Or worse, the police. Pawing through her drawers, pulling books from the shelves, searching Dylan's toys for answers. And would the explanations reveal themselves in the cupboards filled with dinnerware and champagne flutes?

"Take whatever you like," he said. He lifted the edge of a table, pushed it aside. He raised a kitchen stool over his shoulders to show her more at the back of the room.

"The old manager used to chuck it out at the curb." He put the stool down. "Not me. I save the good stuff."

He smelled sweaty, no cologne today.

"I appreciate it. You've been so nice." There was a chair behind him. It was teak, solid and polished, finely turned wood. She'd seen similar chairs before. This one was surely authentic, expensive. "It's a lot to set up a new place."

She chose a simple pine coffee table—it was garbage from Ikea—so it wouldn't be obvious. She didn't want to look too desperate, or greedy. She'd like him to believe the armchair was just an afterthought.

"Do you think it's vinyl?" She touched the seat. Definitely high-grade leather. She knew it was mid-century Scandinavian. Was Henry aware of the value of this chair? He seemed like a blue-collar guy who probably knew nothing about furniture design.

10

October 16, 1918

I left Alice alone in the apartment on Farmdale while I went to teach at Jesse Ketchum School. She is only three, but she is a serious minded child and she knows to stay quietly and wait until I return. To my surprise the school has been ordered closed until further notice, along with theatres and other public places. The influenza outbreak is affecting the entire city and I won't have to go to work. The second graders departed cheerfully, schoolbags stuffed with the subtraction and reading I gave them to do at home.

When Principal Mathers told me I won't have my salary during the closure I was struck with worry about feeding Alice. He isn't aware I have a child. He knows I am not married and so assumes I am therefore not a mother. It would be a scandal if I told him

the truth, and worse if I lied and said I was married.
I would only be cutting off my own foot. Teaching
positions cannot be held by married women.

For Henry, the trip downstairs with Nora was a preliminary test. After he'd been so generous with the furniture, he expected she'd say yes to a drink. Women like her were usually accommodating. Raised to have good manners, return favours. His own family had been full of that type. Very concerned with appearances and social connections. Interested in money and people who had it. Superficial and easy to manipulate because of the desire to fit in. Everything he thought about her was confirmed when she lunged for the Danish chair.

He carried the table up to the eighth floor for her and then went back for the chair. He watched her fuss, moving the pieces, positioning them different ways in her room. Then he suggested a glass of wine and told her to come over in twenty minutes; he needed to straighten up a bit. He left her no choice but to agree to a thank-you drink.

In the building, his apartment was one of the biggest. Hard to believe that former supers, janitors, whatever you wanted to call them—he preferred landlord—lived in the first-floor unit he now used for storage. Single guys without family, easy to shove them into that cramped room. The uncles had tried to put him down there when he came back. He'd said he didn't want the job unless they gave him a better apartment. After what he'd gone through, he needed more. To his own amazement, they agreed.

He could use a shower after carrying the furniture and working all day, but there wasn't time. He had just enough time to set things up before she came over. Nora was dragging something heavy in her place, scraping the floorboards. He heard it clearly through the wall. She better not ruin the wood. Arranging the furniture, no doubt. He brushed toast crumbs from the brown sofa into his hand and some fell on the rug.

He heard the water go on in her place. The old pipes banged together, especially when the hot water started. He wondered if the drain was still clogged in her tub. Should have checked that before renting it again. There were imperfections in that small apartment. His own was fixed up well. He'd done the carpentry and plumbing repairs, used the skills he'd learned when he was away.

The uncles neglected the building when it was theirs. Just another entry in their real estate ledger, hanging on until they sold to developers for a pile of cash. Giving him the job so they could feel good. *Philanthropists* was the word used so often when the family was in the news.

He hoped Nora might enjoy a glass of wine here, with him. It was comfortable, although he might have crammed too much furniture in the sitting room. Two sofas faced each other across a glass coffee table. They didn't coordinate, the blue velvet and the brown twill too dark together, like a stormy landscape. He wanted her to like his choices.

He poured salted nuts into a ceramic bowl and put it on the glass table. He placed red paper napkins beside the nuts. He thought with glee about the last of the uncles dying before selling the building. Now he was in control.

He heard her door close. He looked over the room quickly once more and noticed that the white wicker garden chairs didn't belong in the room. They were incongruous and were piled high with books and papers, impossible to sit in.

She knocked on his door. Well, if she expected silk upholstery and Persian rugs she was out of luck.

At the sound of the knock the cat ran out of the room towards the bedrooms. He scooped the papers and the scrapbooks from the chairs and put the pile on the floor, the diary on top. He opened the door.

"Hi." She had glossed her lips in red. They looked sticky. And the hair, touching her shoulders, loose around her face, was shiny. She'd fixed herself up. For him.

She came over to the long oak table, and he opened the wine. He could put a hand on her face, she was that close to him. The urge to touch her was almost irresistible. Almost.

"You have so many rooms. Even a dining room," she said.

"Glad you like it." The corkscrew was finicky. "Come over anytime." He sounded too eager, yet she wasn't put off. She probably liked the attention.

"Lots of space for entertaining," she said.

He saw how inharmonious the room looked: card table chairs pushed in around the family-sized dining table. There was too much furniture. And he'd set out a platter on which there was far too much cheese.

"Are you having a party?" she said.

He could put a hand on her neck.

"I really like your place," she said.

He poured out two glasses of red wine. She was merely being polite, not criticizing him. "To your arrival at Farmdale Court," he said, raising his glass to hers. "Come sit."

She chose the blue sofa, and he brought the cheese tray with him and placed it on the coffee table. He sat on the other end of the sofa, with newspapers between them.

"You'll like it here," he said.

"Toronto?"

"The building." He offered her a cracker and took one

44

himself, then another. "I'm somewhat of a building historian," he said. "This apartment house is unique."

She held a cracker between two fingers, took a tiny bite and looked at him with interest. "Do you mean the architecture? I noticed the glass doorknobs and the brass kickplates." She stared at him, and he smiled.

Her interest excited him. He reached for the diary on top of the pile of papers. He held it towards her, almost pressing it into her hand.

"This is everything," he said. She raised her eyes quizzically. "What it was like to live here a long time ago." She reached for the diary, but he pulled it back to save it from her fingers, greasy from the cracker. "You can read it later."

"I'd like that," she said.

"You're not from the city?" he asked. He sensed that her interest was a kind of flirtation. A signal that she was attracted to him. He changed the topic to see where he could lead her, and he had a sense of himself speaking a role in an old movie, a man entertaining a woman in some overwrought black and white film. He was self-conscious, now that she was here in his place, after he'd obsessed about it since meeting her.

She shook her head and delicately sipped the wine. He wanted her to like him.

"I hope red is okay," he said. "I know women prefer white."

Did she raise her eyebrows? Like he was a moron.

"Where did you live before?" He really wanted to know. "I bet you've travelled," he said.

But she seemed bored by the question, looking across the room at his art. The tacky oil scene of barns and fields and the poster for Black Cat Cigarettes. He'd rescued both from the trash.

"I meant those ironically," he said. "I know it's kitsch."

Trying to convey that he wasn't just some janitor, that he came from money. Again, the eyebrows arched in mockery.

She took a long drink. "Where are you from?"

He topped up her glass. No longer delicately sipping, gulping it down. She put it away like a sailor. No problem. He'd get her drunk. Maybe wouldn't need to slip anything else into her drink.

"Lots of places, really." He bent to pick up Toffee and put the cat on his lap. The animal immediately jumped off and ran out of the room. "So skittish," he said.

They drank the wine. He was careful not to have too much. She finished her glass and rested her head against the high back of the sofa, her eyes half-closed.

"Have some of this." He put a piece of blue cheese on his fingers and brought it to her lips. She let him put it in her mouth, he had to part her lips to do it, and then he licked the remains from his thumb.

He waited.

He emptied his own glass. Noticed a few red drops had rolled down the stem of hers to the surface of the table.

He tilted the cup so she could drink. The sip dribbled from the corner of her mouth. He put the cup down.

"Tell me about yourself," he said. She seemed to have drifted off. He asked twice to make certain. Her eyes were closed, head rolled towards him. Then he shoved aside the papers between them and brushed a strand of hair off her face.

46

11

Nora looked again at the job listing, unfolded it and smoothed the paper, smearing her fingertips with black ink. She'd torn the post from one of the free community newspapers thrown down at the subway entrance. Most of the listings in the paper were for data entry, call centres or food delivery, not jobs that interested her. Trouble was, she didn't know exactly what did interest her. She'd always been a wife and stay at home mother, with no desire or need to work.

One listing looked like a possibility, something she could do. Barista. Fancy name for a counter person in a coffee shop. She was certainly capable of pouring hot drinks. She folded the bit of paper into a square and tucked it away in her purse. No experience necessary, it said. She would make the long trek downtown to apply today.

She got up early to take a bath in the cracked old tub. She leaned her head against the sloped end and soaked in very hot water. She was tired, her throat raw and sore. She closed her eyes in the bath. Rest was fitful in the discomfort of the confining yellow bed, the mattress too thin and the frame so rickety that it shook when she turned over. It kept her alert in the dark worrying, until she finally fell into a dream-filled sleep only to wake up shivering, the covers fallen to the floor and her head aching, hours before dawn.

With her eyes closed while the faucet plink-plinked drips to the surface, she thought of her daughter. The dripping of the tap made it seem as if Dylan were here, gaily patting the water with her tiny hands. She had loved bathing Dylan in the nursery bathroom at the house, a special mother-daughter ritual to forget daily cares. The nursery bathroom was clean and cheerful; shiny white tiles glazed with ceramic chicks and ducks surrounded the tub.

She opened her eyes to dull cracked tiles around the faucet and a winding thread of black mould in the caulking. She got out of the tub and dripped water onto the black and white floor before reaching for the thin Walmart towel. The tub drained inexorably slow, a soapy ring forming like a reproach.

After the bath she wanted caffeine and went into the kitchen wrapped in the striped bath towel. The stream from the kitchen tap ran warm and she waved her hand through it waiting for the water to cool. The kitchen was hot and dry, the water refused to cool down, and she perspired in the towel.

She could mention it to Henry, have him adjust the thermostat. Remove the bathroom mould too. Look down the drain. She pulled a spoon from the drawer, picked a dry green speck off it with her fingernail. No dishwasher in the apartment to sanitize the cutlery. Living here was like going back in time. Back to a time when women had more work to do in the kitchen.

She would be mindful not to bother him excessively for now. One thing at a time was probably the best way to handle him.

Like she had with tradespeople at the house when they renovated the kitchen. So he'd realize she was no bother and she'd be his favourite tenant. Then he'd do whatever she asked.

He already liked her, obviously. Yesterday when she opened her front door she discovered a grocery store packing carton had been left there. The note on top was signed simply 'H', as if they'd been friends for years. Inside the cardboard box was a toaster, an automatic coffee maker, some melamine dishes in bright colours and a Ziploc bag full of kitchen utensils. The things were scratched and tatty and must have come from the room downstairs, but all of it useful to her. Pre-loved, as they say. There was even a tin of no-name ground coffee. 'Enjoy!' on the note.

He wanted to be a friend. Still, she'd have to be careful. Men so often got the wrong idea if you weren't careful.

She thought to open the fire-escape door to get some fresh air into the kitchen. The door was difficult to push open more than a crack and she gave up the effort. The outside air was too cold, anyway. She drank while standing at the stove enjoying the steam and the warmth of the coffee as she held it in both hands. The mug was pink, like a cup for an infant. Like the hard plastic set she'd had for Dylan. She pictured the cups with double handles she'd used to feed her baby. Bowls with bunnies painted on the oversized rims, short spoons with looped handles.

She put the mug in the sink. It was half full of coffee but she'd lost the taste for it. She scrubbed the cup out vigorously and wiped down the counter until her upper arm was sore. Why did everything have to remind her?

* * *

She came out of the building under an overcast sky and cinched the belt of her coat against the chill. Please just let the rain or snow not happen until she got to the place and applied for the job. Keep her hair smooth and dry. She always felt more confident when her hair looked good.

The massive oaks lining the flagstone walk had dropped their remaining leaves in the rain. She walked under the bleak canopy of gnarled tree limbs, barren branches held fast like claws to clumped empty nests, birds gone for the winter.

Beside the walkway to the curb was a large brown paper bag stuffed with the raked-up leaves. A dog had peed against the bag; the line of urine ran down the paper and along the pavement. She stepped carefully to avoid it.

Henry was across the lawn working under a Norway maple, the rake scratching against the bricks as he dragged it near the wall. He stopped to arch his back, the red of his jacket a wound against the heavy greyness of the sky and trees. She waved to him but he was turned away drinking from a thermos. She reached the sidewalk and a huddle of more paper bags full of leaves. Resting on top of one of them lay the body of a dead squirrel.

She crossed the street and walked by the vacant lot. No construction work was going on, though there were messy piles of rotting wood in the corners and rebar poked out of a hole in the ground. It looked abandoned or even bombed out like after a war. And people had trespassed and helped themselves to some of the material. A lone blue port-a-potty listed to one side beyond a gap in the plywood hoardings.

She rounded a corner to the street of row houses whose backyards were visible from her apartment window. From the eighth floor she'd seen brown chimneys and gentle plumes of furnace smoke, evidence she took of families snug inside. Walking by at ground level the fronts of the houses looked less than neighbourly. They were ramshackle and mean with disrepair.

Paint peeled on sagging porches; windows were covered by

flags rather than curtains. A discarded washing machine squatted in a weed-grown yard. She quickened her step, eager to get to the job interview promptly, as she reached the last of the houses. She felt pity for anyone living in these awful places, imagined voices muttering disdainfully to her: we don't care, what are you going to do about it?

The streetcar stop was in front of a parkette. She waited, stepping out into the road once to see if the blue lights were approaching in the distance. She observed the park. There were swings and a climbing apparatus in the patchy little playground ringed by a low metal fence and gate. A cold wet day, inhospitable for fun in a park, but a boy of five or six straddled the monkey bars. A woman waited at the fence gate, her eyes trained on the road, once looking back at the boy. She called to him to get off right now. He didn't hear or ignored her the way children do, and reached one arm up. The woman strode to the apparatus and barked out his name. Nora couldn't make it out. The child froze in mid-climb. Then the woman lunged and grabbed the sleeve of his dirty snowsuit.

"C'mon," the woman said. "You're making me late."

He tried to shake her arm off and step to a higher climbing bar. He had one boot lifted when the woman seized him hard by the hood of his coat. His head jerked back and whiplashed forward, hitting the metal bar. The woman yanked him to the ground where he lay howling. She slapped his bottom.

Nora was never rough with Dylan. She didn't believe in harsh words, let alone spanking. A child was a precious gift. What a terrible person this mother was. She watched the woman give the boy a tissue to wipe a string of oozing snot, then help him stand up. The woman brushed mud from his jacket. Nora hated this mother.

She turned away from the park gate and the woman and the boy.

A double clang signalled the approaching streetcar. The woman pulled the boy through the gate and told him to hurry. His little body shuddered as he gulped back tears, and Nora fought the urge to take him in her arms. The mother, if indeed that's what she was, glared at Nora as if telling her to quit staring and then pushed the boy up the streetcar steps. Then she spit hard, hitting the toe of Nora's suede boot.

12

Kyle Nowak hoped one of the new recruits would be a drummer. He pushed his hair off his face and tucked it behind his ears. It was growing long quickly, like he hoped, tickling the back of his neck. He'd probably stop growing it out and get a trim at the barbershop when it reached his collar. He drummed impatiently on the tabletop with his hands. Yep, a drummer was what he needed. Naturally, he was going to choose the best candidate for the job of making coffee, but who would it hurt if after hours, that person could also push a mean groove?

He was the lead guitarist and songwriter in a struggling punk band called Unknown World, and he'd been trying to keep the group afloat ever since they met in college, fifteen years earlier. The band played in dive bars while drinkers shouted at them and at private parties where people wanted to hear only classic rock. Once they booked a rave in Buffalo, where the headliner was a guy who'd played with the Sex Pistols. He'd been super pumped for that and driven the van with their equipment across the border in a raging thunderstorm, only to arrive too late to go on stage.

A few weeks ago, his drummer had gotten married and quit the band, even took Kyle aside to suggest it was time he did the same, told him to stop throwing away his youth and money. But he was not ready to give up. Hell, he wasn't even forty yet. Maybe they were never going to earn anything but the free beer they drank at gigs, as he told his buddy, but didn't the friendship count for more than that?

His other job was manager at Lakeview Coffee.

"Dude, do you mind?"

Kyle and two fellow managers were crammed together on one side of a rectangular table, three empty chairs across from them, waiting to begin the interviews. The others scrolled calmly through their phones to pass the time, but Kyle was agitated, impatient to get this process started and find good people. He disliked the inane questions he'd been trained to ask and was pretty sure everyone lied to get hired. He thought these job fairs were impersonal and demeaning, treating applicants like they were scrounging for welfare cheques rather than making important career decisions.

He hadn't realized he was tapping with the palm of a hand on the stack of application forms.

"Sorry," he said. He put down the pencil he'd been using in the other hand to beat the edge of the table. Okay. Stop thinking about music.

It was company policy that the managers wear the same uniform as the baristas, a green apron printed with the pine tree logo, and his was pulled tight over a growing paunch. Too many pizzas and brews with the guys during rehearsals. He tucked his chin-length hair behind his ears again, with more determination this time so it would stay there, showing the sideburns. Friends said he looked like a seventies-era Neil Young. He was flattered in a way, though it wasn't what he was going for.

The applicants were lined up outside on the sidewalk, mostly young girls dressed in shades of black, heads bobbing hopefully, necks craned, eager to be admitted. He thought ruefully that his band would never see such a crowd of groupies clamouring at a stage door.

It was okay though. He was proud of his work at the store. He'd been promoted to manager almost immediately when he'd proved his worth. And the money was fine. Coffee was very trendy in Toronto, and Lakeview Coffee had started it.

He wasn't a fan of this particular location, mind you. Thank goodness he wasn't manager here where the job fair was held, the biggest Lakeview Coffee in the city, a boring spot in the financial district serving bankers and hedge fund guys. The hiring fair was in this barn-sized space because it was large and central, close to the subway. He was in charge of a new location in a funkier part of town near the art college, lodged between a used record shop and a tattoo parlour. He would mention that to the drummer. One of these applicants must play the drums.

Kyle checked his watch, a Rolex like Eric Clapton wore, although Kyle's was an imitation. The applicants outside were restless, peering in through the glass. It was time to open the floodgates and let them flock inside. "Nine o'clock. Let the games begin."

* * *

The interviewees streamed in one after the other, and he questioned each one with mounting boredom, their answers mostly indistinguishable.

"What do you know about Lakeview Coffee?"

"Mm. Hmm. I see you work well with others."

He was tapping on the table again. The girl across from him, perfectly pleasant; what was she saying? Oh yes, studying hospitality. Or physiotherapy?

He could hire any of them. They'd probably work to the end of the Christmas season rush, make enough to travel or return to school and not even care if they were let go during the January lull.

"I'm too honest."

He ran out of questions. "Thanks for coming. We'll let you know."

The two other managers conducted interviews simultaneously on either side of Kyle, the dull staccato of rote questions and answers in his ears. For a moment, the chair across the table from him was empty while the conversations beside him droned on. Work experience. Provide a reference. He pictured Keith Moon sitting down, firing up a joint, "Sure man. Love to play in your band."

A woman stepped forward. She disengaged herself from the gaggle waiting and walked towards him, glided, she was that sylph-like, elegant in a neatly belted tan coat and stylish ankle boots. She pulled the chair out soundlessly and perched on the edge, holding eye contact.

"Hello." She offered a hand to shake. "I'm Nora Davis."

He told her his name. Was about to ask what brought her in today. Her hands rested in front of her on the table, and a soft light fell on her smooth hair from the windows behind her.

"Why are you hiring?" she said.

"Why?" He wasn't sure what she meant. "We increase at Christmas. You'd enjoy the party atmosphere."

"Do people quit? Lots of people moving through, going on to better work?"

"I started as a temp in college. Now I'm a manager. It's a solid career." He defended his choice. He wasn't insulted, kind of unusual to be grilled this way by an applicant.

"What's the pay like?"

"We pay above minimum. Great benefits." No one had ever asked him about money in an interview before, as if they were afraid to raise the topic. They usually presented themselves as lambs to the slaughter, almost begging for a job. This woman was different.

"Is this the store I'd work in?" She moved one hand off the table to her lap. "I'd prefer something closer to the lake."

He was caught off balance by her curiosity. "Oh, the name," he said. "Truth is we have no locations anywhere near the water. It's supposed to be ironic, I guess." He watched her face for a reaction and observed her wry smile. "My shop is on Queen West. It's a cool spot. Art students come in and try to sell us weird paintings, and there's a famous author who sits in the back writing, never orders a thing."

"Sounds very bohemian," she said.

"Well, I like it. I'm a musician so, I like customers who are into the arts." And, hoping she was interested, though knowing he was being too personal, he told her about Unknown World and even, stupidly, asked her if she played drums.

She laughed, but it was a friendly laugh, appreciative of his brand of goofiness, he thought. Her entire face glowed when she smiled.

She was very pretty. Her dark hair was lustrous, and a rose sheen on her lips reflected a glint from the overhead lights. Her application form lay folded in her hand. So what if she wasn't a drummer, or any sort of musician. He wanted to hire her.

The hand holding the application had lovely mauve polish on the nails. He concentrated on the folded piece of paper. He should probably at least glance at it, get her details and a reference or two before he offered her the job.

13

It was worse than she expected. The highlight may have been the green apron, a colour that was hard to pull off, usually too bright or garish to be flattering to anyone. Initially, Nora was relieved to have work and an excuse to get out of the dark apartment. She told herself the long daily commute by subway wasn't so bad. But three days in and she was both exhausted and bored. Her wrist ached from pulling levers on the espresso machine, her skin was red from the steam.

Kyle was kind though. He said everyone was initially overwhelmed. To cheer her up he showed her a YouTube clip. It was an old black and white television show from her parents' time—when she was a teenager, they loved to watch TV and when a classic show came on they howled with laughter, urging her to put down the homework for a minute and join them.

In the clip Kyle showed her, a hapless woman works on a factory assembly line with a furious pace of production. The belt keeps speeding faster while the woman is trying to fill moving boxes with chocolates. She can't keep up, especially since, instead of packaging it, she tries to grab and eat the candy as it flies by.

She felt like that in her barista job: like she was on an assembly line of endless orders that could be done better automatically, by a machine.

Kyle said it would improve and to not let any customer's antics get to her. One day a man demanded six pumps of syrup. His mouth turned down impatiently, and she didn't want to ask him again, pumps of what flavour? She consulted the laminated booklet describing the drinks and the combinations and permutations of sugar, flavour, shots of espresso. The customer cleared his throat loudly, asked her what the problem was. Kyle made the drink and told her by next week she'd be a genius at this.

It was almost Christmas, and they were busy, a locus of the city's collective frenzy to shop and socialize and live entire lives before everything shut down for the holiday. It wasn't only the art students, although they rushed in and out in bunches, their clothes splattered with paint and always in a hurry to get back to the studio. They fueled themselves with caffeine and sugar to complete year-end assignments. Nora admired their ambition. The shop was also popular with clutches of tourists exploring the lively neighbourhood, who held up the line dithering over the drink choices. At least those people were polite and some even tipped.

The customers that annoyed her most were lawyers from the nearby courthouse, grabbing coffee to offset the boozy seasonal lunches they'd indulged in. They were loud, constantly shouting into their phones, and barely registered her presence as they waited for their online orders, alcohol on their breath. They exuded arrogance. Just like Carter. He had been one of those lawyers, once.

She was on her feet all day in a dance of constant motion.

A sore spot burned in the ball of one foot and cramped her calf muscle. For relief, she stood awkwardly on her heels. Her hair frizzed in the volcano of steam erupting from the espresso machine. And the smell of coffee, an aroma she ordinarily loved, now permeated her clothes and hair with a stench that made her gag.

It was always Kyle and his silly sense of humour that saved her, his engaging ridiculous banter that made her laugh.

A guy at the counter said he was going next door to get his baby son's name tattooed on his forearm. He ordered an Americano with extra water. Kyle asked him if he was nervous. The guy said the boy's name was Elvis. Kyle passed her the empty cup, and she wrote the name on it in black Sharpie, drawing an extra flourish for the 'E'.

"Here's what it will look like," Kyle said.

She raised the cup so the man could see his son's name in her elaborate script.

The customer grinned.

Kyle asked him if he was a fan of Elvis Presley.

"Who the heck is that? It's just a name my wife likes. She wants to call the next kid Priscilla." He winked at Kyle, who was by now in stitches and shaking so much he handed off the cup for Nora to pour.

"Maybe you should try writing it on your skin first," she said to the man. "See how you like it."

"Nah. Been waiting for this. Feels like a thing I can do. To show him I care."

On the tip of her tongue, a mother's admonition: then go home and look after your son, keep him safe. He needs your love, your vigilance. Don't get sidetracked and make bad decisions.

Like I did.

* * *

She had a scar on her belly from Dylan's birth, the operation unexpected after such an easy pregnancy. She thought the birth would be easy too. The baby floating inside her like a little seahorse, and she had been so happy, her emotions for nine months smooth as gossamer soap bubbles blown from a wand. Carter was protective for once of them both, marvelling at her rounding body and even staying home with her some evenings. She thought he had changed for good. The surgery was a shock after hours in the labour room, but the baby was perfect. And for a very short time, so was Carter.

"You good there, Sport?" A blue uniform stood in front of her, moustache moving atop a toothy mouth, her reverie dispelled.

Kyle came beside her and handed over a tall cup to the police officer. They watched him take a sip before he turned away, a column of blue bisected by the dark holster at his hip. The black handle of a gun.

"You're shaking." Kyle put a hand on her arm. "Cops have that effect on me too," he said. "I've never been in trouble, but they make me nervous. That's why I don't charge them for the coffee."

*　*　*

Days melted into each other as she worked to a soundtrack of blaring music, rock and jazz versions of Christmas songs, the same tunes on repeat. Kyle jumped and bopped awkwardly to the tunes, never bored with the playlist, weaving around Nora and the others. He was all right, Kyle. Treated her with respect and made sure they all shared tips. Hadn't made her feel stupid once for mixing up orders or spilling syrup.

She started to relax. All the trouble was behind her.

"Having fun?" He grinned. She waved her hand, inky from

marking up the cups. "We're getting a printed label system," he said. "Soon as the computer program is running. Something to look forward to."

She started finding her own sources of amusement in the customers and sharing them with Kyle. Two art students in identical white parkas and turquoise hair, heads inclined together in conversation like conjoined twins, waited for spiced lattes. Very popular choice. They'd given their names as Adele, both of them.

"Decaf vanilla." Kyle nudged her elbow, slid the full paper cup her way.

He smiled all day, his default facial expression. "Foam me to you." He enjoyed bad puns, joking around, acting like a sort of dad figure for his younger employees. Nora was closer to his age than most of the others, and he'd already asked her if she wanted to attend the training seminars the company held to identify future managers, but she wasn't ready for that; she had no plan to stay long-term. She needed to be cautious, keep her head down and earn a living, if only a meagre one. She could be friendly and casual and inconspicuous working in the store. That was enough for now.

And she had made a friend there. Izzy. She was young, only twenty, elfin and pale, with white spiky hair cut short on one side only and fair, nearly invisible eyebrows. Izzy liked to talk about herself and struck Nora as a very courageous twenty-year-old. She had made her way south to Toronto from the remote northern town she grew up in by working in a string of bars and truck stops. Along the way she'd convinced people to let her sleep in storerooms at work or crash on co-workers' couches so she could save all her earnings. And she had done it all alone and without fear. She had landed here in the city, with a steady job and a shared apartment. All five feet and ninety pounds of her.

According to Kyle, Izzy learned everything there was to know at Lakeview Coffee on her first day. She filled several drink orders simultaneously, remembered what the repeat customers wanted and put funny and peculiar versions of names on the cups to amuse herself.

"This is nothing," she told Nora. "I worked in a prison kitchen for a summer. And I was a waitress in an all-night diner. In Wawa."

"Blind River." Kyle's forehead was damp from dancing in front of the hot coffee machine. "The wildest place I lived. Where the van broke down. So we decided to stay for a few weeks. Band played in honky-tonks. Miners and loggers don't like punk music much though. Guy threw a bottle at me." He lifted the hair away from his ear and bent down, so they could have a look. "Eight stitches."

Izzy and Kyle had been in towns with one gas station where bears wandered the main street. Nora's town wasn't like that. A clean and prosperous place in the Golden Horseshoe, with wide streets and impressive brick houses full of families with old Ontario names.

"Who had the craziest job?" Izzy said. She looked up expectantly at Nora. A delicate silver arrow pierced one of her eyebrows, dots of coloured glass glittered in her ears.

"I've nothing exciting to tell," Nora said.

She looked at the floor. The past was the past.

14

Nora returned to her building one day after work as the sun was setting. The dwindling light washed the yellow bricks in a hazy orange, bile-like, ugly, the colour of some animal droppings or human effluence you didn't want to step in.

She held a small table lamp under her arm, which she had bought in a second-hand shop on Queen West, a cluttered hole-in-the-wall on the block where she caught the streetcar. The lamp was displayed in the window of the shop, an orphan waiting for adoption, gathering dust between a plaster garden gnome and a clutch of red votive candles. The parchment shade was faded, some of the fringe ragged, but the ceramic base was adorable, a green unicorn with a white horn. It needed a good home.

The clerk hadn't known how to wrap it up. It stuck out awkwardly from the bag, so she took it as it was, winding the cord around the base. It had made her happy to look at it on the subway as she rode home.

* * *

Henry was in the vestibule when she entered the building. He was with a woman, heads bent close, in whispered discussion. He didn't look at Nora, and she didn't want to ask them to move so she could open her mailbox. It seemed to be a serious conversation.

She had not seen the woman in the building before. She looked to be in her fifties, wore a good wool coat and a fur hat, and gesticulated with a gloved hand at Henry, rapidly moving her mouth, the lips animated by deep red lipstick.

The talk was urgent, so important they didn't want her to hear, their faces close together. The woman angry and Henry's expression flat. Neither one of them acknowledged her as she passed them to ascend the stairs.

She placed the lamp by her bed under the window and turned it so the unicorn's horn pointed into the room. The lime green and pink was cheerful next to the yellow cot. She stood looking at them together and absorbing the effect her things had on the room. She had tried to make the little apartment her own, but it wasn't right, the colours, the feeling in the room was wrong, unsettling.

She flicked the lamp on and off. It was too small and the bulb in it too dim, shedding scant light. She saw then, she knew at once what she had done, what she had created in this one-room dwelling with the fanciful lamp and the small painted bed. She had made herself a familiar yet strange place to live. A child's bedroom.

* * *

She had to go out again to get dinner provisions. Izzy and Kyle were invited to come have a meal that she would cook. They were both working later shifts than hers today, giving her time to arrive home first and get ready. As she buttoned her coat she heard floorboards creak on the landing; Henry must have come up. Nora waited long enough for him to go into his apartment before opening her door to leave. She didn't want an encounter.

*　*　*

At the end of Farmdale Lane, there was a corner store called Lucky Convenience. A retractable metal gate, currently rolled back, protected the front window from being smashed by thieves, and above the window a dirty brown awning stretched out over uneven plywood tables topped with desultory wares. Cheap winter caps were layered in a bin and snow shovels perched in a clump against the wall like pick-up sticks about to be thrown. Some small bushels of produce, bruised apples and potatoes, all of it lightly dusted with frost. Fading posters in the window advertised Vape pens and Pringles.

It was cold inside the store. A television screen by the counter played a soccer game from somewhere in the world where it wasn't winter, and for a moment her attention was diverted by the movement of the players. She followed the men in coloured jerseys criss-crossing the field and thought about seeing kids play soccer at the elementary school back home. Passing by on her walks with Dylan in the stroller, thinking someday she'd be watching Dylan run like that while she cheered with the other mothers. The sound on the television was off, and she lost interest in the silent game, turned her attention to the misshapen squash and carrots in bushel baskets.

She picked up a bunch of salad greens and pressed cherry tomatoes for firmness. The wares inside the store were in better condition than those for sale outdoors, but the prices were high. She brought a bunch of cilantro to her nose for a sniff. It seemed off.

A man at the cash register peered at her over the top of his glasses. He wore a Maple Leafs beanie on his head and a dirty green jacket. He read the *Toronto Sun*, flipping the newspaper with a hand in a fingerless glove, the tips of his fingers blackened with ink.

"Basically, the policy is 'you touch it, you buy it'," he said.

She put down the expensive tomatoes.

"That seems a bit unreasonable."

"New to the neighbourhood?" he asked. Behind him were shelves of condoms and batteries, a jumble of aspirin bottles, lighters and tampons.

"Yes." She chose a bunch of basil. "Still getting to know where everything is."

"Never seen you shopping here before." He turned back to the soccer. "Madrid will win I think."

She searched for garlic and pasta, noting that everything was over-priced, and thought she should have gone to Hunters, a large supermarket. Except it was a longer walk to get there.

"Live close?" he said. A snapshot taped to the till showed a woman and two little boys at a lake. And a graduation photo of a young man, perhaps one of the boys grown up, grinning in a cap and gown. "I can do deliveries." He looked out the window, where a man in a long overcoat was holding a potato. "Goddam it." He darted to the front door as the man scurried off, potato in hand.

"Are you going to run after him?" she said.

"Not worth it for a ten-cent tuber. Besides, I have to watch you."

"Well, I'm not going to steal anything."

He looked at her, the coat, the silky hair. "My apologies." He went back to his counter. "Pick out a chocolate bar. On the house. A welcome gift to the hood."

She put items in the basket: two types of pasta, orecchiette and spaghetti, mushrooms, Roma tomatoes and a bulb of garlic.

"Do you know the Farmdale Court Apartments?" she said. "I moved in there."

He put the newspaper aside and began arranging a tray of lottery tickets, pulling them out and slipping them back in a different order.

She put her items on the counter and he rang them up. She paid with the credit card.

"So, you've heard the stories?" he said. "About that place."

"What stories?"

The door chimes jingled as a woman lumbered in, burdened with possessions. The woman lugged several overstuffed plastic bags and wore ragged layers of clothing, her shoes and socks wound with Saran wrap. A smell of putrefaction wafted in with her. The man shouted that there was no bathroom here. He rushed to follow the woman as she headed to the back of the store.

Nora took her purchases and left.

15

November 16, 1918

Alice and I are restless cooped up in our apart-ment. I am afraid to take her outside while the flu is spreading. I make short trips to the local shops and I have been issued a little face mask to wear when I leave the apartment. A flimsy square of cheesecloth tied with kitchen string that covers my mouth and nose. I tried it on for Alice and she laughed at how silly I looked.

November 18, 1918

The neighbour woman next door is not very nice. This morning she had the audacity to say I make too much noise. It was only Alice bouncing an India-rubber ball. I will not ask that woman to look in on Alice if I am out. She is too unkind.

November 20, 1918

> *Alice will have her fourth birthday next week and I want to bake her a cake. I don't have money for ingredients, and I used most of the flour making ration cakes and mailing them to the war office to feed the men. At least the war is over now and the soldiers are coming home. Those cakes must taste like rocks by the time they reach the men. If I can get more flour and a lemon I could make Alice a chiffon cake.*

> *They say it is the returning soldiers who brought this terrible flu.*

Henry heard her come in. He stopped reading the diary. The rattle of the doorknob, the door closing, her steps receding as she moved about her apartment. The floorboards creaked. Comforting to have someone living next door to him again. He could go over there now and ask if she needed anything. But perhaps it was better to give her time on her own to settle.

He could busy himself enough with the list of building repairs, and he had his own personal tasks to complete. He'd been meaning to collate his collected ephemera. Over the years he had amassed so much. There were articles from newspapers, archival material found online and in libraries, old photos. He was especially interested in miscellany about life in the city in the time during and right after the First World War. The soldiers who returned to Toronto and their struggles to resume civilian life. To find jobs. To find wives. How they put the horror behind them.

The best things, the most interesting items that he deemed worthy of collection, he discovered here in the building. He always looked around if he was in an apartment repairing a leaky faucet or caulking a bathtub, especially if the tenant was old and likely to have hoarded mementos.

Also, he enjoyed snooping in cupboards and dresser drawers.

Some of the best treasures were in the apartments of people who had died. Occasionally there was nobody who came to clear out, no relative or friend. Then he had to do it. And he was happy to. That's how he found a photo dated 1915, of women waving at young men boarding the train for Halifax. And a cookbook advising what to make with war rations. Stuck in between the recipes had been a letter to a woman from her lover. The lady whose apartment it was lay dead two days before anyone realized.

He'd found a photo in a gold frame sitting on top of a bureau and he kept it on his own dresser now. He had no idea who the people were but it was taken in the building's courtyard. A plump young woman smiled under the oak trees, holding hands with twin boys. It was dated June, 1945.

He heard Nora running the water as he picked up a clipping from the *Toronto Star*, February 10, 1919.

> All winter Toronto has been overtaken by disease. Armistice Day 1918 brought the glorious return of soldiers from battlefields, but also a fearsome influenza epidemic the city was unprepared to handle.

She banged a pot on top of the stove. She slammed shut the cupboard door. His kitchen was next to hers where he could hear even better and he went there. The room was too hot. He turned the radiator knob and opened his fire escape door a crack to let in cold air. Time for tea. After he filled the kettle with cold water and turned up the blue gas flames beneath it, he put his ear against the common wall.

It sounded like she was putting things in the cupboard. He could see her in his imagination fussing around in the little kitchen, the way women liked to do. He pictured her slim arm reaching high to put a jar on the top shelf, the curve of her hips as she bent low to retrieve a pot from deep in the lower cupboard, perhaps brushing her dark hair away as it fell with her movements across her face. He visualised himself in the kitchen beside her.

Then the sounds stopped and there was a knock on his door. The glass panes rattled behind the red velvet curtain. He turned off his stove.

Nora stood there in a wool skirt and black turtleneck, black tights, shoeless.

"This may be weird," she said, "but I realized I haven't got a broom or anything."

Her hair was pulled into a ponytail, practical, out of the way, so it would not fall into her eyes. And no make-up, which left her looking more delicate, he thought. Her cheeks were flushed, little holes in her ears where earrings should be.

"To tidy up," she said. "Friends are coming over."

I have been helpful and friendly to you. I have invited you into my place. You consumed my food and my wine. And now you have excluded me from—

"Could you lend me a broom for a minute?"

"You're having a party?" he said. He was furious and stepped back from her behind the threshold, wary of his own anger.

"No. My two friends from work. Don't worry. There won't be noise." She looked at the books and papers that were spread out over his rug and sofa. "You really must tell me more about the building, some other time."

"How late will this party go on?"

74

"Not late at all. And you won't hear a thing, if you want a quiet night."

He dismissed an urge to shake her. No. Flies with honey, not vinegar.

"Just a minute." He vanished into his apartment. The little ginger cat raced ahead of him around the corner and towards the hidden bedrooms. He took his time and slowed down his breath and rummaged in two closets before returning, coming back to the front door holding a Dyson stick vacuum. He practiced looking calm, the way he'd learned. Relax the facial muscles, slow intake of air, slower outtake. Often it worked.

She took hold of the vacuum awkwardly, one hand and then two for balance; it was heavier than it looked, weighted towards the motor in the handle, with a clear cannister at the end. He had passed it over to her gravely, like a bishop offering a holy object with his blessings.

"Take this," he said.

He waited until he heard sounds in her kitchen again. Then he sat down to find something calming to read. He opened the diary.

16

Nora stirred the tomato sauce with a wooden spoon, small circles, larger circles, bubbles bursting and sputtering. Flecks of black pepper and a shallow pool of olive oil dotted the red surface. She poured a bit of wine into the pot, added more chopped garlic.

How many times in her life had she prepared spaghetti? It was one of Dylan's favourites. She always put more sugar in the sauce for Dylan, less garlic. She would cut up the long noodles and let her daughter grab them up with her hands, pushing the slimy pasta towards her face, red sauce like clown makeup smeared on her cheeks, the highchair tray a sticky mess.

This kitchen, with its museum-relic appliances and cracked tile floor, was very different than the one she'd had in her house. That kitchen was special, gleaming stainless steel and white marble. Sub Zero fridge; Wolf range. The more exclusive or elusive the brand, the more Carter wanted it. He sought out and bought the best, loved to show off his supposed wealth and success, and Nora was complicit in raising their mounting debt. She desired beautiful things too.

Although he was a lawyer and worked in a small town on matters that would not have made him rich, wills and real-estate, the occasional divorce, Carter made most of his money from dubious business ventures and other schemes involving shady clients. He did things for a local motorcycle club and a casino. Sometimes he drove several hours down the highway to clients in the federal penitentiary. She didn't question him and tried not to think about it. She hadn't cared what his business was as long as she and Dylan had what they needed.

Nora stirred the sauce and heard noise from Henry's kitchen.

"I told you so." A woman's voice, scornful, and then a garbled reply, angry. Henry's voice rose and fell, rose again, as if he moved back and forth while he spoke.

The trouble begins when you ask questions.

She unlocked the fire escape door to hear more but she managed only to open it a crack. Cool air slid into the steamy kitchen and she felt relief on her forehead and cheeks, her face damp with sweat from the over-active radiators and the simmering pot on the stove. But she heard no more talking. The argument was over, or she had stopped it herself with the noise of her own movements.

It was dark outside, the lane behind the building in shadow and lights blinked on in houses on the other side. A watery yellow glow from Henry's kitchen window fell on the icy slats of the fire escape. Distant traffic hummed beyond the trees and a dog barked in a yard.

She locked the door. The stove clock said it was after six. Izzy and Kyle would be here any minute. The moment of cold outside air had done little to cool the kitchen. Moist heat like a sauna saturated the room and rivulets of condensation rolled down the wall above the stove. She filled a large pot with water for the pasta.

From the landing outside her apartment door, she heard laughter and footsteps and knocking. And Henry's voice behind the wall calling out to his cat.

She opened the door to Izzy and Kyle. The smell of the outside world permeated their clothing, scents from the cold air picked up as they walked from the subway: woody chimney smoke on Kyle's jacket and a whiff of cinnamon from Lakeview Coffee on Izzy's scarf. Both smiled happily.

"I didn't hear you buzz," Nora said. "Did someone let you in?"

"The front door was open," Izzy said. She wore a bright green coat with a fuzzy collar. She was radiant with glittering eye shadow and her spiky white hair poking out from a striped wool cap with a braided tassel dangling off one side. A neon pink scarf completed the look. Kyle, in his heavy parka, grinned behind Izzy, towering over the much shorter girl. He held a crusty baguette in a clear waxy wrapper and a brown paper bag from the liquor store.

"OMG," Izzy said. "Eight flights and no elevator!" She hugged Nora.

Kyle stepped towards her, came in for a hug, raised his arms to show his hands were full with wine and bread. He managed to embrace her, pressing his elbows around her in a friendly squeeze.

She ushered them in and for a moment a brief ember of regret burned through her. She wished she was welcoming her friends, not to this shabby little apartment, but to the beautiful lost house she'd known before.

Izzy went straight to the window to check out the view and then pointed to the unicorn lamp. "I love it," she said. "It's so adorable."

Kyle waited politely in the open doorway for Nora to direct where to put the bread and wine. He could obviously see the apartment was only one room, and the kitchen nothing more than a carved-out alcove. "This is a really nice place." He seemed shy, waiting for her to invite him in, conscious of not wanting to act like her boss.

Nora's skin tingled with happiness at seeing her friends. She was about to take the things from Kyle's hands, show him where to put his coat. He looked handsome, away from the fluorescent lighting at work. She hadn't noticed before how lovely his brown eyes were.

She reached out for the bread in his hand and before she could take it, he lurched forward and lost his footing, bumped hard against her as he was pushed out of the doorway from behind. Someone shoved him aside, pushed roughly and barged in.

It was Henry. He rushed in like a rude passenger on the subway who jumps on the train at the last minute, who barrels headlong through the shutting doors, not caring who he knocks down or injures. He'd pushed Kyle out of the way without the slightest care.

Kyle looked embarrassed. He apologized to Nora, as if he had done something wrong. Henry offered no apology.

"Um, what's the hurry?" Kyle said, recovering his composure.

Henry ignored Kyle, came to Nora, grasped her hand eagerly. She was stunned at his dramatic entrance, and tried to peer around him to signal Kyle, as if to say she wasn't sure what was happening here.

Henry said, "The time got away from me." He gripped her hand tightly. "But I'm here now." As if he was the most important guest.

She didn't remember inviting him to dinner. An unsettling flutter of déjà-vu played in her head. The muddle of people in the room. The strong smell of Henry's cologne in her nostrils.

Izzy and Kyle looked at Nora quizzically, brows furrowed. No one spoke. Nora shrugged, having no explanation. Then Izzy complimented Nora's hair, though she hadn't done anything much to it. Kyle removed his boots, and Nora helped him as he took off his heavy jacket. He laughed when he got tangled in his sleeve.

"I'm hopeless," he joked. He wriggled out and folded the jacket over the arm of the teak chair. He smiled at Nora. Henry watched the interaction.

The four of them stood awkwardly in the room and she felt how small the space truly was. Finally, Izzy introduced herself to Henry. "Call me Iz. And you are . . . ?"

Which roused her to her role as hostess. "This is my land-lord," she said. "Henry." She must have invited him and forgotten. She was over-tired from work. Or Henry had misunderstood her when she borrowed his vacuum, taken her mention of the dinner as an invitation.

Henry wore jeans and a thick plaid shirt in black and red. Work clothes, although clean. His hair had been carefully slicked back with gel, his face a wide square without the usual blond lock crossing his forehead. A pronounced shine revealed that he'd also applied the grooming gel to his dark eyebrows.

Henry said, "This is such a lovely time of year for a dinner party." He held out a bottle of red wine, confounding her further. She nodded at the bottle, acknowledging it, pointedly not taking it from his hand.

It was Kyle who reached out and shook hands with Henry. Kyle was affable and used to making people feel comfortable. He saw that there was something awkward in the situation. He was shorter than Henry and heavier, his body bear-like next to Henry. Henry was tall and muscular. He held the offered hand rigidly, without warmth, and was the first to withdraw. He looked at Nora.

"You must want the vacuum back," she said, still confused. She had used it earlier, and now the dust-free wooden floors glowed in the small patch of light emitted from the unicorn lamp. She would give him his vacuum and he would leave.

He laughed, but the shiny eyebrows stiffened over his green eyes. "Remind me later."

Henry strode into the kitchen, put the wine on the counter and rummaged noisily for a corkscrew. He opened her kitchen drawer like someone who knew where things were stored.

"You decorated so nicely," Izzy said. She looked tiny next to Kyle, a meadow sprite to his forest bulk.

"Place looks great," Kyle said. "And dinner smells amazing."

The living room was too dark with only the light from the unicorn lamp, the corners of the walls veiled in shadow. She hadn't decorated at all, not like the house, with its English wallpaper and coordinating upholstery and silk drapes on the windows. This apartment had nothing but some cast-off furniture and a coat of cheap paint. It hardly felt like a home.

"These old buildings have so much character," Henry said, still rummaging in the kitchen.

"That's what I thought when I first saw it," she said, agreeing with Henry. "A cool building with history." She would fix up the apartment to make it comfortable. "I had a good feeling once I was inside." She smiled at Izzy and Kyle. "I know it's a long trip for you guys from downtown. Thank you so much for coming."

Kyle pointed out the window. "You can see the clock tower in the distance."

Henry said from the kitchen, "That clock tower. Used to be a train station. This wasn't even part of the city. They demolished the station for a condo and the tower is now a liquor store. They ruin everything."

Izzy made a funny face that Henry couldn't see from his place in the tiny kitchen. He opened and closed a cupboard. Izzy whispered, "weird guy," but Nora wanted to think he was only trying to be helpful. He evidently found a corkscrew she didn't know she possessed. He popped the cork and poured wine into mugs and juice tumblers.

"You need wine glasses," Henry said. He handed them each a drink and raised his mug. "Here's to new beginnings." He touched her arm when he said it, a slight squeeze. "Right Kyle? I must get this lady some proper stemware."

She was flustered and could tell Kyle was puzzled, yet too polite to say anything. She didn't want anyone to think she and Henry had something going on. They were landlord and tenant, nothing more. Izzy put a hand to her mouth, tried not to laugh. She knew what Izzy thought, many women would think it, that Henry was acting proprietary, like a boyfriend. Or a husband.

"So, what does being a super entail?" Izzy asked.

"I'm not the super," Henry said. "I'm the landlord. My family erected this building."

"But when the toilet's plugged, you're the man with the plunger right?"

Henry bristled at Izzy's remark. And it was a little rude of Izzy to take him down a peg, when he was only being neighbourly. Kyle smiled and sipped the wine. He seemed oblivious to any tension.

Okay, Henry's pretentious, sure. Yet she didn't want to be mean. Henry *was* the person who took care of the building and she would certainly need him to fix things. Also, he had been only kind and helpful so far.

Thinking back to their exchange earlier in the day when she'd borrowed the vacuum, she couldn't recall exactly what was said. Had she mentioned the dinner? Had she invited him?

Henry sat down next to Nora on the bed. It felt wrong to be on the bed with him. Never had she wanted a sofa more. Kyle stood leaning against the wall and she realized he had deliberately taken his place there, rather than seating himself on the bed, to save her embarrassment. Such a thoughtful man.

Henry looked over at Izzy, who sat curled on the teak chair, her legs crossed underneath, like a school kid waiting on the mat for story time. Nora saw him assess Izzy's child-like frame, saw him dismiss her as inconsequential, staring at her until she rose in discomfort.

"Can I use your bathroom?" Izzy said.

Nora waived her hand to show which door was the bathroom. It was right off the living room, you couldn't miss it. Yet Izzy hesitated as if waiting for Nora to come with her, as if they were in high school. Henry was next to her on the bed. She'd almost have to crawl over him to get up. They could all see the door to the bathroom, slightly ajar. She stayed still on the bed and then Izzy hopped off the chair in a flash.

Henry was too close to her on the yellow bed. So close she felt the pressure of his thigh grazing hers.

"The building," he said. "It's always been in my family."

She inched her thigh away.

"No one intended to insult you man, even if you were a janitor, or whatever," Kyle said. "I'm sure it's a big responsibility to look after a whole building."

"I decide who lives here." Henry cleared his throat. "Everything."

She lowered her eyes, wanted to dive into the red depth of the wine in her glass.

The evening wasn't going as she had intended.

"I suppose you push a broom at Lakeview Coffee for a living," Henry said. He leaned in, his hip pressing on hers. She wished he wouldn't sit so close.

Henry had it wrong if he thought she was attracted to him sexually. And he was having this unnecessary pissing contest with Kyle.

Nora got up from the bed to go stir the sauce. She was careful not to touch Henry's legs, even though he didn't move out of her way. Kyle followed her into the kitchen alcove, handed her the wooden spoon from the counter. They heard the toilet flush.

"This is so different from my place," Izzy said, returning from the bathroom.

"How so?" Henry asked.

"I'm on the twenty-first floor, swimming pool, gym, high-speed elevators in the entertainment district," Izzy said. "The only drawback is two loud roommates to share the cost."

"How can I help?" Kyle said. There was barely enough room for him to be beside her at the stove.

She shook her head and salted the sauce. She felt comfortable with Kyle. She liked standing close to him in the warm kitchen.

"This building opened in 1918," Henry said. "One of the first of its —"

Izzy giggled, causing Henry to break off in mid-sentence. Nora wanted to know about the building's history, but Izzy's reaction said "boring." Her laughter said "stupid."

"What kind of wine is this?" Nora asked from the kitchen. She had to save Izzy and Henry from each other.

"Merlot." Henry sounded angry. "A good wine for spaghetti."

"I brought white. Hope that's okay," Kyle said, returning to the living room.

Choosing wine had been Carter's department. She liked it well enough but was indifferent to its provenance and intricacies. Carter purchased expensive vintages and expected her to be a gracious hostess when he entertained clients. She dreaded those parties, when drinking brought out the worst in Carter.

She took Kyle's bottle of white out of the kitchen when she saw that the red was empty.

"Well, let's open it," Henry said.

She looked at the empty bottle, the red wine Henry said went well with spaghetti. She wondered how he'd known what she was cooking when he chose it.

She worried there wasn't enough so she boiled two boxes of pasta. After the meal, after they had managed to stuff themselves with food and consume all the wine, Kyle was the first to say goodnight. He was so tired, he said, having worked six days in a row and jamming half the night with his bandmates. Izzy decided to leave with him; it was late and she didn't want to be alone on the long subway ride.

Henry lingered in the room as she went to the door with them, waiting as they praised the meal and said their goodbyes. Nora had hoped he would leave before her friends, so she could explain and tell them the truth, that Henry was an interloper, uninvited, just a lonely neighbour who needed company.

Izzy was the first to step out, pulling her hat on while Kyle came out on the landing. He zipped his coat, fumbling when the zipper stuck. Then he bent his head to Nora and kissed her goodnight.

It was a real kiss, with a meaningful press of warm lips on hers, longer than it needed to be for a quick goodnight. Unexpected, yet not unwelcomed.

Izzy winked, then hugged her. She'd noticed the kiss.

Henry waited on the landing until Kyle and Izzy descended the stairs, until they were out of sight down several floors, their voices and footsteps diminished to silence. Nora stood framed in her doorway, she held out her hand to shake his good night, not knowing why he lingered. He didn't take the hand. Her lips parted, about to say good-bye to Henry, but he turned his back on her abruptly and disappeared alone into his apartment.

17

Henry knew he would be awake all night, too angry to fall asleep. At first he tried to lie still in his bed and to empty his mind, but he couldn't stop his swirling rage. Images of Nora kissing Kyle pierced his brain. He kept seeing it like a faulty electrical circuit that continued to spark. He had to do something to stop the vision. This kind of obsessive thinking only led down a dark path.

He got out of bed and sat morosely in the living room feeling sorry for himself and worrying that his plans were ruined. He drank some brandy and looked in vain for the cat.

The woman was duplicitous.

He was so angry he felt he should go back over there right now and give her a piece of his mind.

He opened the armoire where he kept the master keys on a ring. He could let himself into her place.

But that way lay trouble. Instead, he took some lorazepam, two pills. He resigned himself to wait it out until morning, let the anger subside. There would be more opportunity and time with Nora. For now, he could lose himself in his collection. Distraction from negative emotion, like the psychologists had advised him.

Reading the diary was usually diverting. The white, cloth-covered journal felt comforting in his hands, like the soft old books in his father's study when he was a boy, the volumes he was forbidden to touch but often secretly did.

He opened the book and put it on the coffee table in front of him, the frayed silken marker woven into the binding lay on the page he had last read. When he initially discovered the diary wedged behind a kitchen radiator, it was damaged by years of heat and moisture, some of the pages too brittle to handle without tearing. He was incredulous that it had remained hidden for decades, the diarist long gone and subsequent tenants arriving and departing year after year, none of them aware it was there.

He considered the woman's diary a gift left for him to find. She'd inscribed her name on the inside cover: Doris Carr. She had been one of the building's original occupants.

He imagined Doris dipping her fountain pen in an inkwell and recording the events of her days, her most private thoughts. He saw her raise her head in reflection, absently run the silken place-marker between her fingers exactly as he now did.

He started to read a favourite entry. The handwriting was intricate, precise and feminine.

September 15, 1918

I rented a small apartment on Farmdale Lane, which I will move into next week. It is on a pretty street south of the train tracks. Lots of oak and maple trees, and I will be much closer to the elementary school where I teach. The building is very respectable, one of the first apartment houses in this part of the city. It is decidedly not a tenement like my previous place. I will have my own lavatory instead of a shared privy out back. And an icebox in the kitchen!

It will be much safer for me and my little Alice to stay at Farmdale Court Apartments. I had to say there was a Mr. Carr who was overseas with the war effort, or else they would have refused to rent to me. They won't allow unmarried women to move into such a fine building.

Henry could hear Nora moving about next door. It was 2 a.m. He was somewhat gratified that she couldn't sleep either. He should go over there and talk to her now. The medicine was taking effect and he was calm. He would like to lie down next to Nora in her yellow bed.

But better to stay put imagining Doris in Toronto in 1918.

When I went to view the apartment today the main road was muddy and walking there was cumbersome. My new boots, plain brown lace-ups, and the hem of my going-out dress were wet and mud-splattered.

Nora was in her kitchen now. He heard dishes bang in the sink and the hot water pipes groan. Cleaning up after the dinner party. He hoped she regretted humiliating him by kissing another man.

November 21, 1918

This morning I woke up early while it was still dark. I ran to the corner to find a newspaper. The front page said there were 700 new flu cases this week in Toronto and that anyone who coughs in public is worse than the German Kaiser. I hurried home to Alice. There were two men smoking pipes on the front stoop on Farmdale. I don't know what they thought I was doing out before light but I felt them staring at me with contempt.

I am not sure I like the people in this apartment house.

Alice was awake and so happy when she saw me come in. She had set up her rag doll at the table and put a teaspoon of porridge in the doll's bowl. Alice is such a treasure, the delight of my life.

After breakfast we pulled the kitchen chairs over to the front window and pretended to be at the pictures. We are on the fifth floor and have a nice view of the courtyard and front walk. We watched people leaving the building, men in fedoras and Ulster coats. And two women with white nurses' caps on. No one wore the silly face masks. I hope they don't catch the flu. Or bring it back to Farmdale Court.

In his socks and his robe, he went to his front door, pinching the velvet curtain ever so slightly so he could peek out. The landing was empty. He adjusted his eyes to the light from the hallway and listened to the air whoosh under his door. He heard nothing else. Then her door swung open and she appeared in pyjamas and her ankle boots, arms laden with bags of garbage. He jumped away quickly and let the curtain fall back, afraid she might see him.

She made considerable noise right outside his door, dropping one of the bags on the floor, cursing as the contents spilled, bottles and cans clinking together. Then he heard the hard click of her heels descending the steps. He waited a moment.

He opened his door slowly and inched out to the landing. She must be taking her garbage to the disposal chute, which was one floor below on seven, midway down the corridor. He gave her a second or two to get there and then he followed her down, silent and undetected in his padded hiking socks.

There she was going down the dim hallway. He hung back on the seventh-floor landing and observed her walk away from him down the narrow hall. She stumbled against the wall, unbalanced by the bags she carried, or maybe a little drunk from the wine. Her shoulder brushed the wall, rubbed the faded brown roses on the wallpaper, and a wine bottle fell out of her grasp and rolled onto the carpet.

It was against the rules to take out garbage this late at night.

He could admonish her. Put her in her place.

Her shadow fell intermittently beside her as she passed the apartment doors under the single bulb lighting each one. Then she reached the garbage chute at a point in the hall where the wallpaper was stained with greasy handprints. When she bent to put the bags on the floor—the spot of carpet there was similarly marred and filthy—he was afraid she would turn her head and catch him watching her.

He fled upstairs as she opened the closet door containing the chute. It screeched as she pulled open the metal trap to slide the first bag down. By the time the garbage fell to the basement, clanging and banging against the inner metal walls, by the time she had taken the last batch and shoved it down, he was already home, catching his breath behind the velvet curtain.

DWELLING

He felt her when she returned on the landing, inches away from his sweating palms and his rapidly beating heart.

18

The bright full moon was visible through the uncurtained window over the yellow bed. Not until clouds formed in the sky and obscured the moonlight could Nora fall asleep. She slept fitfully, intermittently waking up too hot under the duvet and then too cold after she tossed it to the floor.

Nora dreamt and in the dream she flew through the rooms of her former house. A strange disquieting version of the house she had known. She flew through walls and the roof, looking down at scenes altered beyond reality, rooms missing fourth walls as in doll houses, with incongruous furniture and unfamiliar inhabitants. And a sense that she could not stop flying, could not land if she wanted to.

She flew through the white kitchen, over the marble worktop where coloured shapes like spilled paint oozed on the counters and into the dining room where her husband Carter sat at the table, bleeding from his mouth.

She flew over a king-size bed, the bed in the room on the second floor overlooking the garden, the room where she had slept with her husband. She saw herself naked and writhing in the marital bed.

Not a dream; a nightmare. If only she could wake and make it stop. She would fly to Dylan. Fly to her beautiful baby in the nursery. Cornflower blue walls. White curtains luffing softly like sails in a breeze. Music box playing happy rhymes. Sunflowers sprouting towards a white crib as the nursery morphed into a field.

She flew to Dylan, safe in the white crib.

And then the crib was gone and there was no baby Dylan anymore. Only Carter staggering towards Nora with his blood leeching all over the sunflowers.

Nora woke violently and lay shaking in the little yellow bed. Her heart pounded, head throbbed. The house was gone to her now. She was awake in the apartment on Farmdale.

She had saved herself from Carter.

* * *

Every time Carter hit Nora he'd said *he was really going to hurt her this time.* He preceded each beating with shouting and yelling as a prologue before the physical attacks. She still heard his voice, felt his words vibrate like a sensation in her own throat. She could hear him yell that she was to blame for all that happened to sweet baby Dylan.

As if Nora could have prevented the child's illness.

As if he hadn't started hitting Nora years before they ever had a child.

Bitch. No one will miss you when I kill you.

* * *

She sat up. She was dizzy and disoriented from the dream, but she knew where she was. It was the middle of the night. Carter was dead and baby Dylan was gone too.

She put her feet on the floor and got slowly out of bed. She switched on the unicorn lamp. The teak chair was close to the bed, a heap of laundry on the seat cushion. A tea-stained mug on the table. This one-room apartment was her home now.

She noticed a low, irritating, insistent noise somewhere in the walls.

A sound like fingernails scratching on wood.

No wonder she slept poorly in this place. The old walls thrummed with sound. Wood expanding or contracting, water dripping.

She got out of bed and steadied herself with a hand on the wall. The plaster felt cold and she realised the heat had gone off.

The scratching was louder.

The only illumination came from the unicorn lamp. Why had she bought the silly thing? She really needed a brighter source of light.

She was thirsty from too much salt at dinner. Some warm milk would help her get back to sleep. In three steps she was in the dark kitchen.

Scritch. Scratch. It could be a mouse between the walls. She put an ear to the surface but heard nothing.

She opened the fridge and listened to it hum. There was no milk left.

The noise started again.

The scratching came from the closet and the thought that occurred to her was it must be the cat from next door. The cat was always running out of Henry's place and was probably hiding in her closet. Rubbing itself on her clothing.

She couldn't stand the thought of cat hair all over her wool skirt and her coat.

She opened the door, annoyed. This was the reason she never

wanted pets. She pushed aside the hanging clothing, her coat, pants, skirts, more unwashed laundry on the floor.

There was no cat hiding in the closet.

Henry's vacuum cleaner was still there behind her coat, lodged in a corner. The noise, the incessant scratching, came from the vacuum's clear plastic canister.

Nora snatched it from the corner. She felt the thing vibrating. It buzzed with something trapped and alive. Something desperate to escape.

In the dim light she could indistinctly make out a tangled black mass in the canister.

The mass writhed.

She screamed and held the vacuum away from her like a contagion, afraid to drop it on the floor. She darted to the fire escape door. She shoved it open with her shoulder and climbed out.

Her bare feet froze on the metal slats and she was afraid she might slip and fall in the darkness. It was freezing cold outside. She wanted only to open the canister and dump the hideous contents over the railing. She raised the vacuum higher. It was heavy and it unbalanced her. The black mass moved against the canister walls like a creature in a cage. In a panic she lost her grip.

The vacuum fell from her hands. It fell over the railing and down. It crashed and shattered on the laneway pavement, eight floors below.

19

Henry made his morning coffee and drank two cups of it while he read the diary.

November 22, 1918

I went to the school office to ask Principal Mathers when I could return and was told that female teachers must work as nurses with the Sisters of Service. The Toronto Daily Star reported that there are so many bedridden patients, temporary hospital wards have been set up in school gymnasiums and church basements.

I am to go for training tomorrow at St. Clement's Church. I have never cared for a sick person in my life, except Alice when she had a fever as an infant.

He made toast and buttered it lavishly. He spread extra marma-lade and relished each bite. The food and coffee roused him while he read and waited for sounds from Nora's apartment. He heard her run water in the kitchen and knew she would soon leave for work.

November 23, 1918

I attended for nurse training. I left a cheese sandwich and some apples for Alice. I told her to play quietly and that I would be home as soon as it got dark. The darling girl seemed happy enough with her blocks and doll but I was worried. What if someone came knocking at the door? I truly wish I knew a friendly woman in the building who could look after Alice.

He finished his breakfast. All was silent in Nora's kitchen. He went to his front door and listened behind the velvet curtain for steps on the landing. He wanted a chance to talk to her before she left.

December 6, 1918

Sadly, three patients died today. It was an enormous shock and I had to wait out back for the hearse to come from the funeral home. When the men arrived with stretchers, they looked very sombre and tired.

The driver told me they had been back and forth "doing collections", as he called it, all night.

He asked for a cup of Bovril, which I gave him, and then directed him and his assistant to the right beds.

We had left the dead resting in their cots as if they were simply sleeping. The poor deceased souls were removed discretely from the hall before we wrapped them in sheets outside the church, so we wouldn't alarm the other patients.

He grabbed a rag and broom and went out on the landing. He polished his doorknob with the rag and then he began on hers. She opened the door and he stepped back.

"Oh," she said.

"Just getting started on the day," he said. "Nice surprise to see you."

"Yes." She came out in her black ankle boots, tying the belt of her coat. She looked at the rag in his hand and the broom he'd propped against the stair rail. "Oh," she said again. "Your vacuum. About that—"

"I'll get it later."

She made no move forward; she seemed to be waiting for something more. She wore the shiny lip gloss.

"Do you need to borrow anything else?"

"I don't know. Maybe." She pulled a clip of some sort from her pocket and gathered her hair into a ponytail, smoothed the hair with her hands and pulled it back. It was an intimate thing to do right in front of him while he watched. He took it as a sign of her interest in him.

"Come for a drink. I can show you more of the diary."

"Maybe." He took it as a yes. She slid past him and he let her go down the stairs.

December 7, 1918

Today I did not have to report for work. It was a relief to get away from sadness and illness. I took Alice for a walk outside. By chance as we were going down the stairs I ran into the Robertson twins. I taught the boys a few years ago and had no idea the family lived at Farmdale. Mrs. Robertson insisted we stop in for tea. So she met Alice and now my secret is out. Mrs. Robertson did not comment.

Their apartment was a flurry of activity. The boys were jumping with excitement and Mrs. Robertson was very distracted telling them to get off the furniture. There was a man there with all sorts of tools and wires, installing a telephone in their apartment—the first one in the building. I don't think the twins have any inkling what a telephone is. They never paid the slightest attention to lessons when they were in my class.

I thought of asking Mrs. Robertson to take in Alice while I am working, but she already has her hands full with those boys.

I brought Alice outside to walk around the building courtyard. Then we walked in the back laneway where a strange thing happened.

I had an eerie sense that someone walked behind us and when I turned around I saw a large, mangy dog running fast towards us. I moved Alice away because I didn't want her to be bitten but when I looked back the dog had vanished and a man stood in its place, leaning against the fence.

He came out of nowhere and I was frightened.

20

Nora found excuses to take extra shifts at work. It wasn't simply for the income, though she needed the money. There was comradery in the busy store, especially with her friends Kyle and Izzy. Ever since the dinner party, she'd felt closer to both of them. And with Kyle, especially, a delicious but subtle sense of attraction grew. They held hands, they kissed. It hadn't progressed further because he was being considerate. She could tell he was waiting for her to make the next move.

Izzy asked her if they had hooked up yet and expressed astonishment at how chaste the relationship was. Nora was too circumspect to admit she'd only ever been with one man. Who would believe such a thing? And beyond the embarrassment of limited experience was her reluctance to talk about her marriage.

Besides, while she and Kyle continued acting as if they were innocent, there remained the excitement of possibility. The delectable anticipation.

She took her breaks in the back room at Lakeview Coffee. Someone who'd been in the room earlier had left the air saturated with smoke. Smoking was prohibited, but in the cold of December people were loath to duck outside and stand in the frigid air. The room often stank of cigarette smoke and weed. Though Kyle asked people to smoke both outdoors, the armrests of the couch she sat on were pock-marked with burns. She put her finger in a hole and ripped the imitation leather a little more.

Henry was a smoker. She'd seen him with a cigarette walking in the laneway or standing in back of the building. The other day he'd come up from the basement just as she went through the vestibule. He had a heavy-set man with him, an exterminator, Henry said. Both of them reeked of smoke. We fixed a problem, he'd told her, the whole city was infested.

Kyle came into the break room, his face flushed and his hair a little stringy from the previous hours of steam at the counter.

"My turn for a rest," he said, holding out his hands to help her up from the sagging couch.

Nora said, "I guess I should forget it."

"What?" Kyle said.

She laughed. "I'm having a conversation in my head. You don't want to hear it."

"Sure I do." He plopped down on the couch and put his phone down beside him.

"It's about bugs."

"Please tell me you didn't see any in the store."

She changed the subject. "How's the songwriting going?"

He was working on something for his band, which he talked about constantly, thinking she was interested, even though she had ducked his invitation to hear them play in a bar.

"Want to help me?" he said. "You can take an extra ten minutes and write some lyrics."

He sprawled out on the couch and patted the seat. "Come here," he said.

She sat back down next to him, snuggled against his shoulder. He smelled of laundry soap and coffee. They all smelled like coffee while they were at work.

They kissed.

"Seriously." A long face atop a skinny body appeared in the doorway. It was one of the new hires Kyle had taken on for the Christmas rush. She couldn't remember his name. "We need help out there." He pulled his head out of the doorway and was gone.

Nora started to get up but Kyle tugged gently on her arm, keeping her on the couch. "I'm the boss," he said. "Not that guy."

"I want to go help Izzy," she said. She'd had enough of him for now.

* * *

Izzy seemed never to get tired. She didn't stand behind the counter, she danced, bopping between the shiny copper espresso machine and the industrial fridge. Kyle had laughingly reminded her to be careful more than once, saying the espresso maker cost as much as a car. Izzy twirled a pirouette. Nora said she'd take over the register and prodded Izzy away. Izzy stepped back, raised her arms in a stretch and arched her back like a high diver about to plunge off the board.

"Ah, that's better," she said, releasing herself out of the stretch. She gave her arms a shake. "It's been madness."

"Yes," Nora said. "Also, I love your hair."

Izzy had a new purple streak running along one side of her bright white hair and had cut it into short spikes. She looked like a pixie, Tinkerbell.

"Did you and Kyle lose track of the time?" Izzy teased. "Did it finally happen?"

"I had a little nap," Nora said. "Really, I needed it. I never sleep at night anymore."

Izzy scooped ice and poured milk into the blender. People ordered cold coffee all year.

"Why can't you sleep?" Izzy said. "I'm out the moment I hit the pillow."

Nora wasn't certain what kept her awake, what prevented sleep despite her exhaustion. It was partly the nightmares, but also the noises of the old building waking her, wood swelling and settling, pipes banging behind walls. How chilly the apartment was in the dead of night.

* * *

Some days after work Nora wandered the streets of nearby Chinatown, not really needing to shop for anything, but wanting to delay the commute across town to Farmdale Court. Today was such a day. The evening streets were busy and cold, and she strolled from store to store.

She held a knotted end of fresh ginger and considered whether to buy it. There was jasmine tea for sale in colourful foil packets, but she had a full box of Earl Grey in her cupboard. She couldn't spend more money on tea. She walked under red paper lanterns and imagined them hanging in her apartment.

A bar of sandalwood soap covered with intricately patterned paper was only a dollar. She turned it over in her hand, inhaling the aroma. In the end, she put it back on the shelf.

Nothing would make the cramped apartment as beautiful as her house had been.

In a place called The Bamboo Emporium she examined delicate blue and white porcelain rice bowls and white soup tureens, brass Buddha figures and jade carvings. She bought none of the wonderful things.

There were shelves of inexpensive toys. Little wind-up gizmos smaller than the palm of her hand, tin ducks that quacked and four-piece wooden puzzles. She wound up a badly painted beagle that took a few steps before falling over and considered a net bag of silver jacks and a jump-rope with musical handles.

She had loved buying toys for Dylan, and collecting beautifully illustrated books that she had ordered from bookshops in England and arranged on white shelves in the nursery.

When she thought of Dylan's toys and Dylan's pretty room, it was as if her daughter was right there. A plump healthy baby who'd never contracted meningitis. She wished she could return home right now and hold her sweet child.

She left the store in a daze and found herself in a small produce and kitchen-goods market next door. Mechanically, she selected a bamboo vegetable steamer and wooden chopsticks. She chose a bunch of bok choy, and a slab of firm tofu. Cooking would distract her from her thoughts, from her bitter resentment that her new city life had not expunged sad memories of the old one.

It was too dark now and bitterly cold. She passed a store with a display table on the sidewalk, trinkets and small items arrayed for sale. The world was taunting her with these baubles. Reminding her that factories went on making things even when babies died.

She grabbed a little plastic coin purse, pink, with the face of Hello Kitty on the front. Certain that she was unobserved, she dropped it into her pocket.

21

Nora boarded the Dundas streetcar, managed to find a seat half-way to the back and tried to peer out the dirt-streaked windows. At each stop, a passenger pulled the cord signaling the driver they wanted to get off. When someone left, other riders waiting on the boulevards and curbs clamoured on. By the time they reached Spadina, the articulated streetcar was at maximum capacity and the driver flew through the intersection without stopping, despite several passengers angrily ringing the bell and yelling. Nora sweated uncomfortably.

"Move to the back," the driver shouted, even though the back was already packed with passengers. At the next red light, the doors nearest her slid open and a little girl climbed up from the street, her father assisting by boosting her up slightly from behind. The girl, entombed in a thick pink snowsuit, walked with stiff legs. She made straight for Nora, little round face beaming in delight, and held her arms out to be lifted to Nora's lap.

The young father, burdened with a knapsack and bags of groceries, tried to stop her.

"No honey, that's not Auntie," he said. He stuck out a foot to steer his child away and said to Nora, "Sorry. So sorry. Did she get mud on you?"

The little girl looked at Nora and her father in confusion.

"It's okay," Nora said. "I'm a mom too."

The child clamoured to get onto a seat. A woman with white ear buds and a computer open on her lap refused to budge, and the child whimpered until an older man rose and offered his seat to the little girl.

The father sat the child down and she immediately kicked her legs at the woman beside her. Nora suppressed a laugh. The father apologized and positioned himself in front of the child so she wouldn't kick or try to climb down from the seat. The little girl poked her head around his legs, staring at Nora. Nora smiled, causing the child to burst into tears.

"She had a tough time at daycare today," the man said. "A lot of kids sick with colds." He gave the child a cookie. "And she misses her Auntie."

The fat little cheeks reddened with tears, the chocolate cookie squished and melting in the girl's hand.

Nora felt strangled by the heat in the overcrowded streetcar, all the voices, the smell of camphor on winter coats newly taken out of storage and raw fish carried home from shops, the takeout McDonald's consumed on the streetcar, the lurching stops and starts. It was overwhelming. She thought she might vomit. She stood up and felt dizzy. She might faint.

The windows had fogged up, everything outside was a blur, she was unable to see where they were. It might be Church or Victoria already, past where she needed to get off. Distracted by the child and the heat and her urge to leave, she missed her stop and the connection to the subway.

She pressed the 'stop request' button, pressed it two or three times until she heard the electronic bell that told her it had registered, and without knowing or caring where she was, rushed to the exit.

Out in the cold air, she felt almost as desperate. Exhaust fumes from traffic, the cacophony of trucks and cars that rumbled over ruts and potholes, tires splashing through puddles, sprays of brown water hitting her legs.

She moved with the surge of pedestrians, the city inhospitable to them as they navigated the sidewalks. She walked north up Yonge Street, clutching her shopping bag until she passed Dundas Square, where she had bought the yellow bed. The music was loud and obnoxious, the billboards flashing above solitary seedy men and packs of aimless young people huddled in the cold, smoking, waiting for the next fix, the next whatever.

Nora walked, head down, passing cannabis dispensaries, bars, fast-food joints. She knew enough about Toronto by now to understand that eye contact in some neighbourhoods, certainly in this one, only invited people to approach you, demanding money. You had to walk with purpose, even if you had none, to be left alone. She walked north several blocks.

At the intersection, while she waited with the crowd to cross, she saw she was in front of a red brick building. Bright light emanated from inside and spilled on the pavement. It was the central reference library at Bloor Street. She decided to go in.

The entrance to the building was a wall of heavy glass doors where people surged in and out. A beggar held the door open for her, standing beside it like an imposter doorman, providing a service no one desired. She was halfway through the door as he reached out his arm imploring her for money, impeding her progress. She slid around him. He was thin, unshaven, black gaps in his open mouth from missing teeth. He thrust out a battered paper coffee cup—Tim Hortons—for donations. She averted her eyes.

It wasn't that she was unsympathetic to the man. He might be one of the unhoused, people who roamed the city with nowhere to shelter. She understood that home could be a precarious thing. It wasn't the man's fault he needed money, but she had none to spare.

"You have a nice day," he said.

The library was crowded and overheated. She was sorry now to have come in. The large lobby of the library contained a make-shift encampment, prone bodies everywhere. People appeared to be living there and had set up private areas with tarpaulins and cardboard boxes marking territory. There were red picnic cool-ers and dirty blue duffle bags, blankets and sleeping bags piled everywhere.

She stepped around a tent, the flap open, revealing a woman lying inside. Plastic bags were strewn on the floor, people slept on the carpet, their bodies covered head to toe in blankets. Beside some of the human bundles lay unopened Styrofoam meal boxes or sandwiches in plastic wrap, crumpled paper bags from take-out joints, clean rolled socks. Someone must be helping the desti-tute people by providing these disparate offerings.

Nora wondered what it would be like to have no home of her own. No place to go at the end of a day, just a dubious and temporary claim to space in the foyer of a public building.

Carter never gave money to charity, even though he could have afforded to. She felt a pang of guilt for her former lifestyle. She had been selfish. Taking a small yellow cabbage out of her shopping bag, she placed it near the head of a sleeping man. Next time I'm here, she told herself, I'll bring them some McDonald's.

114

She should really turn around and go home; she was tired now. But she was propelled by some urge into the library, into the vast computer room. Tiered rows of tables topped by dozens of screens blinked in the semi-darkened space, placards on the tables announced free internet for anyone who wanted it.

People bent forward at the long tables, hunched over keyboards. The low lighting, absence of windows and muffled sound lent the room a reverential tone. No one spoke, except one man talking loudly into a headset. Beside him was the only empty chair in the room. She took it.

She lodged her bags under the desk and logged on. The computer was grimy, smudged with fingerprints and grease from multiple users. People in the room coughed and sneezed. She told herself as she tapped the sticky keyboard to keep her hands away from her face, not to let her germy fingers stray to her eyes or mouth until she had washed her hands.

She entered her query into the search bar and looked around the room before making her selection from the results. The man beside her had turned away from her, he was in his own bubble of intensity while he spoke into the phone. No one was interested in what she was doing.

She entered her town's name.

A schedule of away games for the high school football season. A newspaper article about a land dispute between a local farmer and a First Nations band over the unearthing of a sacred burial site. A wedding announcement for someone she barely recalled.

Nervous, she went to another tab and stared vacantly at the Google logo. The teenager sitting on her other side watched a movie, his chin down on his forearms, headphones as large as earmuffs. He certainly was not interested in what she had on her screen.

She typed in her question. To be sure nothing had changed. And found the town paper, *The Sentinel*.

The article said the police were investigating the death of local lawyer Carter Birmingham. And the disappearance of his wife Nora Birmingham.

Nora was too warm in the crowded library room. The man next to her spoke into his phone.

Autopsy results were inconclusive.

Police had interviewed neighbours—

"C'mon man," the guy next to Nora said. "Once in a lifetime opportunity." He spoke too loudly into his phone. He punched at the keyboard while real estate listings scrolled by on the screen, his face reflecting yellow and blue.

"You're an idiot if you don't buy." The man winked at Nora before turning back to his screen.

The police were working on the theory of suicide. Neighbours hinted at financial problems.

The computer users were very close together. There were several rows of people behind her. She didn't want anyone to see what she was reading.

She had rented the apartment and taken her job using her maiden name, Nora Davis. Maybe that had been stupid. Should have concocted something entirely new.

The man beside her spoke forcefully enough that spit flew onto his screen. "I've got the perfect property for you." He was the only person talking so loudly. Everyone else observed the current library etiquette—not complete silence, just low murmurs.

She should leave, go back to the apartment, forget the past.

But there it was a few clicks away on her screen. An anonymous source had told the police about "problems" in the marriage. A photo of Carter showed Nora smiling beside him;

116

they looked like a normal, happy couple. She wondered who in her circle knew anything about problems in her marriage.

The man on the phone beside her said something about a house in a great school district. She thought of her friend Bila from the playground, how she noticed things Nora wanted to hide. She scanned the article. There was no mention of Dylan.

She couldn't think with the man's voice blathering while she read. She wanted to leave the library, to be home. Quickly, she cleared the search history. She got up abruptly, moving her chair over sharply until it collided with the man on the phone and he rocked sideways, dislodging his phone cord and losing his connection.

She ran to the exit.

22

She welcomed the cold air, and by the time she reached the sidewalk on Farmdale Lane she felt better. Everything looked almost pleasant covered in snow, like a path in a country field. But it was deceptive. The snow disguised uneven pavement, the divots and holes. Nora tried to step in the footprints other walkers had already made, but she found this hard-going and slippery, the sidewalks were perilous with ice and snow forged into uneven ridges where it wasn't trodden down. With each tentative step forward, she slid one back. Her ankle boots were a fashion statement not meant for winter weather.

No one had bothered to lay down salt to melt the ice, a task the city left up to individual property owners to save municipal costs. Evidently, people didn't care about their neighbours' safety around here. Decorating for Christmas was still on the agenda, though. A few residents had made the effort to hang red and green lights from their eavestroughs. In some yards, a few strands of tiny white bulbs were wound unevenly on spindly trees.

An elderly woman stuck her head in and out from a doorway,

like a bird pecking at seeds. After some tentative pecks, the woman emerged fully in bedroom slippers and a nightgown and walked in small, halting steps to the sidewalk from her porch. She peered inside a black mailbox mounted on the shaky wooden fence, found it empty, and tottered back. She lost her balance and Nora was sure she would end up splayed in the snow. She stood clinging to the fence, looking bewildered, as Nora walked by.

If she'd been a good neighbour herself, she would have offered the old lady assistance.

Her building had snow blown against the bottom bricks. The walkway and sidewalks in front had been dutifully cleared with a small snowblower, which stood against the near wall. Henry was out front making finishing touches, moving snow off the front stoop with a shovel. The dull scraping of the metal blade against concrete grew louder as she came closer, his efforts echoed off the wings of the building and around the courtyard. A few lights glowed in upper windows and smoke from the furnace rose into the early evening sky.

The building had not been decorated for Christmas. Nora thought of remarking on this to Henry and asking if there was a box of lights in the basement to string up or if he'd be putting a tree in the front vestibule. Motivate him to spruce up the place for the holiday. Coming home to festive decorations would be welcoming.

He might not be interested in such things, or there could be budget restrictions. She would get something to hang on her own apartment door, some inexpensive seasonal items from the Chinatown shops.

At home every Christmas she'd always put up a real cedar wreath on the front door. And a small wooden angel with gossamer wings under the window, nestled in the shrubs. Dylan loved the little angel. And of course, a glorious tree in the living room.

At least Henry was mindful of safety. The stones on the walkway leading to the front door were cleared of ice and snow right down to the pavement. No one would trip and fall here, even her thinly soled boots gave her some traction as she stepped along the path to the door.

Henry looked up and watched as she came towards him. He wore a thick flannel jacket with a leather collar turned up against the wind, and dark green work gloves. He removed the gloves when he saw her and pushed back his cap, resting his hands on the handle of the shovel. His blonde hair was damp with perspiration.

"Hello," he said. "Don't you just love this weather? So invigorating."

She preferred warmer weather, but why bother to explain?

"Yes. Feels like Christmas is around the corner. We've got the decorations up at work already." She didn't know why she mentioned it, wanted to swallow back her words when he looked strangely at her. She was fixating on holiday ornaments.

"I'll string lights. Eventually," he said, and looked up to the sky. "Have to dig out the box from last year."

She followed his gaze up to the roof where presumably he would hang his Christmas lights. Up to the eaves where the snow collected in solid chunks. She squinted against the glare of a streetlamp and saw long icicles hanging from the roof edge. Long pointed daggers of sharp ice.

"I wouldn't stand directly under those," he said. "They could pierce a skull."

It hurt her neck to look up at that angle. She moved out from under the icicles. What an odd thing for him to say. "Will you knock them down?"

He laughed. Then scooped up a handful of snow and tossed it up into the air. It landed by her feet. "Too high to climb."

She started up the steps to go inside.

"You're only coming from work now?" He stepped on the fallen snowball, smooshing it down. "Where is it you work?"

She had told him where she worked. She wondered why he was pretending not to remember. "Downtown," she said. She was not going to tell him again that she worked at Lakeview Coffee. His initial reaction when she had first mentioned her employment weeks ago had been condescending, as if her job was contemptible. Which was rich, considering he was basically a janitor.

"One of those temp jobs, right?" he said.

Didn't he remember their conversations? He seemed always eager to engage her, ask her about herself, but then he acted as if he wasn't paying attention to her responses, like he was testing her out. Trying to catch her in a lie.

Carter had spoken to her that way, and it had bothered her, but it wasn't the same coming from Henry because she wasn't married to him. She almost wanted to laugh at his feeble attempt. She deflected by changing the topic. "I find the building a little cold at night." She was careful not to sound reproachful. It was important to stay friendly so he would be helpful. There were other issues in the building she needed him for: the pilot light on the stove went out often, the window rattled.

Henry resumed his scraping, using the shovel to pick intently at a patch of ice.

"That's just the nature of old buildings," he said. "The insulation is basically newspaper and horsehair."

She was chilly standing still out in the cold.

"But I'll turn up the furnace a little for you."

"Thank you," she said. He wasn't an unkind landlord. "Well. I'll see you."

"Listen, Nora," Henry's body blocked the width of the path in front of her. He stopped chipping at the ice, put a foot on the edge of the shovel and waited for her full attention. "I'm going to bring you a few things, might be useful, this evening."

He said it like a command, not asking if she was free or wanted whatever things he might bring. Her evening plans were to eat and go to bed. She was exhausted. But perhaps it was only another way of expressing kindness, helping her.

She told him she would be free after dinner.

He returned to shovelling.

As she moved forward, a slab of snow and ice broke off from the roof. It slid down and landed on a withered oak limb, severing it from the trunk.

"A big one," he said. He pulled his cap lower over his forehead. "That branch was dead anyway. Saves me some trouble lopping it off." He resumed his slow scraping. "See you later, then."

*　*　*

In the vestibule, the two facing radiators were turned up full blast, creating too much heat for such a small space. Nora almost went back to Henry to point this out, the incongruity of overheating the foyer while leaving her apartment too cold, but he and his shovel were no longer in sight. She hastily unbuttoned her coat and removed her hat and gloves. The hat had flattened her hair and her nails were dry and brittle. It had been ages since she'd been to a salon for a professional manicure or hair treatment. One nail was broken with sharp, ragged edges.

Metal mailboxes hung on the wall over one of the radiators. A symmetrical arrangement of eight horizontal rows, one for every apartment, each box locked tight. Her own tiny mailbox key dangled from a small heart-shaped ring, along with keys to her unit door and the building. Each mailbox had a little open-slotted window revealing whether or not there was mail inside. Even without a key, you could prod a finger into the slot of any one of them, if you were nosy and intrepid and unafraid of the finger getting stuck. She imagined children must do that all the time, if they were tall enough to reach the boxes.

She hadn't received any mail since moving to Farmdale Lane. Although she checked her box every day when she returned home, it was always empty. Not even a utility bill; the rent covered all that. She never saw the credit card bill. She'd kept it going by paying the minimum balance at the bank in person each month. She assumed the bill was still arriving in the mail at the house. Odd that it hadn't been cancelled. There must be thousands owing by now.

And there was no personal mail for her. No one knew where she was.

She opened her mailbox and swept her hand to the back of it. Empty.

Other people had loads of mail. There was always a curiously interesting pile of unclaimed or misdelivered mail splayed haphazardly on the shelf on top of the radiator. Magazines, junk mail flyers from the supermarket, letters. She liked to rifle through it, telling herself it might be hers. She always made sure she was alone in the vestibule and no one watched.

She read the names on envelopes in the pile of unclaimed mail. The mechanical whir of the snow blower outside told her Henry was occupied on the sidewalk, away from the front door. She picked up a pale blue envelope with a handwritten address and an American stamp. It was for someone on the seventh floor.

She slipped it in her pocket.

She could always return it to the pile later. Or crumple it up and throw it away. Whoever it was intended for had obviously moved out. No one would know.

It wasn't fair that she got no mail.

She'd loved getting mail when she was a child. Writing a letter and dropping it in the mailbox for someone else to receive was fun too. She'd never have the chance to make handmade cards with Dylan, to teach her daughter how to properly address an envelope. She would never hold a Mother's Day card lovingly signed by her child.

A shadow passed through the vestibule as light filtered through the wavy glass of the front door. Henry bent over to drag the broken tree branch to the curb. She picked up a cream envelope addressed elaborately in gold embossed cursive. It looked like a wedding invitation.

She rubbed the thick stock between her fingers, then dropped it in the pocket of her coat to join the blue envelope, a used Kleenex and a subway transfer.

23

Nora woke up on the yellow bed. The grocery bag, partially unpacked, still held the tofu and vegetables and gave off a faint scent of celery and onion when she stirred against the bag, where it rested on the end of the bed. She had meant to unpack it in the kitchen and lie down for a moment before cooking her supper.

She must have dozed off. The last thing she remembered was looking out the window over the bed at the orange December sun, watching while it sank quickly and the room darkened as the light dipped below the horizon.

She was awake now, and her apartment was dark.

It felt strange to wake up alone in a bed, after so many years of sleeping next to Carter. In the room in the house overlooking the green lawn and the neighbour's garden with its ancient rose bushes. Now she was alone in her own small apartment. It should feel victorious, but it didn't.

She got out of the yellow bed and switched on the unicorn lamp. It cast a narrow arc of light above and below the lampshade. The rest of the room was dark.

This apartment, this crumbling building, was her refuge now.

No more the terror of waking up next to Carter and unwittingly setting off his anger.

She straightened the duvet and smoothed it down over the bed. Dust flew up under the lamplight.

The beautiful house had not shielded her from a violent man.

She took the grocery bag into the kitchen and put the frying pan on the stove. The fridge hummed softly and when she opened the door to look inside, the motor knocked as if greeting her and then turned itself off. There was nothing inside the fridge she wanted.

She had been reckless staying in the marriage with Carter, had let the big house and the money blind her to what he really was.

This little alcove of a kitchen was hardly large enough for one person to cook in. She could reach the fridge and the stove and the sink without moving an inch. She poured oil into the pan and lit the stove. Her movements made no shadows under the single hanging lightbulb.

The kitchen in the house had been completely renovated, the appliances imported from Europe and the marble from a quarry in Italy. It hardly seemed real now, her former life. Had it all been just shadow and illusion?

The tap dripped in the sink.

The vegetables languished on the counter getting warm in the heat from the radiator, the celery stalks wilting in the plastic wrapping. The block of tofu sweated and looked like a lump of unappetizing modelling clay. It seemed too much effort to wash and chop and fry it all.

She looked in the cupboard for something easier to eat. There was a jar of pickles and a pot of raspberry jam. A tin of lima beans. She reached to the top shelf and found tomato soup in the red, white and gold can. The soup she'd grown up eating, served by her mother when she came home for lunch on school days. The same soup she'd fed to Dylan. She doubted the design on the can had ever changed in all the years of manufacture. Soup for the ages, she thought. And a source of comfort.

She pierced the lid with the slightly rusty and stiff can-opener from the collection of kitchen implements Henry had given her. He may have given her the can of soup as well. For all she knew, like so much else in this decrepit building, the soup had been in the back of the cupboard since 1918. She scooped out the thick blob of red puree, dropped it into a pot and added a tin-full of cold water.

She ate the red soup from one of the pink bowls where it looked garish in the clash of colours, and it was both too salty and too sweet yet tasted so amazing. She gulped down more of it straight from the pot, standing over the sink. Then she felt full and nauseous. Her head throbbed.

There was a knock at the door. She wasn't expecting anyone. Be still, ignore it until they go away.

Then she remembered her conversation outside with Henry. He knew she was home, was probably standing there behind the glass-panelled door. The flimsy curtain she'd put up was translucent and did little to shield her. He'd notice the lamplight.

When she opened the door, Toffee darted in and flew across the floor, furry tail whipping up dust motes. The cat slunk along the perimeter of the room and then crawled under the bed to hide. In the doorway were two figures: Henry and a woman.

The woman stepped in first. She was tall like Henry, large-boned and solid, poised somewhere in her mid-sixties, with a big, square face, handsome but not beautiful. Her wide brown eyes were nice enough; it was the mouth that robbed her of true beauty, a small, thin-lipped track. A hard slash of bright red lipstick rendered the lips even thinner, like a streak of angry underlining on a page.

"I am Esme," she said.

The woman and Henry both stared at her, mirrored looks of concern on their faces.

She had meant to tidy up before Henry came by.

"I was just eating," Nora said. "Excuse the mess."

Esme wore a thick tweed skirt and jacket, soft mauve flecked with gold and white thread, classically elegant, like a matronly woman in a society photo from the nineteen-forties.

Nora picked up a sweater and a scarf from the teak chair so the woman could have a seat.

Esme wore a hat. Incongruously. An outdoors hat, meant for the cold. A Russian-style fur hat, rich and luxurious, the exact colour of the woman's hair, tawny brown. Nora was fascinated by the hat and knew she was staring at it. It was at least four inches high with straight sides and probably mink.

Esme smiled with her thin red lips. She indulged Nora's gawking. Then she removed the hat, lifting it straight up like removing a crown. Her thick, dry hair swirled in a top-knot and was secured firmly with a tortoise-shell comb.

"Oh, we won't stay, dear," Esme said. She came towards the window, cradling the hat in both arms protectively like a baby. "What a charming room."

"Here are the supplements," Henry said. He gripped several cloth shopping bags, and he held them aloft as if asking where to put them. Every surface in the apartment was covered with stuff. He glanced at the pile of clothes on the floor and the dirty mugs on the table, and Nora was ashamed to be so slovenly.

The gold filaments in the cloth of Esme's suit shimmered and seemed to trail off into the air. Henry put the bags on the kitchen counter. "Make yourself useful dear," Esme said to him, nodding her head. The pile of hair shook a little as she nodded, strands came loose from the clip. She winked at Nora, co-conspirator against stupid men. They took things out of the bags. Jars and jars came out. One glass jar was filled with green powder.

"This one brings lucidity," Esme said. She unpacked more jars.

Was this woman going to sell these things, charge money for products she hawks? In her old town, lots of women did this to make extra money. Pushed cosmetics or vitamins to other women at afternoon get-togethers. There was an unspoken obligation to buy some useless item just to keep a friendship alive.

Esme waved some twigs in the air, then brought them under Nora's nose.

"Breathe deeply."

She wasn't going to buy twigs. But she inhaled. It was pleasant: rosemary and lemon. Her shoulders relaxed, the pinched feeling in her neck wafted away. Perhaps there was an herb or spice here she could use after all.

"Dear, Henry tells me you have been tired. Not quite yourself."

Had she mentioned that she was tired? She must remember not to tell Henry anything. He was too interested in the details of her life that were none of his business.

Nora picked up a small glass pot of dried leaves. Esme took it from her hands and lined it up precisely with the other jars on the counter.

"I'll tell you what everything is later."

"I can't possibly buy all of it."

"My dear. Don't be silly. No one wants your money. This is a gift from Henry."

The red lipstick was smooth and creamy. Beige powder nestled in creases around the red mouth. A scent of lilac perfume in the twist of hair.

Henry had been at her elbow, reaching for the jars. Now he was doing something in the other room. He unplugged the unicorn lamp and moved it to another electrical outlet. "There's a short circuit," he said. "We've got illegal wiring, apparently." He laughed. "I'm supposed to fix it. But in the meantime, this lamp is a safety hazard."

She noted the way he took over her space and acted like it belonged to him. It was strange being a tenant, at somebody else's will. It was so much nicer when you owned your own home.

Esme fussed in the kitchen arranging her apothecary. The fur hat was back on her head.

"Where can I plug in this blender?" she said.

"We might blow a fuse," Henry said. "But let's plug it in here."

So that was it. They would ask her to buy an expensive blender.

"Don't go to any trouble. I've nothing left to spend because of Christmas shopping."

Henry took hold of the black cord and plugged in the blender behind the stove.

"Ah, Christmas," Esme said. "I'm not asking for money, dear girl. This little gadget will be needed for all my mixtures."

"You look a little undernourished" Henry said. "Supplements will help." He sat down on the bed. He put his feet up on the coffee table.

"I really don't need it. It's nice of you."

"Nonsense," Esme said. She held a cup full of green liquid. "I hear that young people live off kale smoothies. My nutritional supplement is much better. Taste it. Delicious."

Nora took a sip, to be polite.

"Very nice," she said. And it was. Faintly woodsy, with notes of honey.

"It helps you sleep," Henry said.

She drank it down.

24

Nora put her head on the pillow and pulled the duvet to her shoulders. As she slept, the wind ripped across the roof of the building and rustled frayed shingles. Some tore off and fell to the ground and skated on the icy pavement. The harsh December wind was so loud it woke her and drew her to look out the window. It was late. The city was sleeping. The back lane behind the building was lined on one side with maples, and the wind made the branches tremble. Under the dark trees behind the building, she saw a small child walking alone.

And then Nora slept again and dreamed she was back in her house. There was Carter sitting at his wide desk in the den, two computer monitors glowing in the corner. The tapping of his keystrokes as he enters data on a spreadsheet. Soft clicks like the toenails of mice.

And there Nora was with Dylan, holding sunflowers they picked fresh in the field. The stalks, too big for little Dylan to hold. She wants Carter to help Dylan with the flowers but the blinking computer monitors are very bright, and Carter yells at

Nora. *Get out, stupid slut.* His hand hits Nora in the face.

Her jaw hurts.

Dylan is sick now. The child is very sick, and it is all Nora's fault. She knows she is to blame because Carter tells her so, repeatedly.

It is your fault Dylan is sick. Carter yells and yells.

Carter rains down more blows on Nora, and Dylan cries. She tries to comfort Dylan and stop the crying.

Nora's face is bleeding, and her wrist is broken. She cannot lift Dylan out of the crib.

* * *

Nora was wide awake now. She opened her eyes and she was in the yellow bed. Someone was crying in the kitchen.

She threw off the hot duvet and went into the dark kitchen where the only sound was a slight vibration of the two-burner stove and a dull hum from the curved refrigerator. A crescent moon was visible through the window of the fire escape.

Esme's little jars of powder were lined up on the counter, and the soup pot was in the sink. Nora's arms tingled from sleep, and she rubbed her cold skin. There was no crying. Only the cat Toffee up on its hind legs, front paws clawing at the wall.

"You woke me from a bad dream," she said to the cat.

The clock on the stove showed it was two o'clock in the morning—too late to knock on Henry's door and return his troublesome pet. She didn't want the animal to disturb her sleep anymore tonight. She opened her front door and let it dart out onto the landing. Let Henry worry about where it went.

She closed her door. She stood in the dark. She felt the touch of small fingers on her leg.

Dylan, honey, what are you doing out of bed?

25

Nora married Carter after he graduated from law school.

Her father hadn't liked Carter. He never really said why. But he was glad enough to see his only child settled after she married, and he hoped for grandchildren. He'd never stopped grieving the death of his wife, and he told Nora children bring happiness. He died from a heart attack while she was pregnant with Dylan. Both her parents were gone then.

In a way, a small mercy that he didn't live to see what happened.

Sometimes, wiping crumbs from the counter of her apartment kitchen reminded her of cleaning up in the big house. When she had a family.

The smell of coffee invoked memories too.

"I have a busy week," Carter said. He leaned over the kitchen counter, eating the toast and coffee Nora had made for him, dropping globs of jam and crumbs onto the marble, avoiding her gaze. One eye on his laptop, the other scanning his Twitter feed on the cellphone.

He straightened up, flipping his tie back over his shoulder to the front. He spoke of a hearing or deposition, whatever he had on for the day. She was too distracted by the baby to listen. And he wasn't speaking directly to her, anyway, only pronouncing to the room, commandeering the household so everyone would focus on him. A lawyer, he talked incessantly.

She fed Dylan in the highchair or tried to feed her. The child turned her head away from the spoon and clamoured to get out. At fourteen months old, Dylan could messily feed herself, but Nora loved to do it. "One more sweetie. Then the park."

Dylan mashed cream of wheat into her face and grabbed for the red baby spoon.

"Here Dylan, let's make this fly." She curved the child's pudgy fingers around the handle. "Up in the air and—"

"You listening?" Carter said. "I won't be home much."

Carter's father, Ray, came into the kitchen. He was stooped and hobbled with arthritis. He shuffled towards his son. Ray was dressed in a suit, ready for the office, but he'd chosen wrong, and the shirt was mismatched with the tie. So were the socks, one blue and one grey.

Because of Ray's failing health, Carter gave up his plan to work in the city and instead assumed his father's law practice. The office was a storefront on the main square in town, a one-man operation, the same as Ray had done it, and Carter spent long hours at work. Ray liked to trail after his son, for something to do, and because he failed to acknowledge his cognitive deficits. This enraged Carter and embarrassed him. He often slipped out of the house before Ray noticed that he was gone.

"Let's go, son," Ray said. "We have that motion today. Must get to the courthouse."

"No. That was last week," Carter said. "You should stay

home. This is ridiculous. Nora, you watch him."

"But I have Dylan. You know how your dad is."

Ray needed constant vigilance and supervision, like a toddler. He left the house without shoes, wandered into neighbours' houses, left the stove on.

Once, when Nora was distracted by the doorbell, she returned to find Ray trying to feed Dylan hard pieces of walnut. Dylan didn't have enough teeth to chew nuts, and she would have choked if Nora hadn't intervened.

"It's your job," Carter said.

Ray was the reason they had the big house. He had been the town's only lawyer for decades and very successful until dementia felled him, the one thing he couldn't argue his way out of. The house on Mackenzie King Street was where Ray and Carter's mother Joyce had raised their son. Carter had never wanted to live here with his wife and child.

"Carter. Ray. Someone." A voice came from upstairs. It was Joyce, waking up. Ray sat down with a coffee, oblivious.

"I'm out of here," Carter said.

Dylan pushed her bowl onto the floor, laughing. Joyce called out again.

"Ray, promise me you'll sit here for a minute. Don't take Dylan out of her chair. Promise?"

"Promise," Ray said.

Joyce was in bed on the third floor. She was much stronger, physically and mentally than her husband. Nora suspected she'd chosen to be an invalid, rarely leaving her room.

Joyce had not forgiven Nora for deposing her from the large master bedroom on the second floor, refusing to believe it had been Carter's idea. And although she felt guilty, Nora loved the bedroom she and Carter occupied, with its tiered crown moulding, dark hardwood floors and walls painted a lovely shade of heritage blue. A bay window looked out to the garden. Dylan's sunny nursery was on the same floor.

She was grateful to have the house and the prestige of living on the best street in town.

She wished Carter's parents weren't such a burden. They occupied most of her day, tied her down even more than the baby did. But she loved the house. It had been her childhood dream to live in a beautiful house like this. To have the perfect family.

Too bad it was her parents who were dead and not—

"Nora. I need breakfast," Joyce's raspy, grating voice.

"But it's only nine. You told me, breakfast at 10."

Joyce propped herself up against the headboard. She was a small woman, diminishing as she languished in bed. She smoothed her grey hair into place. Old, but still vain.

Nora opened the heavy chintz curtains and picked up last night's empty teacup from the bedside table, straightening Joyce's pile of books. A cloud lifted in the sky and sunlight inched into the room.

"Roses blooming in Wilson's yard," Nora said.

"I don't care about roses," Joyce said. "I only want to know—"

"Yes, yes," Nora said. She picked up Ray's flannel pajamas from the floor and moved out of the room.

"—if you're keeping my son happy."

* * *

In the kitchen, Ray pressed buttons on the microwave. He had let Dylan out of the highchair, against Nora's admonition, and the child stood wobbling next to it, holding the chair with both hands to stay upright. Her tiny bare feet were like blobs of beige Play-Doh. She'd only started to walk a few weeks earlier.

"Doggie," Dylan said, apropos of nothing.

"Yes, sweetie," Nora said. "We will go to the park and see doggies. That's a good idea."

The microwave beeped. Ray was befuddled.

"What's in there, Ray?" She picked up Dylan and lodged her with one hand against her hip. "Let's see what's cooking."

Pieces of bread lay on the turntable, and she took them out. They were rock-hard and inedible. "Do you want toast, Ray? I'll do it for you in the toaster. Then we'll go for a walk, okay?"

She wanted to be kind to Ray. It wasn't his fault he was so befuddled and she pitied him. It must be difficult to fall from a pillar of the community to … to what he was now, a man in an ill-fitting suit and bedroom slippers, unable to make breakfast, reviled by his son.

When she first met Ray, as she and Carter dated in high school, he made her feel stupid. No matter what she said back then, on even the most inconsequential topics, he told her to explain herself. Say what you mean with precision, he said. She'd get flustered, intimidated by his vocabulary and wanting to impress him and Carter so much.

He and Carter liked to bait her for their amusement. Maybe that's what her father had noticed. The easy and casual cruelty of the Birmingham men.

*   *   *

They made an odd trio walking to the park. Dylan in the stroller babbling nonsensically and Nora singing to her while pushing. Ray traipsing along with one hand on the stroller handle for safety, the way an older sibling would do. If she kept Ray close and attached to them, he wouldn't amble into the street.

Passing walkers stopped to greet them. It was that kind of town, where most people had known Ray in better days. He had been everyone's lawyer if they ever needed one, and now

Carter held the same level of esteem. Or scorn, depending on the outcome of their legal affairs.

At the park, Nora could ignore Ray. There was a fenced and gated play area for the children where mothers were careful about keeping the gate closed. She sat Ray down on a bench opposite the swings and the movement of children swaying back and forth calmed him, and he dozed off. She pushed the stroller closer to the other mothers near the play structure.

Dylan fell asleep in the stroller, and Nora scanned the park for mothers she recognized.

She saw Bila running to catch up after her son Muskoka, chasing a squirrel. Bila was okay. She was a prairie girl—Saskatchewan—who lived on the nearby army base where her husband was stationed. Bila didn't like the other military wives, so she came into town often. She and her son had the same black tufted hairstyle. Bila was the first new friend Nora had made in years.

"I see you have the old guy again today," Bila said.

"He needs his own mama to look after him," Nora said. Saying mean things was bonding.

Bila offered an open bag of Goldfish crackers. "Does Dylan want some?"

Dylan was awake. She held up her arms to be extracted from the stroller. Nora pulled her out, kissed her and let her down to stand on the grass. They took the kids to the sand pit.

"Know why he's like that?" Bila said.

"Muskoka? Like what?" Bila's son was a robust little boy, much sturdier on his feet than Dylan. "No—the old guy," Bila said. "The brain fog." She pointed to Ray, snoring on the bench. "Because of childhood vaccinations."

Bila was one of those. People with wacky opinions. A conspiracy theorist who insisted, laughably, that the moon landing was fake, and fluoridation of water was mind control. Nora had heard her say all these things. Of course, Bila was an anti-vaxxer.

Nora didn't want to get into it. She needed a new friend, and Bila was the only candidate. Besides, her own husband Carter, despite being an educated man, was also a vaccine crackpot. In fact, as Nora would never admit to anyone, Carter had a problem with modern medicine itself.

Muskoka threw a handful of sand at Dylan. None of it landed in her eyes.

Carter distrusted doctors because he wanted to be the smartest person in the room. He had a counter-argument for everything Nora tried to say on the subject. So, she shut up, like he told her to.

He had forbidden her from giving Dylan the routine baby shots. Nora secretly drove the child to a pediatrician in Kitchener for a six-month check-up. She was scheduled to return for vaccinations. But she was frightened, looking in her rear-view mirror the entire trip, thinking he was following her, and then worrying that the doctor's office would call the house and Carter would learn of it. She didn't take Dylan back after that, in case Carter somehow found out.

She didn't like to admit she was afraid of her husband.

It seemed okay. Dylan was thriving.

The children played in the sand. Bila talked about something on television, a reality show about dating. Dylan tried to fill up a pail, digging sand with an orange shovel, but she didn't have the dexterity, and the sand spilled. The boy grabbed at the pail.

Dylan and Muskoka were head-to-head over the pail, breathing in each other's faces. There were things kids caught she knew about, like measles. And there were lots of other diseases Nora had never heard of that Dylan wasn't inoculated against. Muskoka could be sending all kinds of germs her way.

She didn't want to think about it. But she said, "Don't you worry he might get sick?"

"No. It's just big pharma," Bila said. "Selling poison."

Too many toddlers were playing in the sand now, and Nora said, "Let's move to the swings."

Ray was on the bench talking to a woman who maybe was someone's grandmother. He looked almost normal, smiling and having a friendly conversation. Maybe she could talk to Ray about Carter. His temper. His beliefs that kept Dylan away from the pediatrician. Maybe Ray could talk sense into him. Ridiculous idea, she knew. Ray began waiving one arm and the grandmother got up and walked away, quickly, like bees were after her. Ray shouted.

Nora put Dylan in the baby swing. Ray sat on the bench and seemed to have calmed himself down. Carter hadn't always hit her. It only started after the marriage, because of the pressure of running the law practice and paying for renovations to the house.

He said it was her fault for wanting so much.

Nora didn't tell anyone about his temper, his lashing out. She gave the swing a gentle push as Bila next to her did the same with her boy. Bila noticed the bruises on Nora's wrists. Still purple from when Carter had grabbed her yesterday. A few green spots from last week. She pulled down the ends of her sleeves, tried to cover the marks.

"That shit's common in the military," Bila said. "Just give him what he wants. He'll leave you alone."

Maybe it happened to Bila too. Did all women have to endure it? All she had to do was be everything he wanted. Read his mind, anticipate his every need, stay out of his way. She could try her hardest. And maybe everything would be fine.

26

Izzy had inadvertently smeared blue paint on her nose. She laughed when Nora told her and added a bit of red to her chin. She was bound to end up with more smudges on her face; no reason to clean up yet. She and Nora were having a girls' night out after working the afternoon shift. They wore paint-splattered artist's smocks and stood in front of six-foot easels, trying to get more colour on canvas than on themselves.

They were in a small art gallery near Trinity Bellwoods Park. It used to be a working-class area. Now it was hip. There was an actual park full of trees where Izzy knew people went to drink and party and the streets around it were all funky Victorian houses and laneway cottages. She'd love to live in a cool part of the city like this, but even though it looked shabby, it was expensive. Everything done up now for rich people. The streets full of trendy shops and impossible-to-book-a-reservation bistros.

The little art gallery was a former shoe store called Silver's. All the display shelves were gone; the walls whitewashed to showcase art. The original sign was still in the window though: a gilded illustration of a lady's one-strap pump circa 1920. At least that's what the gallery clerk told them.

It was Izzy's idea. She signed them up for a painting session called Tipple and Tint, the Facebook event listing promised a glass of wine along with the art lesson, and she paid for both of them to attend. She'd been worried about her friend. Nora dragged herself around at work and looked worn out. Izzy hoped to cheer her up.

She knew that Nora was careful with money. So no expensive night out at a club with fancy drinks, which Izzy would have preferred. She made the same money Nora did and didn't mind spending it on fun things. But would Nora even like a noisy bar with house music? She was older, after all. Thirty was not the new twenty. Still, Nora was great.

When the ad for the painting class flashed on her computer screen it seemed perfect. She paid the low promotional price for two tickets. She told Nora it was an early Christmas gift. She'd never pry and ask Nora why she worried about money or if anything was wrong. That never got you anywhere except shut out, if the friend was as private as Nora was.

Izzy was very good with money. And she knew about people keeping their troubles close. She grew up with an alcoholic dad and a mom who was silent and withdrawn; both of her parents were relieved to have Izzy take care of her younger twin brothers.

She'd done a good job of it. Made sure they graduated high school two years after she did and got jobs logging. They would travel across the country and live in company trailers and make good money. Only then did she move down to the city from the north, leaving her parents to live, somehow, alone with each other.

Still, she didn't abandon them; she took care from afar. She transferred what small sum she could each month, depositing it directly to the account she'd set up in her mom's name only. At least it wouldn't be poured down her father's throat.

The room buzzed energetically with tipsy painters. On the bright white walls, there were enormous air-brushed portraits of celebrities, the work of a local artist. The paintings were for sale, each priced higher than what Izzy earned in a week.

Izzy sipped her wine and lathered paint on her canvas. Some random stuff was put on a stand in the middle of the room to create a still-life composition. A skull that looked pretty real, fabric roses and a pile of old books. Who said a painting needed old books? The skull though, that was awesome. She gave up trying to make it look authentic and resorted to streaks of neon colour. Nora's painting wasn't half bad.

The instructor came over, squished paint out of tubes and gave her a fresh brush. She heaped praise on Izzy's mediocre effort. Izzy was happy. Feeling good, having fun. That was the whole point. Drake and Beyoncé tunes blasted from speakers. She hoped Nora liked the music.

It was almost too loud in the room for conversation, unless you shouted. Izzy noticed that Nora's wine was barely touched. Nora rested her brush on the easel tray and stepped back to appraise her work. Nora's roses had subtly variegated blush petals and crinkly green leaves, and there were realistic shadows on the skull. All the proportions looked right.

"You're talented," Izzy said. This night out would hopefully bring Nora out of her funk. Lately, she wasn't even bantering with the customers.

"I don't know." Nora's face grew long. She sighed and picked up the brush, touched it to the painting and immediately put it back down. "I'm not loving it."

When you grew up the daughter of an alkie dad and a depressed mom you knew about temperamental attitudes. Mercurial was the word. Izzy had read many self-help books on the subject of dysfunctional families. Nora's moodiness was nothing new. It reminded her of her mother: defeated and unreadable.

Izzy was the one who woke up her brothers for school, made the peanut-butter sandwiches for lunch, faked her parents' signatures on permission slips. It was easier to do things herself rather than remind her folks to do them, when they were so unreliable.

She could help her friend.

She squirted bright pink onto her canvas. "Isn't this a riot?" she said.

"Truthfully?" Nora said. "I'm not enjoying it. I don't feel great. I haven't slept a whole night in I don't know how long." She shouted over the music. "My apartment is always too hot or too cold." She leaned closer, lowered her voice. "Plus, period cramps." Nora grabbed the widest paint brush and slathered it with thick acrylic. Then she slashed a brutal streak of blood red from one corner of her work to the next, ruining it.

"That's how I feel," she said. She burst into tears.

Izzy was shocked, but she didn't give up on people.

This was exactly the sort of unpredictable behaviour she had seen at home.

"Aw, listen," she said, "why don't I come stay with you tonight? I'm done painting. We can get take-out. There's that new Mexican place."

"Do you really want to come all that way? I live so far out. And after I ruined our night."

"Sure. My roommates are having an all-night poker game anyway. They'll be drunk and obnoxious. You're doing me a favour. And you didn't ruin anything. Except your own painting."

Izzy took her painting from the easel, put the caps on the tubes of paint she and Nora had used. "I'd love to hang out with you. Really," she said.

On Queen Street, they walked by a vegan cafe and a shop selling handmade candles. Izzy wanted to look in the windows, but Nora kept moving as snow fell lightly. They waited under a bookshop awning for the streetcar. When it pulled up and stopped with a clang, it was crowded with happy, chattering passengers.

She handled her small canvas gingerly. The paint was still wet and sticky, and she didn't want to get any on her winter jacket. She sat beside Nora on the fuzzy red seats, and she held the artwork at arm's length on her lap. Nora had left hers behind. Izzy wondered if she regretted destroying her work.

"Yours is really nice," Nora said, nodding at the stripes and blobs of pretty colours. "It's abstract."

Izzy smiled. "I like making stuff. At school, I was on every decorating committee—prom theme, stage shows, band concerts. Even posters for student council elections."

"Wow. I was not popular like that in high school."

Izzy laughed. "I never said I was popular. But I got involved in all of it."

Nora took a compact out of her purse to apply lipstick. Izzy leaned in, her pale hair and glitter eyeshadow reflected back to her with Nora's pretty face, whose usually perfect skin had dark shadows under the eyes.

"We need to do more fun stuff. Get out and see the city," Izzy said.

Nora said: "I was good at interior décor. I did my entire house."

"Do you have photos?" Izzy said. But she'd pounced too eagerly on this rare morsel of information. Nora clammed up, retreated to her usual reticence.

"I don't know, Iz. Feel like I could sleep for a week."

She would let Nora have her secrets. Draw her out eventually. Friendships had to simmer.

"Me too. Kyle is putting us on too many double shifts. We need a holiday."

Izzy pulled her painting in closer and squeezed back on the side-facing seat, to allow more room for a blind man to pass with his service dog.

"Let's get some good food, forget take-out. We can make a veggie bowl, or healthy quinoa," Izzy said, "Instead of those green smoothies you always talk about. That might be the problem."

"What problem?" Nora said.

"I only meant—"

"They help me sleep." Nora crossed and uncrossed her legs on the cramped seat. "This woman, Esme, who brings me protein powder." There was another new morsel. Some person Nora had never mentioned before. Nora was guarded and careful about what she said. Izzy wanted to ask her questions, wanted to know Nora better, but she didn't want to pry. A person is entitled to privacy. She let it drop.

27

Nora didn't want to stop in at Lucky Convenience. She had soured on the place because the proprietor had recently switched to cash only, and using cash meant having to be organized enough to keep some in her purse. It also meant depleting her paycheques quickly. She preferred running up the balance on Carter's credit card, since she wasn't paying the bills. She'd begun making the longer trip to the supermarket where she could use the Visa. A twenty-minute walk from the apartment each way.

Izzy seemed excited when she saw the convenience store.

"Look at all the junk in the window," she said. "Is that a bust of Elvis beside the apples?"

They were so close to the apartment, and she had things in the cupboard to eat—surely there was a box of crackers—but Izzy was like a kid.

"I love quirky shops," she said. She took Nora's arm, dragged her inside.

The door chimes jingled as they entered.

The owner was alone, as usual.

"Ah, it's you again," he said when he saw Nora. "And a friend."

"Well, you never close," Nora said. Izzy might think she was being rude, but she was trying to be chummy. Maybe he'd extend credit.

"I keep hours that are convenient," the man said, and laughed at his own wit.

"Blueberries are in from Peru." He pulled a stack of magazines off the rack. "Nobody reads this crap."

Izzy nudged Nora down the aisle towards the back and whispered, "Guy is so strange."

Nora didn't see anything she wanted to buy. Nothing looked fresh, and the displays were messy, tumbled together. Lettuce wilted next to potatoes sprouting green shoots.

Izzy appeared to find it all amusing. She danced down the aisle.

"Isn't it fun?" Izzy said. She raised a plastic pint of wizened blueberries to eye level. "Long journey to Canada?" she said to the fruit.

The man must have heard her. "I can give you two for one."

"See," she said quietly. "That's why I love these places."

The man followed them as they went through the aisles of vegetables. He dragged a hose and pressed a spigot to spray the produce. Nora felt a soft cold mist on her cheek.

"Did I tell you about my son?" he said. "Almost made it to the 2010 Olympics. Vancouver."

Nora ignored him, but Izzy said, "What was his sport?"

He tore the tops off some carrots and handed the bunch to Izzy. "One dollar. He was a figure skater."

Izzy put the slightly dry and flaccid carrots in the basket. "What happened?"

Nora wished he would leave them alone. She took the basket

152

and moved away from Izzy and the man.

"My wife spent all our money on coaches and lessons. We had to get a divorce. And that was that."

Nora brushed past on her way to the cash counter. "We're done," she said.

She waited and looked at the photos taped to the cash register, all of them of two boys standing together smiling into the camera. There wasn't one of a boy twirling on the ice. Izzy came to the counter with containers of dried fruit and nuts. Those things were expensive. The man rang up the items.

"Anyway," he said. "It's a sport for girls."

"That's a bit sexist," Izzy said. "What does he do now?"

He didn't answer.

Izzy gave him packets of ramen and the man rang them up. Maybe Izzy was being practical. Fruit and vegetables had to be washed and prepared. Izzy likely knew instant noodles would end up as their meal. And nuts to snack on. It was late and she was too hungry to cook.

She took whatever bills were in her purse and put them on the counter. Izzy made up the rest with a twenty pulled from her pocket and gave it to the man. He held the bill between two fingers, his mouth tightened with concentration, and the momentary silence caused Nora to recall an earlier, unfinished conversation with the man.

"You told me there were stories about the Farmdale Apartments. What are they?" she said.

"What?" He seemed puzzled, distracted as he repeatedly tried to scan a pack of walnuts. The red light flickered, then stopped. Finally, he looked up the price in a notebook he pulled from under the counter. "Five dollars," he said, along with a low whistle, shocked by his own prices.

"You mean the woman who died?" he said. "All kinds of theories."

"What, when?" said Izzy.

"Running out of plastic bags," he said. "Next time bring your own."

"Oh my God," Izzy said. "What woman, what happened exactly?"

"Plastic is pollution," he said.

"No," Nora said. "Who died?"

"This celery is also good," he said.

Izzy was trying not to laugh. Nora thought the man was looney and she giggled herself. Izzy scrunched up her face and covered her mouth, but laughter escaped, her silver arrow brow-piercing dancing with each guffaw. It felt good to laugh; her shoulders relaxed with the release of tension.

"A woman died," the man said. "Murdered I think."

Nora stopped laughing. Was he saying a woman was murdered in her building?

"It's an old place," Nora said, thinking aloud. "A little creepy at night, sometimes."

"People love to imagine weird stuff," Izzy said.

"Tenants moved out in droves after it happened. They had to lower the rent to get people back in."

"How did she die?" Nora asked. "Was it a long time ago?"

"I don't know. It was the '90s, they say. I didn't have the store back then. I was an accountant in Etobicoke." He laughed emptily, whether at his misfortune or good luck, it was impossible to tell. "You could ask that caretaker fellow. I think he knows the details."

28

Henry watched them come around the corner. He switched off the lights and held himself rigidly still as he spied on them from the front window in his darkened apartment. He was a guard dog, alert and jealous of his territory. Wide sightlines from the window afforded a good command of the courtyard and the street. The two women were the only people walking.

He waited as they came down the block. They carried bags and the smaller one had something square she held out away from her body. Snow fell on their heads.

He stepped back from the window as they came closer to the building. Nora walked with the shorter woman he recognized from the dinner party. What was her name again? It sounded like a scratch in the throat, an irritation ... Buzz, Sis, something idiotic. A tiny nobody, who'd had the audacity to look at him sideways. He didn't know why Nora would befriend such a person.

At least she wasn't coming home with that repulsive man. Kyle. What a stupid long-haired goof.

He was going to initiate the plan tonight, but she was late. And she wasn't alone.

He had waited for her to return from work. He had expected her hours ago, as usual. He even knocked off early, had a shower, left a host of maintenance tasks for tomorrow, then stationed himself at the window in time. Wearing the oxford-cloth shirt.

He'd planned to be ready when she came back to the building. He hadn't taken into account contingencies like this. She was a creature of habit and he knew her schedule, or so he'd thought.

He thought of himself as meticulous, as quite astute. He'd been praised for those qualities at school, had he not? He followed instructions, teachers always said, he figured things out easily. Well, he'd figured out Nora. That was simple when she lived right next door. He'd done it by noting the sounds she made: her kettle whistling on the stove in the morning, the heels of her boots on the wood floor, her jangling keys as she unlocked her door in the evening. He'd learned her schedule. It annoyed him that today she was much later than usual.

And she wasn't alone.

The women came up the walkway under the oaks and he moved far back so they would not see him, and he lost his view. He couldn't see Nora and the small, silly girl who'd been so rude to him. He stayed back from the window, but he knew how long it took to walk through the courtyard. They must have reached the stoop by now.

He should have put surveillance cameras at the front door. He'd considered security systems for the building, but they were expensive, probably unnecessary. He still might put in a camera or two; they might prove useful. It would be fun to follow her progress through the building on camera. However, he wasn't convinced of the need for external support. He could use his own excellent abilities to watch her.

He knew they were inside now, so he moved away from the window and waited at his door behind the red velvet curtain and heard them coming up the stairs. They paused on a lower level for a moment—the wood stopped creaking—and then they were on the landing inches away from him. He was invisible behind the heavy velvet. Nora's voice was soft. She was quiet in the moments the other one laughed. The small one who talked too much.

He had intended to invite Nora in for a drink tonight.

She liked to drink he thought, alcohol made her quite malleable. It had gone well the other time. And he had dressed in the pale blue shirt, perfect with his green eyes.

He had wine and whiskey on the sideboard and had considered what music to play. Miles Davis? He liked jazz but had no idea what she liked. He didn't care, really, what music she liked. It was advantageous to inculcate a woman to your tastes, rather than cater to hers.

She was inside the apartment with her little friend, spoiling his plan.

He had dusted and swept and shut up the cat in the other bedroom. Nora didn't much like the cat. What a chump he was standing there listening behind the wall. Wearing the oxford-cloth button-down with the collar that chafed his neck, thinking he looked good. What was he expecting?

The shirt had hung in the closet unworn for years and the loose fit was out of style. And it made him think of his old school uniform. He recalled staring from the dormer window in his room at Upper Canada College. After meals in the wood-panelled dining hall, up in his room alone. The great lawns stretched beyond the windows of the lower-school residence hall, green grass dotted with elms. Other boys running across the lawn to games before evening study hall.

The window with a ledge wide enough to sit on. And it was still light because supper was so early and it was almost summer. The sunlight streaming through the dormer warming the carpet. Two narrow beds separated by a desk. Alone in the room while everyone was outdoors.

His roommate Jack so busy with teams and activities that he was never there. Jack rushing in after class to dump his books and grab his cleats and jersey; he barely ever acknowledged Henry. They were roommates only, never friends.

The school's red-brick buildings, the famous clock tower looming over Avenue Road, expansive grounds with clay tennis courts and soccer nets arrayed on the manicured grass in the middle of tony Forest Hill. Many of the boys living at the school were the sons of diplomats or overseas business tycoons.

He boarded even though his family lived in an ivy-covered mansion only minutes away from the school. His father's explanation was that because he and his second wife travelled often, he would be alone at home with the housekeeper. Far more character-building to live among other boys. He'd only cried and begged to come home the first term.

So much of his life spent looking out of windows.

Nora and the little one chattered and giggled and he heard the hot water pipe bang in her kitchen. He could go over there with the wine and drink it with both of them. But what would be the point? The friend would interfere and annoy him. He wanted to be alone with Nora.

He stared across the street at the construction hoardings and the row of houses beyond. Was there anything sadder than a snow-covered back yard in December? Pathetic plots of rusty lawn chairs, the Canadian Tire kind so cheap and ugly no one put them away for the winter, scraggly bushes and raccoon tracks in grey snow. Garbage bins overflowing at back doors.

He wondered if Nora found the mail today in the vestibule.

He kept replenishing the trove. Seeding old Christmas cards from his collection so interesting he had debated whether to use them at all. Leaving treasures on top of the radiator. Envelopes of thick paper the colour of old lace, watermarked with the imprint of venerable stationers. Letters he could probably sell to antique shops. Some of his favourites had King George VI postage stamps.

Nora was fond of the mail, he knew, fond of other people's mail, although he doubted she would pocket any letters while her friend was there to witness. He'd planned to tell her more about the building's history. She was interested in that, had seemed intrigued by the diary too.

He put his ear to the shared wall and listened. Two voices rose and fell in Nora's kitchen. They laughed at a joke he couldn't hear. The little friend had ruined his plan.

29

Nora said they were not going to eat ramen for dinner. Even though Nora didn't have much of an appetite, she wanted to reward Izzy for coming all this way. She could give her eggs and salad. It was practically as easy as noodles and more nutritious.

They unpacked the fruit and vegetables and nuts from Lucky Convenience. The small, curved fridge didn't have space to store much, and this frustrated Nora as she shuffled things around, moved jars and leftovers to the back. The tiny freezer compartment needed defrosting, excavating really, before she could make use of it. A thick layer of ice reduced it to a narrow cave.

"I have never had to defrost a freezer in my life," Izzy said. "Who does that anymore?"

"Same," Nora said. At the house she'd had a double Sub Zero, a restaurant sized fridge, but saying so would be uncouth bragging.

"Mind you, it's so cute," Izzy said, "With the retro design." She put the last of the plastic bags under the sink and patted the curved fridge. "I wonder where you buy one."

"Henry says this is original, from the nineteen forties," Nora said. "And that's an upgrade from the ice chest they used in here a hundred years ago."

"Even in the trailer we had a self-defrosting," Izzy said. Nora registered surprise.

"I'm sorry, Iz. I didn't realize."

"Yeah, it wasn't bad. No need to be sorry. Lots of kids to play with in a trailer park." She had two eggs in each hand. "And we had a double-wide."

Nora washed lettuce, which was limp and not very fresh. Not so lucky or convenient. She put the leaves on a tea towel to dry. Poor Izzy, living in poverty it sounded like, while she and Carter enjoyed such luxury.

She cracked the eggs in a bowl. "Scrambled or omelet?" she said. She wasn't hungry, but she thought Izzy was. The hand motions of cooking for other people were automatic; she didn't need to think.

"Scrambled, that's easy."

She'd made scrambled eggs hundreds of times. She whisked eggs and milk together with a fork and set aside the bowl. "We should pare the apples first and get them in the oven. For that dessert I told you about."

Why did she mention baked apples to Izzy? Dylan's favourite, warm mushy apples drizzled with maple syrup and raisins. And come to think of it, her daughter loved scrambled eggs just as much. Any food soft and sweet and easy to chew.

She was making nursery food for dinner.

She put the heavy cast iron frying pan on the stove, using two hands to lift it from the bottom shelf. She banged it onto the gas ring. A corresponding bang echoed in the wall.

"Did you hear that?" she said. She'd heard a thump, a

cupboard door closing in another kitchen, perhaps.

Izzy said, "In my building the walls are concrete. Completely soundproof."

Henry must be in his own kitchen, banging his own pots on the stove. Then she heard a woman's voice, older like Esme's. In a way, it was comforting to know other people were there.

"I worry that I bother people," she said. "It's pretty quiet mostly, but when I move around I hear other noise through the walls. It's like they know exactly when I'm in here so they decide to make noise too."

"I know someone who rented a place," Izzy said. "From one of those creeps who spies on tenants." She ran her hand over the wall by the stove. "Have you heard of that? Like with a little pinhole in the wall."

Nora laughed. "That sounds like a movie." She put butter in the pan. "Or one of those awful stories you tell around a campfire to scare yourself. There's no hole in the wall." No holes, but certainly noises travelling through flimsy walls lined with horsehair and paper.

She turned down the flame under the eggs and handed Izzy an apple and a paring knife, and Izzy began carving off the skin in a thick curl. The paring knife wasn't sharp enough and kept slipping off the shiny surface of the apple.

Izzy jerked open the warped utility drawer next to the stove and rummaged for a better knife. She groped under the packed cutlery and cut her finger on something razor-sharp. She cried out in pain, blood gushing from the soft flesh of her finger-pad.

"Oh Iz," Nora said. She turned Izzy to the sink. She held a tea towel against Izzy's wound. Red splotches swelled on the blue and white gingham.

"Look what I've done," Izzy said, distressed at the

blood-stained cloth.

"Never mind that," Nora said. "Your finger is what matters. Press on it till it stops bleeding."

She took Izzy by the elbow to the yellow bed. They sat in silence in the dark room, watching Izzy's hand, waiting for the blood to clot.

A car drove through the laneway. They both heard it down below.

The sound of the car's engine muffled the creaks of the old building. When the car was through the lane and gone, the building took up its complaining again. It groaned and sighed.

She brought Izzy a Band-Aid from the bathroom and said she was sorry the night was turning out this way. She went back to the kitchen where the eggs and butter smelled burnt. She turned off the stove and oven. She held the bloody tea towel in her hand.

30

The towel would be ruined if she didn't take care of it. You had to wash blood out immediately before it set in the cloth.

The laundry needed doing anyway. A pile of it gathered dust on the closet floor, tights and the black turtleneck she wore to work. Her underwear. She'd been avoiding the effort of going back and forth to the basement and the boredom of waiting for the machines to do the work.

"I'm all better." Izzy turned in the kitchen, holding a bag of potato chips in her bandaged hand. "Found these. Hope you don't mind."

Nora dug into the bag and ate a few chips, the salt and oil, delicious!

"Do you mind coming to the laundry room with me?" she said. "Before we finish cooking. This may sound weird, but I don't like going down there alone."

"It's in the basement?"

Nora found her coins in the drawer, careful not to cut herself on whatever had nicked Izzy. She nodded, yes.

"Then not weird at all," Izzy said. "Who doesn't have a fear of basements." She smiled. "Although, we didn't have one, growing up. Everything I know is from TV."

Nora thought again of Izzy and her family crowded in a trailer, maybe like the ones she'd driven by on secondary roads outside her town. She stuffed her towel and pajamas into a cloth laundry bag, already so full she was unable to draw the cord. The bundle was the size of a small child and she wrapped her arms around it. She gave Izzy the coins.

Izzy said, "I remember when they made the two-dollar coin, before anyone called it the toonie. We set up in the K-Mart lot behind the store, where the trucks unloaded. My Dad knew the manager." She jiggled the money in her palm. "We roamed the lot between cars for dropped coins and used them in the store."

"I'm sorry," Nora said.

"No. It was fun. My brothers were wild, and we had the run of the place. Huge parking lot empty at night where we could play ball. And woods nearby for exploring. It was a disappointment when we moved into public housing, even though they gave us a whole townhouse."

"It must have been safer and better though. I mean, where you live is so important. For kids."

"It's not the place so much. More the people you live with," Izzy said.

* * *

Nora could not find her keys. They were not in her purse or coat pocket where they would normally be. She'd have to leave the apartment door unlocked while they went downstairs. This made her uneasy. But she decided no burglar would come all the way to the eighth floor, when there were easier choices nearer the escape of the front door.

They went out to the landing, both women wearing socks without shoes, like they were going downstairs inside their own house, neither bothering to put their winter boots on.

On the fourth-floor landing Izzy picked up something on the floor. A sock or other thing fallen from the laundry bag. She held it out to Nora, but it was nothing that belonged to her.

It was a child's mitten, bubble-gum pink and bright as a Barbie Dreamhouse.

"Where's the other one?" Izzy said.

Nora laughed. "They only lose one at a time."

Dylan had lots of mittens and it was an effort to keep them together. Nora stored them in a wicker basket in the front closet, along with hats and scarves. Various methods were used to keep the mittens from going astray. There were fuzzy white ones sewed onto a long string, the string went into each coat sleeve and behind the neck; soft blue ones with red stripes held to jacket cuffs by metal clips. A pair bought at a church bazaar by Nora's mother and that Nora herself had worn as a child before passing them on to Dylan. Where were those little hand-knit mittens now?

"Put it up here," she told Izzy, indicating the top of the newel post. "So the mother can find it."

Izzy laid the mitten out like an artifact displayed on a plinth. It was so brightly pink it could be seen from downstairs. But who would want to reclaim it? It was one of the cheap nylon things piled in bins at the Dollar Store. You bought them in packs of three, and they were scratchy and unravelled in the wash. Barely thick enough to offer any warmth. And this one had a hole in the thumb where the child had sucked right through.

* * *

They came to the vestibule in the dark. Someone had switched off the overhead light and the lights outside above the door were out as well. The mailboxes looked flat and cold. Nora stepped in an unseen puddle and dampness seeped into her sock. They rounded the corner to the left to a final steep, narrow set of stairs lined with a worn carpet. The stairs descended to the basement.

A button light switch at the top of the last flight lit the way. Nora pushed on the button switch with her shoulder, her arms full with the bag of laundry. The light at the bottom of the stairs was a single bulb hanging from the ceiling. Izzy halted at the top of the stairs.

"Do we dare?" Izzy said, grinning.

A musty smell rose up from the basement.

"Cut it out." Nora said.

She began to walk down, shifting the laundry bag to her hip. There was no banister to hold and the unpleasant sensation in her wet foot caused her to favour it as she stepped down.

She felt unsteady on the shortened treads and uneven risers of the staircase. It was crudely built, as if by an unskilled carpenter who neglected to measure. She leaned for balance against the narrow walls.

"Don't go in the basement, girls." Izzy said, using a shaky, horror-movie voice.

"Stop it, Iz."

Really, Izzy was so childish.

There were two doors at the bottom. One bore a brass plate that read 'Mechanical Room' and was closed tight with a clasp and heavy padlock. Across from it a second door, propped open with a rubber door-stopper. Darkness and silence beyond it and the smell of mildew. A faint dripping of water in a pipe.

Izzy stepped in first and found the switch, flooding the space with harsh overhead fluorescent light. "Wow," she said. "This is where they do the dissections."

"I swear. If you don't cut it out."

They entered the basement laundry room. The cinderblock walls were orange, the concrete floor red, painted surfaces that glared under the bright light in a manner much as Izzy conjured, a sinister laboratory. Over the white machines, framed posters hung on the wall—yellow and orange tinted scenes of dancing can-can girls.

"Who dreamed this up?" Izzy said. They burst out laughing.

"Why is it so bright?" Nora said. She could hardly speak for laughing. "I need sunglasses."

The room was entirely underground. A lone small window clutched at the corner where the ceiling of the room met the ground level of the building's foundation. Along the wall outside the building, a window-well was cut into the lawn to let natural light through the glass. This would have made the room more pleasant during the day, but it was pitch-black outside now, and the glass in the window darkly opaque, reflecting back the garish colours on the walls.

A metal bar stool was shoved in the corner directly under the window. Izzy perched on the red vinyl seat, her feet hooked on a rusted chrome bar, and took her phone from her back pocket. She poked at it while Nora loaded the washing machine.

Whites, darks, she couldn't be bothered to separate them and do the wash properly. The sharp paint colours bright like flames in the stark white glare of the lights. The thought of waiting here until the washing was done gave her a headache. So did the alternative prospect: multiple exhausting trips up and down eight flights of stairs. Nine, counting the basement.

She emptied the laundry bag entirely. She wondered if any of the bloodied things would come clean. There weren't enough quarters for separate loads. Cramming everything into one machine, overloading it, Nora closed the lid and was about to suggest to Izzy that they wait upstairs. Izzy stared at her phone, head down, swinging her legs a bit, her back to the wall.

She fed quarters into the machine as Izzy looked at the phone.

She thought to ask Izzy for the time so she would know when the wash began, and she looked away from the clothes stuffed behind the glass door of the machine and up to Izzy.

And above Izzy, over Izzy's head where only Nora was looking, above in the dark cold pane of the window. A movement.

Outside in the hollow of the dug-out window well.

Nora saw it behind the glass, moving. While Izzy continued to stare down at her phone. A dark shape stirring out of the black and taking form in the glass.

The washing machine rumbled and filled with rushing water.

A little round face in the window. Eyes, nose, mouth.

Izzy sat on the stool under the hard light, staring at her phone.

"There's no reception down here," Izzy said.

The little round face outside in the dark pressed flat against the window, squished and distorted. Cheeks pushed into the glass, tongue stuck out. A child's game, making an ugly face.

"Not even one bar."

Izzy held her phone in the air to show Nora, the screen glowing.

And for a moment Nora's gaze was diverted away from the window to Izzy's glowing phone screen with its little coloured squares of apps and icons.

The washing machine pumped and banged, releasing a surge of hot water.

The little face was gone.

Why is a kid outside in the dark? In a hole in the ground,

alone. Why is there no protective grate over the dugout to keep a child from falling in?

Nora said, "It's dangerous to play in window wells."

And Izzy looked with confusion at her friend. "What?" she said. A film of worry clouded Nora's eyes as she fixed her gaze above Izzy's head.

Izzy swivelled around on the stool to see what compelled Nora in the window, but there was nothing, only blackness that mirrored the black of Nora's pupils.

Nora couldn't look away from the window. She wanted the little face to return. She felt the anguish of longing.

A child was out there, someone's child who lived in the building or in a house nearby. A child who should be inside warm and snug; not out in the dark, alone.

31

Nora woke in the yellow bed lying on top of the covers, fully clothed in jeans and a sweater. Her forehead was damp with perspiration, a strand of hair pasted across her brow and one eye. A rank smell from the pillowcase under her cheek.

The room in darkness. An empty bag of chips crumpled on the table by the bed and a spoon on the floor. Pebbles in her throat and burning when she swallowed.

In the kitchen the dull, insistent hum of the refrigerator motor cycling on and off. And traffic outside, cars and trucks moving steadily north and south. And then penetrating the single-paned window above the bed, the scream of an ambulance and the Doppler effect as the siren rose and fell, racing off with grim cargo.

She was certain he was dead. There was no need for an ambulance.

Someone was in the kitchen. Carter in the kitchen getting himself a snack.

She had made scrambled eggs with Izzy. It seemed weeks ago.

Her stomach was hollowed out, and it was sore like her throat. She was hungry, yet her body was leaden, too heavy to move. Trying to rise brought an ache, the beginning of some larger pain to the left side of her head; it throbbed, and she put a hand there to quell it and lowered her head back down.

"Could I have a glass of water?" she said.

But how could he bring her water if he was dead.

She fell back to a kind of sleep. And she was in the big soft chair in the baby's room nursing infant Dylan under a stream of sunshine. Her baby sucked at her breast, the tug of infant gums as Nora looked down at the small heart-shaped face she loved so much, that she could gaze at for hours, the little eyebrows delicate as feathers.

The initial impossibility of nursing in the first weeks after Dylan's birth. The searing pain tearing her nipples apart when the baby tried to suck and failed to latch, but she persisted, determined, nipples raw and cracked and the baby unhappy and hungry and then, one day, one day when no one was in the house, only Nora and the baby, it simply worked.

And after that it wasn't painful anymore. Feeding her child became so easy, so calm. A private communion between mother and child. She fed the baby whenever she wanted, no matter where they were. Their quiet, slow time together.

Carter didn't like her to do it when she was out of the house, embarrassed that someone might see his wife's exposed breast, as if the most natural act should be hidden as shameful.

The image of her husband's angry face dissolved the lovely dream.

She was in the yellow bed, her body heavy, breath catching in her sore throat.

Someone in the main room, walking on the wood floor

towards the bed and at the same time the crash of a dish dropped in the kitchen sink.

Two people then.

Nora tried to say, please leave it, I'll clean later, but her jaw didn't work, too stiff for speech.

Two people in the room, a man and a woman, near the bed. And she thought Izzy is still here. Izzy and someone else who walked in heavy boots and smelled of cologne.

They whispered, and Nora tried to understand what was said, a dream of whispers.

The woman said shush, she's sleeping, and the man said, so what?

In the bed they moved, grunting, clothes coming off arms and legs, a belt buckle hitting the floor. Right next to her in the bed, slip and slide of skin, grunting. She felt the bodies, heavy, pushing overtop her own and making it difficult to breathe. Smell of sex and men's cologne.

She tried to yell, stop, tried to wriggle away from the bodies, and she was against the wall, limbs fixed to her torso, immobile, until they finished and there was no human sound, nor scent, only the refrigerator urging its mechanical humming and the seep into her lungs of the apartment's stale air.

* * *

In the morning Esme was there.

"I like to wear good wool clothing in winter," Esme said. She opened the kitchen window a crack, to get some clean air into the place, she said, and came to Nora in bed.

"Natural fibres are the warmest in cold climates," Esme said. She wore her tweed suit. Her hair twisted and pinned at the top. Esme pulled at the bed cover. "These sheets are damp and heavy," she said. "These are sick-bed sheets, they want changing."

When had she let Esme into the apartment? The conversation about weather-specific clothing a puzzle seemingly started in the middle, without her. She was so thirsty, and the room was too hot.

"Toronto winters are long and dreary," Esme said. "But not as bitter as the ones I endured in childhood." She picked up a plate from the table by the bed. There was a crust of bread left on it. "Now, that was a cold country. At least here we have reliable heating."

Nora tried to sit, found it too strenuous, and propped herself up on her elbows instead. Her forehead was greasy, her hair lank. She needed a shower and tried again to move out of the bed but fell back down hard, her head heavy as a twenty-pound sack of rice.

Esme was in the kitchen, heels on her shoes clacked on the floor, a spoon scraped in a glass. "This will do the trick," she called out to Nora. The blender whirred as Esme mixed the green powdered supplements with frozen berries. She turned the blender to a high pulse that Nora felt in her forehead, poured milk from a bowl into the mixture.

"Henry and I have been keeping an eye on you." Esme filled a jar with liquid and put it in the fridge. "Do you have a pen to label these, dear?"

"Am I sick?" Nora said. She felt weak, disoriented. "I thought Izzy was here last night. I'm confused."

Esme came out of the kitchen holding a box of chocolates.

"A get-well gift from Henry." She put it on the bed next to Nora. Laura Secord. Not the best kind. "Be sure to thank him. Every gift should be acknowledged."

Nora sat up slowly. Cold air from the open kitchen window roused her. She looked vacantly at the proffered candy. The thought of eating it made her gag. Esme turned away.

"It has been snowing for days," Esme said.

Snowing for days. How long had she been ill?

"You're not well enough to get up," Esme said. "You know, chocolate lasts for years."

She could see the laneway from her window where the branches were pocked with snow and roofs of houses also patched in white as the snow melted from chimney heat.

"Everyone loves chocolate," Esme said.

"Esme, are there many children living here?"

Esme put on her fur hat, as if poised to go outdoors at any minute.

"Why do you ask?"

"I saw a child the other night." Was it only last night? "And I found a lost mitten."

"I don't know who lives here, dear. That's Henry's department. But it stands to reason."

Esme's suit was mauve and grey and woven with strands of gold.

"You should rest up a few more days."

"I have to go back to work," Nora said. "I've missed my shifts, haven't I? Kyle and Izzy must be wondering where I am."

"You've had the flu," Esme said. "I'm sure they'll understand."

"I don't have a phone to call them." She felt panic at the thought of losing her job, her friends. Acid rose in her gut. Were they worried about her? "I need to go."

"I don't have a cell phone with me," Esme said. "There's one—a landline—next door you can use. Just ... let's not tell Henry. He wouldn't like it if I let you in when he isn't there."

Esme stroked the red ribbon on the box of chocolates.

"We should open these so Henry knows you appreciate it."

"How did you get in here?" Nora said. She'd been sick in bed, hadn't she? She had no memory of getting up, answering a knock at the door, admitting Esme.

"Don't worry. It's just little old me. You don't mind."

"I locked the door."

"We were concerned. You aren't well, dear."

"Did Henry let you in?"

Nora swung her legs over the side of the bed. She wanted Esme to leave. She'd show her out and get dressed and take the subway to work. She must be so late for her shift. She stood up.

She spiralled down and fell on the sour sheets.

32

Kyle decided to walk home after work. It was a cold crisp evening, and the air would do him good. He crossed Queen's Park, the tree-lined expanse of ground behind the provincial parliament buildings, passing several people walking their dogs. A runner in a lime green jacket ran ahead of him on the snowy path, tossing up puffs of snow with each heel strike.

His phone vibrated in his pocket, and when Kyle pulled it out he saw that the call came to him as "unknown". The phone screen glowed brightly under the dark tree canopy, and he let it ring until it stopped. As a general rule, he didn't bother to answer unknown callers. They were either wrong numbers or telemarketers selling him something he didn't need or even worse, scam artists in far-off countries out to bilk him of money.

Surrounding Queen's Park, segmented by a circle road of whizzing traffic, was the campus of the University of Toronto, where Kyle had studied economics. At the time he thought that he would follow in his father's footsteps and become a city politician. But by his fourth year of study and part-time work, he was burnt out. No way was he going into politics.

Playing in the band and working his way up at Lakeview Coffee was just the right level of ambition. Much to his father's chagrin, Kyle had settled where he was.

His ears burned in the cold as he walked. He'd left his hat in the backroom. Which reminded him he needed to get someone to fill in tomorrow for Nora. She'd left without giving notice three days ago. He wasn't surprised because employees sometimes did that; it was the nature of the work. Better opportunities or a yen for travel took over, and people simply failed to show up, sometimes forgetting to pick up final pay cheques.

But he was mystified all the same. He thought he had something going on with her.

It was his own fault for hiring Nora. Hadn't he had his doubts right from the beginning? He'd picked her because she was pretty, ignoring the absence of references. When she didn't show up this week and didn't call in sick, he asked Izzy if she knew where Nora was, if she'd heard from her.

Izzy told him Nora had no phone.

Who doesn't have a cell phone?

He had checked her employment file and found that she hadn't provided an emergency contact. Or her social insurance number for income tax.

The snow was coming down heavily now, streaming under the streetlamps.

His phone rang again. Unknown. Probably the same caller. He answered.

"Kyle. Thank goodness I found you."

Nora.

He felt wary. It wasn't only that she hadn't shown up at work. He was embarrassed, even a little hurt, that she'd been missing in action. They'd never moved beyond some initial kissing since her dinner, but he'd been interested. Thought there was potential.

Now she was on the phone, her voice was plaintive.

"I was unable to call," she said. "I've had the flu I think. I'm still weak."

And then he felt guilty.

He should have been worried about her, not indignant at her failure to commit to the job. He assumed she'd found a better one. Thought she didn't belong slinging coffee. There was a certain attitude she showed sometimes when she thought no one was looking. He'd seen her with an expression on her face, a sneer, like she was bored serving customers. He wiped snow from his cheek. And it turned out she'd been sick. He'd been wrong to assume she'd quit work without giving proper notice.

He had been selfish, hurt because she'd never let him go farther than a kiss. He trudged along the snowy path and decided he would not be so immature. He was a better man than that.

Izzy was the one who had realized something was wrong, who worried about Nora. She had wanted to go to the apartment building to make sure she was okay. Nora was a woman alone in the city, and who knew what could have happened to her? He'd dismissed Izzy as a naïve girl, over-reacting. Now, he felt bad for that.

"Kyle. Are you there?"

He could hardly hear her voice above the din of traffic as he tried to cross the road. He was at the Royal Ontario Museum. The road here was curved and vehicles rushed both ways without a break, white and red car lights streaked the pavement. There was no break in traffic for him to dash across. There was no pedestrian crosswalk.

"Are you okay now?" he said. "Do you need anything?"

Her words were garbled by the vehicle sounds. He heard her say "tomorrow."

Another voice in the background said, "You're too weak."

He dodged a UPS truck careening at speed around the crescent.

"Who is that?" he said. A feeling of jealousy hit him. She was with someone.

"I'm at Henry's, using his phone. I don't feel very well."

She was calling from that guy's place, the janitor. Her voice was muffled by the cars curving around him as he dodged his way across like a human pinball.

He made it safely to the other side.

"I know it's a lot to ask, but could you come over?"

* * *

Kyle arrived with cartons of food from Green Mango, his favourite take-out place: curry chicken, Pad Thai, and coconut rice. He hoped the meal would be enough of an apology to Nora for his unfounded belief that she had run out on him. He berated himself as he rode the subway and continued the self-admonishment until he got to her apartment. He felt so guilty for thinking she had selfishly quit and disappeared.

And all the time she had been sick in bed.

It took forever to get to her place. And he had cancelled on the guys, on a rehearsal he had looked forward to. But here he was. He apologized for not checking in on her and not realizing she had no phone. He said he was sorry it took so long to get here.

Her apartment had that smell of sick rooms. Like hospitals and the retirement place his grandmother had gone to. A sweetness tinged with something acrid, the air tight and fever-burned. Kind of gross, actually.

She was pale except for a flush across her cheeks and neck.

"The subway shut down," he said. "So crazy. We had to get off at St. George and wait for shuttle buses. Must have been six hundred people trying for one bus."

He removed his boots, placed them neatly by the door. He took off his jacket and wondered where she wanted him to put it. It was a heavy hunting coat he'd bought in the army surplus store on Parliament Street. He'd never hunted a day in his life and never would. He liked the style, the epaulettes and multiple deep pockets. The dense cloth of the jacket still carried the sensation of cold night air, and he felt the cold on his shoulders as he stood waiting for her to tell him where to leave it. It smelled also of the Thai cooking fumes absorbed while he waited in the restaurant.

He looked around at her main room, the few pieces of mismatched furniture and the solitary window.

"In the closet?" he said.

She frowned. She said she didn't want the food odour permeating her things.

She gagged and turned her head away and he realized his mistake. The food and its heavy scent were too much for a person who'd been ill. He'd brought it because he thought she liked spicy food, and he was trying to do something nice.

She took the jacket, held it away from her body, and folded it over the teak chair. She wiped her hand on her jeans.

"A suicide?" she said.

"What?"

"The subway. Is that why it shut down?"

Her thin, weary face, the long hair still wet from washing, dampening the shoulders of her blouse. Jeans hanging loose at the hips. She looked unwell.

"On the subway," she said again.

He wondered why she was asking about death on the subway.

He wanted to be kind, had thought bringing a meal to consume together would be a friendly gesture, but she seemed changed, distracted, not the fun co-worker he knew. He was uncomfortable around sick people, the frailty and neediness he didn't know how to address.

He should not have come without Izzy; she would know exactly how to help a sick person. He felt useless, and it was a long inconvenient trip from downtown. He would make it a short visit, have the meal with her, check on his phone to ensure the subway was running again, and leave as soon as he could.

She hugged him. He was uncertain if he should kiss her hello so he moved out of her embrace and took the food into the kitchen. She followed and stood by as he placed each carton on the counter.

He asked her if she was hungry and she said yes, though unconvincingly. He apologised again for not visiting sooner.

"This is very kind," she said. "You're a considerate man."

Nora excused herself and went into the bathroom, and when she returned her hair was pulled back neatly with a clip and she had applied a pale, shiny lipstick. Small gold hoops were in her earlobes.

"I feel better already, just seeing you," she said.

They sat on the floor, backs against the bed and legs under the coffee table, and she asked about the store, what had happened this week while she was gone. He described the hordes of tourists and Christmas shoppers.

"Izzy will be happy to see you back."

"I miss her."

"Her hair was green and pink the other day."

He ate some chicken and felt her leg move against his under

the table. He thought it was accidental until she hooked an ankle over his shin. He swallowed some rice and she did not move away.

"She says she's getting another tattoo," he said. "Of a fawn."

Nora said, "You're really nice to do this."

They sat side by side at the coffee table and it was odd talking without facing each other. She put a hand on his thigh. He thought if he turned to face her she might move her hand away. He wanted it to remain on his thigh.

"I. I'd like to get to know you better."

"Me too."

He felt the warmth of her hand on his thigh. He thought she was sending a signal.

"I need to ask you something," he said. He put down his fork. "This is awkward."

"I was married before," she said. "And it didn't work out."

Kyle was startled. He was only going to ask if it was difficult with him being her boss and potentially, maybe, something more.

"You don't have to tell me," he said. "But I'm confused, I have to say." He shifted slightly away. "At work. In your file. So much information is missing. You're kind of a mystery."

There. He'd said it.

She looked down at the uneaten food on the table, chicken now congealing in the yellow sauce.

"He wasn't a good person," she said. "He was abusive."

He moved his body so that he could look at her then, her head was turned down and she pushed rice around on her plate.

"Did he hurt you?"

She laughed. Then said she was sorry. She was nervous talking about it. He held her hand.

She told him that it was horrible to talk about, but that he deserved to know the truth. He listened to her while she told him the story and then they lay down in the yellow bed. He held her, offering comfort, and she kissed him. She put a hand on his face, on rough stubble because he hadn't shaved since the morning, and he drew closer. They kissed again and went on. They didn't stop.

33

In the morning they got ready for work together. Kyle made coffee for her in the little kitchen while she dressed in the other room. She had a kettle and French press, and the coffee was good, strong. He was hungry but she wasn't, so they didn't make any breakfast. He gobbled down some left-over noodles straight from the fridge while she was in the bathroom.

He felt so close to her now. And protective of her.

They were a couple, he thought. Comfortable in their routine and off to spend the day at work. And it wasn't only because they'd had sex, though he was pleased to have crossed that barrier. It was because she had opened up to him. She had explained why she was so careful, so private. And it all made so much sense.

He hoped he hadn't pushed her into sex too soon. It was often weird on that first morning after you'd been intimate with someone you hardly knew. It was dark when he woke at seven, and he didn't know what woke him without daylight or an alarm. Probably the discomfort of the cramped little yellow bed. He'd hardly slept.

They left for work together. On the landing outside her door as he stood and waited while she was locking up, he thought of reassuring words he would say to her later. So she'd know her secret was safe with him.

She turned around after locking her door. He waited behind her and he was going to speak. He smiled at her, looked down at her pretty face and she looked up at him at once happy and a little sad, or contrite, as if about to make a confession.

He kissed her. "I'm so happy you feel better," he said. "And thank you for telling me everything."

They met Henry coming up the stairs. He stepped loudly in steel-toed work boots, lugged a red toolbox in one hand and in the other gripped a large wrench.

For a crazy second Kyle saw the wrench and thought Henry was going to use it to slug him. That Henry was going to raise the wrench and strike him hard.

Henry stopped immediately below them on the step. He put down the toolbox and lay the wrench on the lid. Kyle told himself to get a grip. That he was feeling paranoid because of the conversation with Nora and because he'd had no sleep. And because Henry was a strange, weird guy.

"Good morning," Henry said.

Kyle said, "How's it going?"

Henry ignored him, looked through him and said to Nora, "I need rent tonight."

Nora, flustered, said, "It's still December."

"And you were late with that too. I want January now."

"She'll get it to you man. When it's due on the first."

Kyle took Nora's hand and squeezed reassuringly. He decided to give her an advance on her wages, in case she was forced to pay her rent early. He put an arm around her and drew her close.

*   *   *

At the streetcar stop, a notice was affixed to the pole saying that the route was temporarily suspended for track repairs. They would have to walk to the subway station, several kilometres away.

"First the subway goes out yesterday. Now this," Nora said. "How are we supposed to get to work?"

They walked to the main cross street. He slowed to keep pace with her as she favoured one foot, limping slightly.

"Are you okay?" he said. He had never felt this protective of anyone.

"I guess I shouldn't refuse his invitations," she said.

They passed a falafel place, shuttered and empty, and an electronics store, closed, the windows soaped up and a "For Rent" sign on the door. Kyle thought he understood now why she'd chosen this non-descript neighbourhood. Outside Tim Hortons, a red-faced man huddled on a piece of cardboard, a mottled-grey dog shivered beside him. No one would look for her in such a crummy place.

"Who?"

There was a smashed mess of dog shit on the sidewalk. He stepped over it.

"Now he wants the rent," she said. "Well, I do owe it to him."

She was talking about her landlord. He didn't like the guy bothering her.

"Is he pestering you?" he asked.

"Henry? Oh, he's okay. Not a pest."

She squeezed his arm and leaned into him.

"Maybe if I agree more often to his drink invitations, he'll give me a break on rent." She laughed.

"No, I don't think you should."

They walked by a massage parlour, green neon flashing in

an upstairs window, a recessed doorway where a ragged swirl of paper and cigarette butts fluttered in a vortex on the pavement. A sign offered 'Gentleman's Special'.

She laughed again. "You're so sweet to be jealous," she said. "But there's no need. He has a girlfriend, you know."

No, he wasn't going to be that kind of boyfriend. "This part of town is run-down," he said. "It wasn't always so seedy. Back in the day, it was all record stores and theatres. And places to hear live music."

She seemed lost in thought. Was he even her boyfriend? He wanted to distract her. Stop any worries. He could tell walking was hard for her, there was something wrong with her foot. He held her arm.

"Look, a pet store," he said. They stopped to peer through the glass. "They sell ferrets," he said, reading a placard.

"Not sure what that is," she said. "Like a weasel? Not a pet I'd give Dylan. I was planning to get her a puppy when she was older."

She seemed mesmerized by the pet store, and she went on talking, staring into the window of the shop as if he wasn't even there, not looking at him while she talked.

"Who's Dylan?" he said.

He was confused by Nora's talk, the bits of information about a past, a difficult past. But if he was going to be with her, he would have to get over it. He would protect her.

Then his attention was drawn away by two mounted police-men on huge chestnut horses cantering down the street.

She stopped talking. He thought she was overtaken by the beauty of the horses as he was and he bent in for a kiss. And she responded and pressed her body against him, and she pulled him into a dark doorway, and he thought how much he liked her.

She kissed him for a long time, and the kiss did not end until the police were gone and the clip-clop trotting was only a faint echo from far down the road.

*   *   *

Kyle knew he and Nora had a special bond. She'd confessed everything to him. How she had to keep herself safe and hidden. How she had to conceal information about her past because she was running from her abusive husband. Her lawyer told her secrecy was the only way to stay safe until the divorce went through. She must never let him find her.

34

Izzy saw them walk into the store holding hands. She raised her eyebrows at Nora and smiled. Obviously, something good had happened. She was so happy Nora was back and hadn't ditched the job as Kyle had thought. Kyle helped Nora put on the green apron like they were a happy couple. She had a million questions to ask Nora, and she waited impatiently for a moment alone with her. Kyle stayed out front longer than usual. He handed Nora cups to fill when she could easily grab them herself; he touched her hair. Wow, clearly, they were a thing.

She wiped down the counter. A woman had spilled a sugar and spice latte, and Kyle was about to make a replacement. The grin on his face gave it all away. He should be at work on the computer in the backroom like usual–not hanging off Nora's every move like the lovesick dope he surely was.

She was happy for them, Nora especially. Kyle was always fine in his own silly way, but Nora walked with a dark cloud over her head. She deserved something nice. She threw the damp rag in the sink and gently nudged Kyle aside.

"Let me do it," Izzy said, waving him away. "Don't you want to go calculate our Christmas bonuses?"

"You wish," he said. But he left her at the counter with Nora. Right away she asked for the truth.

"I like him," Nora said.

"I'm not surprised," Izzy said. "You guys are made for each other." She wiped the milk spigot with a damp cloth. "But why'd you wait so long?"

Privately, she thought Nora might have been distracted by her landlord. Henry was good-looking, though there was something off about him.

"How is the sex?" She said it under the noise of the milk steamer. Nora didn't answer.

Izzy used dating apps on her phone. People were very casual, and sex was easy and available. Maybe Nora wasn't like that.

"Hey, can we talk about our sex lives?" she said again, making a joke of it. "Or are you the type who marries the first guy you sleep with?"

Nora didn't respond. She filled a cup with ice and water and handed it to her, though she hadn't asked for it.

"You want the details?" Nora said.

They were alone during a lull in customer traffic. Outside the big front window, the sky was grey, laden with sleet that would soon fall. A streetcar went by without stopping at the corner. Nora looked at the ceiling like she was thinking what to say, like she had something to say that needed attention. It felt like they were back at high school, in the girl's bathroom on the second floor, skipping math and gossiping. Izzy loved those talks among girls—it was how you made friends.

"Kyle's a great guy," she said.

"He is," Nora said. "I'm not used to that."

Here was a detail Izzy hadn't known.

"I'm just glad you didn't fall for that creep—"

Nora looked off dreamily. She dumped out the cup of water and ice, though Izzy wasn't done with it. She talked, but she wasn't paying attention to her own words.

"You're young," Nora said, "you wouldn't get it."

So, Nora thought Izzy was inexperienced? There was a ten-year age difference, but Izzy guessed she'd been through a lot more than Nora had. She'd practically raised her own brothers.

"I've had my share of bad boyfriends," Izzy said. "So many guys are nothing like their online profiles." Nora wasn't wearing lipstick. That was new. "But about Kyle, I bet he's real cuddly."

A family came into the store, stomped their wet boots on the matts. They only wanted to use the bathroom for the kids and didn't order any drinks. Nora talked a little. Kyle had been gentle. It had been fun. That was the main thing Izzy learned. Then, after the family trooped outside, Nora said Kyle would help her get the memory of Carter out of her mind. She needed to forget he had ever existed.

What? That was the thing about Nora. Just when you were having a normal conversation, in came some unexpected comment. Before she had a chance to ask, the door opened and they took the next order. A woman with long, thick false eyelashes wanted ten pumps of sugar syrup in a latte. Ten. How gross. She made the drink and Nora took the cash.

Nora said, "I'm picturing a man on white marble floors with blood seeping from his head." She wiped up a drop of milk on the counter.

"Okay, creepy. Is that from a movie?" Izzy said.

"Yes," Nora said. "A movie about a terrible marriage. It sticks in my mind." Freezing rain began to hit the sidewalk and ping off the window. "I'd never stay with an abusive man. I'd kill him and walk away," Nora said.

They both laughed at the satisfying, though absurd, fantasy.

35

As the only Lakeview Coffee for blocks, the store was often busy.
A wild early morning rush preceded a brief mid-morning respite;
then another crush of customers at lunch. Today there had been
no lulls, no time for a break in the back, so there was no time to
hang out on the sofa with Kyle. He had warned them it would
be a crazy day. He said they would sling more hot chocolate in
the morning than they did in most months. And he'd been right.
They'd run out of kid-size cups an hour ago.

All because of a parade.

The families arrived early, hours before the start time. The
dads set up lawn chairs and blankets, camped out on the sidewalk to save spots and wait in the freezing cold for the start of
the parade. The men stomped their feet to keep warm, and then
when the moms and children arrived, the parents took turns
running into the store for the bathroom. They bought hot drinks
and gave them to kids to warm frozen fingertips and throats. The
floor was sticky with spilled cocoa.

Nora tried to watch from the store's big windows, to catch a glimpse of the winter parade through the steam and fog on the glass. She couldn't see much, too many people pressed against the windows blocked her view. She could hear the music and the announcements, and each opening of the door brought a flood of voices from the street.

The line-up for service snaked around tables to the door.

"Holding up okay?" Kyle said. "This is great for business. But I'm glad the Santa Claus Parade is only once a year." He handed her a cup of tea, and she took a sip.

* * *

It was Izzy's idea that they go outside to watch the end of the parade. Nora was tired and hot, and her feet were sore from standing so long, but she thought the cold air would feel good. Kyle said, of course, go outside as soon as the line ends. He kissed her cheek.

The swell of customers diminished. The espresso machine became silent, wooden chairs sat vacant and pulled out haphazardly at tables, the floor was scuffed and wet from departed boots. For a moment the store was eerily silent except for the slap of the mop hitting the tiles.

"Go now," Kyle said. "It's almost over." There was a blast of tubas and drums from a marching band.

Izzy was as excited as a child. "I've never seen it!" She tugged at Nora's arm. "Only on TV."

Nora had been taken to the city for the annual Santa Claus Parade when she was four. She had a vague memory of being hoisted on her dad's shoulders so she could look over the sea of heads. They had driven the two hours to Toronto on the 401, windshield wipers going furiously against the blowing snow. She only knew this because her father told her. It was a story for Christmas gatherings. How the heater broke in the Ford and their toes had gone stiff in the cold on the way home. How she had sat huddled between her parents and her mother wrapped her in a blanket to keep her warm.

She had no memory of the parade itself, or of being in the happy company of both her parents. And she had never taken Dylan into the city for any reason at all. Not even when it really mattered, when she should have brought her to the big children's hospital.

"You guys should go out." Kyle nudged her, his hair was pushed behind his ears, his wide smile framed by sideburns.

Izzy beside him, clasped her hands together in a prayer of glee.

"The rush is over," he said. "Go watch. I'll man the fort."

They put their coats on over the green aprons, and she and Izzy went out into the crowd on the sidewalk. Nora wanted to stay back, she didn't like being in a crowd, but Izzy took her hand and moved them forward, gently pushing through the bodies. The families were a mass of bulky parkas, solid forms reluctant to move, unwilling to give up claims they had staked hours ago and fought for in the cold.

Izzy was persistent and pressed on, pulling her foreword.

"I don't really care," Nora said. "We can see from here."

But Izzy couldn't hear her above the horns and bugles and chatter of the crowd, and she was shorter than Nora and wanted to be closer where she could see. Izzy pressed on, eager to get to the front where they would have the best view. And because Izzy was so small and her touch so gentle as she prodded their backs with her small hand, people assumed she was a kid and let her pass.

They made it right to the curb with the crowd behind them and nothing to block their view of the parade. Izzy clutched Nora's hand, bounced with excitement. They watched the marchers.

Boys in red, white and blue stepping high like tin soldiers come alive. At the curb, the spectators were separated from the marchers by waist-high crowd barriers. Yellow metal rails set up to keep order during the parade.

It was very cold and the air Nora breathed in through her nose was sharp and icy. She put her hands on the rail and realized she'd forgotten to put on her gloves. The metal was too cold on her skin and she quickly put her hands in her pockets.

A man beside her wearing a maple leaf tuque munched Timbits from a cardboard box, compulsively stuffing his mouth with the small donut pieces. When she looked at him, he held the box out to her, offering globs of dough with chocolate glaze and sprinkles.

She'd let Dylan have such treats sometimes from the bakery in town.

She shook her head at the man. Hairs grew low from his nostrils.

"Drum majorettes!" someone shouted.

The people were excited. Girls marched by in formation sprung on tip toes. Small girls around Nora tried to emulate the majorettes, jumping and jostling each other. Nora was pushed a little, knocked into the metal barrier, but she smiled at the children. She watched the high-stepping and twirling, admired the costumes: gold epaulettes, red velvet skirts and immaculate white caps. Silver batons flew into the air.

The man chewed his donuts. Had she poisoned Dylan with too much junk food? Is that why she got sick?

The Mother Goose float appeared. A car, a convertible with the top down, covered over in papier mâché to look like a giant goose, the car mounted on a flatbed truck. The Mother Goose in the back seat waved, and children dressed as sheep clamoured all over the float. The contraption crawled by slowly as the flatbed moved along on massive wheels, high off the ground.

Families pressed forward for a better look. A sea of puffy jackets and striped scarves, hats adorned with rabbit ears, dinosaur crests and pompoms. Everyone pushing forward to get a look at Mother Goose and the children climbing over her.

The float jerked and stopped for a moment when the marchers in front of it suddenly halted. One of the little sheep-children lost her balance near the side of the flatbed and fell precipitously close to the edge. The truck moved on.

The next contingent was bagpipes and men in plaid kilts. Four fat men held a banner aloft with a message: The Rotary Club Salutes Santa.

Nora was cold. Izzy had slipped off somewhere into the crowd.

The families clapped and cheered and tried to push ever closer. Santa must be coming.

Nora's ears tingled and stung in the cold.

Down at her feet a little boy sat alone on the curb. He'd managed to wedge himself in an opening between two of the metal barriers and he sat, solemn and alone, his feet in the gutter. He looked five or six. He wore running shoes, no boots, and he was hatless in the cold.

Dylan was always dressed beautifully.

Someone in the crowd yelled 'he's coming' and fathers with kids on their shoulders surged forward for a better view. People shouted for Santa. Impatient in the cold, ready for the main attraction.

She would go back to the store as soon as the parade ended. She would go right now if she could turn around and get through the crowd behind her. Her hands, feet and ears were numb with cold.

Recorded circus music preceded a line of clowns.

The line formed in the distance, a hazy orange and yellow blur that moved closer down the street making everyone laugh. She wanted to find Izzy but where Izzy had been there was a burly dad pressing his pudgy son out in front of the crowd. He elbowed Nora out of the way, and everyone behind her also pushed harder now, pushed forward to get themselves into the street.

Nora saw police. Mounted officers decked out in parade regalia of blue and gold, riding high on imposing police horses.

Her instinct was to flee.

The police brought the horses to a slow walk close to the sidewalk and the crowd of people; the police used the size of the horses to keep the crowds behind the barricades. But the people kept moving forward, spooking even the trained horses.

The riding officers signalled to each other and pulled the reins on the horses and turned them away from the crowd. They moved off down the street, leaving the crowd to itself.

The yellow and orange clowns seemed to have grown in number. They acted victorious. They danced and made mocking gestures at the receding police.

She wanted to leave. The ugly clowns were frightening and had shifted the mood of the crowd. The crown behind her would be impossible to wade through.

Emboldened and heedless, people moved onto the road. The clowns encouraged them. They weaved and bobbed through the people on the street. They dashed up to the barriers.

The uncanny clowns unsettled the crowd. The costumes were upside down: bulbous heads at the bottom where legs should be, with knees and clodhopper feet on top dangling high. The children especially were mystified, confused. They laughed and screamed.

The fathers loved it, were drawn to join the mayhem. Clowns

walking on their hands, how hilarious. They had to get photos and rushed headlong into the street. The grotesque clowns egged them on, their low-hanging heads bobbed, each upside down grin a frozen grimace.

The metal barriers crashed to the pavement, and the men ran out into the street, berserk and reckless. Mothers held small children close, clutched them on the sidewalk to shelter them from trampling feet.

The children were frightened. They screamed and cried.

Nora thought, Dylan must be terrified.

The little boy sitting alone at the curb tried to stand up as people clamored. The rush and tangle of heavy bodies held him down. A boot struck the side of his head and he cried out.

She reached for the child but he was torn away by the surge of people.

A man collapsed in the street, he tripped while taking a picture with his phone, and the phone flew out of his hand and he lay dazed. He groped for anyone's arm or a leg, something to help him right himself.

Nora watched in horror as the clowns converged on him, they really let him have it. The clowns stomped on his hands and kicked and kicked at his ribs until he stopped moving and then they ran off, howling in a blaze of orange.

36

Henry hated the days following Christmas. The holiday itself didn't affect him. By now, all these years after his trial, he'd resigned himself to his status as family pariah. They wanted nothing to do with him and that included holidays and celebrations, when most families tolerated unloved relatives. He didn't miss aging uncles or cousins. Most of them were gone now, anyway.

It was the period of time after the holiday that disturbed him. The city shut down, shops closed, work was suspended. You were supposed to relax and spend time with someone you cared about. He always longed for someone special at this time.

He thought this year things might have been different. A faint whiff of possibility that he might be able to live like everyone else. That he would at least have a woman. To be with someone.

But Nora had turned her back on him.

The hours inched by like cracks forming in the wall, each day endless and empty, the sky perpetually grey. He sat in his apartment and was annoyed by the ticking clock, the wind rattling the windowpane, the cat's claws striking the floor. He thought of ways to punish Nora.

No sound came from her apartment. He'd used his master key yesterday and gone in, walked through and looked for signs. He'd pulled open drawers and felt inside the sleeves of a red top. He'd run her brush through his hair.

He was hollowed out and let himself brood. When he felt sorry for himself he thought about his time at Penetanguishene.

He had felt acute loneliness there. The problem had been the opposite of his current situation. The centre—they called it a hospital but to him that was a laughable misnomer—the centre contained too many people. He was constantly surrounded by them. The guards and the keepers and the other wackos. The crazies.

And not a woman in sight. So naturally, what he mostly did there was obsess about them.

The guards disgruntled, angry at working such shitty jobs and taking it out by tormenting the inmates. Stealing his food, hiding his books. It was supposed to be a progressive place, with an emphasis on treatment, but the doors and windows were locked tight. The windows you could not open to expel your own stale breath, the bolted doors admitting no visitors.

Not that he would have had visitors.

You longed to get outside for even a minute, even in the cold, to feel the wind roiling the water in Georgian Bay, to pick up a chunk of broken ice and throw it away with all your strength. He was young then, with energy that needed burning off.

They kept you inside and occupied with projects and busy-work, to distract and ensure you didn't think or feel anything. All the little wooden boxes and model planes you hammered together, but you weren't allowed to keep.

And always the other nut-jobs slobbering too close and talking too loudly.

His lawyer said being sentenced to the treatment centre was a better deal than prison.

The tools were locked up at the end of every session, so they couldn't use them as weapons to attack each other. And he still did that, a habit he couldn't break: locking up his tools. Which reminded him, he could distract himself from these negative emotions by finding tasks in the building. He had lists of needed repairs. That was one of the therapeutic techniques. Distraction.

It sometimes worked, distracting and calming himself with simple activity. He would tackle a few easy items on the job list. There was a patch of torn carpet on the fifth floor. One of the washing machines knocked and banged. He should fix that before it leaked.

He walked through his sitting room and felt how cold it was. The temperature had dropped since Christmas and the interior of the building was uncomfortable.

The cold air inspired a suitable punishment for Nora. He would make her uncomfortable. He would turn the furnace down low, ever lower until her apartment was unbearably cold. That would teach her not to spurn him.

Where was the damn cat? The creature was always hiding somewhere. He put the kettle on. The woman who'd owned Toffee had spoiled the animal—that was the problem.

He imagined Nora having sex with Kyle, who was ordinary, not even good-looking. Nora was selfish, aloof. More like Lucinda every day. She might try to evade him completely by moving out of the building unless he did something about it.

He made Earl Grey tea and put on a sweater to keep off the chill. He sat down to work on the scrapbooks.

DWELLING

TORONTO TELEGRAM

September 20, 1918

Mayor Attends Ribbon Cutting

Toronto Mayor Tommy Church was the guest of honour at a ceremony to officially open the Farmdale Court Apartments. This edifice represents a transformative housing alternative for the city, ideal for small families and returning servicemen.

"Our boys coming home from battle in Europe will fill these affordable units," proclaimed Mayor Church. According to His Honour, it took some doing to convince him and the city governors that Farmdale Court would not be a tenement, overcrowded with the poor.

The developer, Mr. Weston, parcelled off land from his own estate to build the project, and promises he can generate more property tax revenue for the city with his apartments than with single family homes on the same amount of land.

One of the very first tenants is Miss Doris Carr, a teacher at Jesse Ketchum School, who is over-joyed to have modern kitchen equipment, including an ice-box to keep food fresh, and the convenience of laundry wash tubs in the basement.

He pictured Doris Carr attending the event with other tenants, standing in the courtyard, the shadows of the oak trees falling on the lawn while the reporter wrote down what she said at the ribbon-cutting ceremony. The concept of apartment buildings new and exciting at the time.

He had found this clipping at the library newspaper archive. The paper yellowed and brittle and already a century old. He almost shouted out to the room that he knew Doris Carr. She really lived in his building.

He suppressed his joy. The librarian would take him for another crazy patron, a lunatic spending his time in the reading room, so delusional he thought it was 1918. He would have to explain that he knew full well what year it was, that he had read and re-read the diary of a long-dead woman so many times she had become part of his inner life.

Far better to enjoy this discovery privately by waiting for the librarian to disappear into the stacks, then take it for himself. Use the gloves so thoughtfully provided to him by the library for careful perusal of the archives and gently lift the newspaper clipping from the library folder and drop it into his briefcase.

He mounted the article carefully on acid-free paper. He imagined Doris living here in the first early days, leaving a dank, filthy rooming house with a privy out back, marvelling at her new apartment, the crystal door knobs, brass kick-plates, porcelain toilet. Her good luck at having been approved to live in such a beautiful place.

He got up to relieve his stiff back and walked to the armoire in the dining room to find the diary. The door stuck a bit, the old wood bent and swollen, and was never properly closed. He opened it and found the cat curled up inside on the bottom shelf, asleep.

November 11, 1918

Armistice Day! It is almost midnight and I am still so full of excitement I cannot go to bed. Is the Great War truly at an end? The streets were thronged all day with revellers. I took Alice out into the crowds and she was thrilled. We joined the pandemonium at Christie Pits. People were cheering and waving flags and climbing on top of trolley buses.

I was so happy I took Alice to buy a new toy at Eaton's. She looked for a long time at the jigsaw puzzles and the rubber balls, but finally chose a tiny dish cupboard for her doll. The doors have real hinges and can open and close. We didn't buy any toy dishes to put in it though.

We have both settled in nicely at the apartment. I made macaroni for dinner and baked butter tarts in honour of the day. The people in the new building keep to themselves. I mused about bringing the neighbours tarts to make friends. Alice asked me to read from her book of fairy tales. I read one of a gnome who steals babies and another of a talking goat under a bridge. I find the stories macabre, but Alice loves them. I decided not to give tarts to the neighbours and let Alice devour two herself.

He felt chilly in his living room. Sometimes when he read the diary he was almost sorry for poor old Doris Carr. She really had been too obsessed with that child.

37

Henry put his hand on the wall behind the sofa. Icy winter air seeped through the poorly insulated wall. Someday he would rip it all out and renovate.

He found the photo he used as a marker between pages in the diary—the pink ribbon was already serving as a reminder for a later entry—and looked at it fondly.

The photo faded to grey tones, a man in a bus driver's cap, the peak partially shading his face, a woman in a flowered house dress and white apron in the courtyard. He didn't know who they were but they had lived at Farmdale Court once. The man's arm was around the woman, children out of focus on either side of the couple, not looking at the camera, fussing and moving around too much for the long exposure.

A comforting image of a family, whoever they were.

It was becoming too cold in the apartment, giving him that aching feeling you get with the flu. He'd have to get used to it if he was going to keep the heat turned off.

In the old photo, lilac bushes bloomed against the brick

building and the trees lining the walk were full and leafy. It must have been summer.

He would find additional ways to get Nora's attention, devise a smarter plan.

At the photo's top edge, on a window sill grainy and unfocused, hard to make out, a flower box lush and blooming, maybe geraniums.

* * *

In the basement, he unlocked the mechanical room door and opened the tool cupboard behind the hulking silver water boiler. He pulled aside the split doors and of the cupboard to see the yellow peg board with marker outlines drawn for every implement. Jars of nails and screws, rulers, files, pliers, hammers.

He'd organized the collection of tools himself, shortly after he was released from Penetanguishene. He was pumped full of Thorazine and Risperdal back then, in a state of awe and disbelief that Lucinda's family gave him the job. Well, they were his family too, weren't they? Let him come back to the building they owned. They said they wanted to forgive him.

They would forgive him even though he killed Lucinda, his cousin. But it wasn't his fault, they said. It was a disease.

Over the years he had added to the tool collection, buying from catalogues and dealers in Britain and Europe, shoring up the original cache of workaday implements with antiques and hand-crafted tools, expensing it all through the building's operating fund. The family could afford it.

And over the years he'd tapered off all the medications. The anti-psychotics. He didn't like the side-effects.

He kept this cupboard locked and didn't often need to remove tools from it. The frequently used pieces, the hammers and screwdrivers, were in a portable red toolbox he carried into the units when he made repairs. He stored the box upstairs in his apartment.

He was disconcerted to see that a nineteenth-century German wrench was missing from the pegboard, the empty space outlined in marker like a crime scene. He'd done a lot of online research before ordering it, and it was more a museum piece than a tool. He didn't think he'd ever used the thing but he liked owning it. Maybe he'd taken it out of the tool cupboard and left it upstairs.

There was work to be done. The winter had crept up on him, caught him out, had permeated the building by stealth while he went about thinking it was still autumn. Things seemed to fall apart more often in winter as if the building too suffered from the grey skies, the cold.

In the old days, tenants wore thick winter clothes even while they were inside. They put bowls of water on the heaters to moisten the winter-dry air. Discomfort in winter was expected. You took care of it yourself, instead of moaning about it to the landlord. You put on a sweater, an extra blanket on the bed.

But now tenants were more delicate. They expected everything to be new and modern and they complained of the slightest deprivation.

Nora, in particular, did not shy away from asking for repairs the minute some minor broken thing revealed itself to her. She knocked on his door last week when a knob came loose from her bathroom cabinet. Looked so helpless because she didn't have a screwdriver to reattach it. He stared into her eyes for a long time, willing her to beg for his help.

She was definitely acting more like Lucinda. Had he learned nothing about women since then? Lucinda had been open to his kindnesses and affection. He had been fooled. Now Nora had asked him about the building, wanted his attention.

Like Lucinda, she signalled that she desired him.

Then Lucinda found other men, brushed him off. Reminded him they were distantly related. Shamed him.

They were the same.

But he tried not to think about Lucinda.

Nora expected him to repair the knob. She treated him like a janitor, nothing more. He would make her wait. Let her pry open the cabinet with her fingers.

* * *

The furnace was next to the garbage room at the rear of the building, down a hall leading out to the back door and the laneway. Removal trucks pulled up there to haul trash away, and sometimes he stood in the doorway with the men from the trucks, smoking and talking. The hall was quiet and empty now, the back door closed. The trucks didn't come during the holidays.

The furnace was ancient, a huge metal contraption that often broke down and was tiresome to adjust. Yet, it still did the job. He felt the thick casing, resting a hand on it here and there like a doctor palpating a chest. It was stone cold.

He couldn't leave it turned off for long. Without heat the water pipes would freeze and burst. Some better plan to get her attention would come to him. He went into the garbage room to inspect the bins, ensure that all was in order there. Perhaps he would step out to the laneway for a smoke after that.

The garbage room reeked. He yanked angrily at the shovel attached to the outside of the bin and clenched his jaw. Everything stank. How dare she ignore him. And someone had stolen his wrench.

He considered the open maw of the bin. Deep in the layers of garbage lay clots of rotted potatoes and rancid meat. If the wasted food hadn't already attracted rodents, it soon would. It was a problem for Henry every fall when the weather cooled, and mice burrowed into the building's foundation seeking warmth for nesting. He tried to keep them out of the concrete and out of the garbage bin, an exercise in futility; the lid on the massive bin had to be left open during the day to catch garbage thrown down the chute from upstairs. And he didn't always come here at night to close the lid.

He propped up a ladder to climb and peer over the edge of the blue metal bin. He gagged from the stench. He lowered the shovel and prodded tentatively in the muck and nudged at something black. Could his wrench be there, discarded by the thief?

The pile moved. A pointed snout poked out of a greasy pizza box. He followed the animal for a while as it burrowed, the tail surprising and disgusting, like a sidewalk worm left after the rain. It was a rat, sooty black and much too large to be a mouse. Henry watched it chewing into the trash, and he contemplated smashing its head with the shovel, but he couldn't be bothered.

38

Nora had no money to take a taxi.

She wasn't earning enough as a barista, clearly, to cope in this expensive city. After-work drinks with Izzy and Kyle and the little trinkets she purchased to give them as holiday gifts had set her back financially. And now she was walking in the cold and desperately wished she could afford a taxi for the last mile of her trip back to the apartment.

The streetcar to her neighbourhood was out of service, the route suspended indefinitely while the transit commission ostensibly completed interminable track repairs, and they hadn't bothered to replace it with a bus. Nora suspected that they were never going to reinstate the service. Her route was seldom used and easy for the city to neglect. Each day after work she rode the subway as far as it would take her, then got off at the terminus where she was often the last passenger. She walked the rest of the way home.

The cold today was the bitter wet kind that seeped through her bones to the marrow.

Her gloves were too thin. She balled her hands and clenched

her fists, fingers curled in a rictus of frozen pain. The suede ankle boots, once so stylish and perfectly matched with her coat, were also not meant for winter weather. Inside the boots, her feet were soaked as the wet snow seeped through. The suede was ruined, stained with a jagged white line of road salt.

As she walked by Lucky Convenience and saw that it was closed, deep sadness overwhelmed her. She'd become used to the quirky owner, a familiar person in her new neighbourhood, and she'd learned not to over-spend there. The lights were off and the store shuttered in utter darkness. The trash can out front spilled over with empty soda cans and folded cardboard boxes. A hanging sign in the door erroneously said 'open', as if the truth were immaterial.

Wasn't this supposed to be a joyful time of year?

The last time she celebrated Christmas, really celebrated as if it meant something to her, was before Dylan died.

Snow fell on her head and melted in her hair, dampening the shoulders of her coat. She'd forgotten her hat somewhere between work and the moment when she realized she wasn't wearing it. She tried to conjure an image of it on a hook in the back room or lying on the subway seat. She came up with nothing. Her hair was stiffened with ice at the ends.

Before Dylan died, when the little girl was sick and listless, and Nora was concerned, Carter insisted that whatever was wrong with Dylan would heal itself. Proclaiming that doctors were charlatans and fools. She could still hear his voice as he made this pronouncement, his words an invasion in her head.

Nora walked by a house with a sagging porch, broken chairs lined up under the window. A mongrel dog chained to a chair lunged towards her, barking furiously and dragging the piece of furniture across the porch. The chair caught in the railing, restraining and enraging the animal even more but giving Nora time to hurry past the house. Someone in the window above the raging dog pulled aside a torn curtain and watched her go.

She could hear Carter shouting. The animal's bark called forth her husband's raving anger, his voice screaming in her head. When she said she was taking Dylan to a doctor he threatened to take the child from her. But she was already in the car and on the way to find medical help.

The dog growled and barked, saliva dripping from its jowls. She heard it for half a block until she finally reached her building and saw the oak trees in the courtyard and felt safe.

The front walkway had not been shovelled. She picked her way across crusty snow to the front door, each step painful on frozen toes. She stepped cautiously, because she'd already gone over once or twice on her ankle. It was unlike Henry not to have cleared the ice from the path. He was usually so diligent, so busy at his tasks.

Your fault, Carter had screamed, you let the hospital kill her. But he had it all wrong, backwards.

She used her key to open the heavy door of the building, her fingers so stiff from the cold she fumbled and fought to grip. It was oddly cold inside the vestibule. She removed her gloves and massaged the blood back into her corpse white fingers. The rubber weather strip under the front door had come loose, peeled off at one end and it lay useless on the floor like a sloughed-off snakeskin. Icy air licked its way in underneath it.

A haphazard pile of unclaimed mail lay on top of the radiator.

Her fingers tingled as they came back to life and she picked up a letter and felt the smooth paper, then put it back down. She chose another, a red one with a Christmas postage stamp on it. A square envelope, the paper cheap and bent at the corners from its travels. It was addressed in blue marker in a child's uneven print-ing to Miss M. The street name was misspelled and the apartment number missing.

Perhaps a Christmas card for a Miss M., whoever she was, a person who lived on Farmdale Lane. A card mailed a few days too late to arrive in time. Nora looked up at the steps to the first landing and over her shoulder to the walkway outside. She was alone in the vestibule, and no one was approaching.

The red paper was discoloured by a drop of moisture near the stamp. She slipped the envelope into the pocket of her coat and went upstairs.

She hadn't received any Christmas cards, nor had she sent any.

During her marriage, the Christmas holiday had been a big deal. In the house she would light candles, display all the greeting cards on the mantle, and decorate a tree in the living room. They entertained lavishly during the season, and Carter invited half the town to his annual Christmas open house. It was his way of drumming up more business for his legal practice and showing he was a pillar of the town. He played the loving husband then, acted sweet to her while people were there to observe. He always drank too much at the parties, and later, when they were alone, he got rough.

Nora walked up the eight flights to her apartment, and at each landing she paused and turned, putting Carter further out of her mind. She was moments away from a hot bath, a restful evening alone, a nice glass of wine.

* * *

The apartment key wouldn't turn in the lock. She pulled it out and inspected it to see if she'd used the right one, scrutinizing the notches as if they held a secret code. She turned it over in her palm. It was her apartment door key, marked with red nail polish to distinguish it from the identical-looking building entrance key. Strange to think that this small piece of steel was the armour keeping her safe from the world.

She slid it around the heart-shaped fob until it nestled with its front door mate. She had used the right key. The other two keys were differently shaped: the heavy square Lakeview Coffee key that she'd only had to use to lock up once and then forgotten to return to Kyle, and her mailbox key, tiny, insubstantial, no more secure than a pin, symbolic, like a key to a diary.

She took the key marked with red nail polish and tried again to unlock her apartment door. She shoved it in the hole and tried to move the cylinder, and turned the key quickly and hard. It jammed part-way and would not turn. She kicked the door in frustration.

At Henry's door Toffee's head popped up under the red velvet curtain.

She knocked on his door. The cat jumped away but there was otherwise no response. She thought she heard the radio playing, indistinct and low, voices of a call-in show at this hour. She often heard music or the weather-report through the walls or behind his door, and suspected he left the radio playing because he was one of those people who abhorred silence.

She knocked once more, but it was obvious he wasn't in. She wondered if it might be useful to see if a neighbour could help. Get someone else to try the key, insert it at another angle, use a different motion to twist, or apply some grease to the mechanism. She knew that sometimes when she did things in anger or haste it was her own insistence thwarting her, keeping the solution out of her grasp. She didn't have much patience and was certainly tired enough right now that maybe she couldn't see what she was doing wrong with the key.

A neighbour might know where Henry was. He was probably around the building somewhere. She went down to the seventh floor where the hallway was cold, air whistled through a vent. She knocked on the first door in from the landing. No answer. She tried a few more doors, knocking and calling out "Hello, anyone home?"

How annoying this was. She thought she sounded polite. How rude of people to ignore her when she simply wanted to lie down and rest on her own bed. The hallway lights burned low, casting long shadows on the dirty green carpet and the faded cabbage roses of the wallpaper that looked like wizened old faces.

It was 7 p.m., Monday. She knew without question that people must be home making dinner, watching something on TV. Faint light spilled out randomly beneath a few doors, and there were smells, even under the scent of dust and damp, the lingering odors of other people's cooking.

Cautiously, she crept up to a door, it was 708, and rested her ear against it. She held her breath and listened. She thought she felt someone on the other side, listening for her to go away.

She returned to the landing to try another floor and remembered Henry had told her about a suite he was renovating on the fifth floor. She'd try looking for him there.

As she rounded the corner from the stairs and entered the fifth-floor corridor, a flicker of light, a reflection from the turning of a crystal knob, shone briefly on the threadbare carpet.

She rushed to the apartment door. 502. She knocked.

"Hello, Henry? It's Nora. I'm locked out. Please could you help me?"

She wondered if this was the right unit. Was it another number he had mentioned?

Her head spun a little from running down the hall and she

felt empty with hunger. She needed to get into her apartment and to eat something.

"Henry," she called out. "Where are you?"

Behind the door there was a soft sound. A child giggling.

She rattled the glass handle. "Please open the door," she said. "I'm your neighbour." She leaned in hard and pushed. The door was locked tight and failed to yield at the thud of her shoulder.

Her head throbbed. Was she shouting?

The soft sound behind the door, within, not laughter. Sobbing. A child crying.

She'd upset someone's child.

"I'm sorry I frightened you," she said. "Are you alone in there?" She backed away from the door. "You're right not to answer if you are all alone."

What had gotten into her? Shouting in the halls. Frightening someone's kid. She hurried away.

39

When she returned to the eighth floor, the landing blazed with light. At Henry's door the red velvet curtain had been pulled aside and she could see his living room; all his lights were on, the yellow glare from the chandelier and the harsh white of his reading lamps spilled out through the glass and onto the hardwood floors and the rug. A Glen Gould recording played on the stereo, the same CD Henry seemed to play over and over, the Goldberg Variations he'd said it was called. She remembered because she'd found the music haunting, the sound of the pianist humming over the notes disconcerting.

She put her hand on the glass knob and turned. The unlocked door opened and she entered Henry's apartment.

A window behind the ridiculous white wicker chairs was open a crack, the curtain fluffed lightly where there was no screen, and from down in the courtyard the sounds of traffic on the snowy road were sucked up into the room and mingled with the music.

"Henry? Hello?"

She was alone in front of the armoire. She pressed eject on the CD. She listened for Henry.

And then the rustling of tissue paper and heels clicking on the floor. Esme bustled into the living room, fussing with fancy paper shopping bags from the high-end boutiques on Bloor Street. Nora gazed with envy at the stiff bags with designer names. She watched as Esme pulled at ribbons and packing material and extracted elegant things from the wrappings and examined and clucked over them.

"Beautiful, beautiful," Esme intoned softly. She made a pile of folded tissue paper and bows.

Nora went to the blue sofa, where the beautiful items were being arrayed and Esme spoke to her as if it were the most natural thing in the world to find Nora alone in Henry's apartment.

"So many sales this time of year," Esme said. "My dear, come see what I've got."

"Did you just get here?" Nora said. "I knocked a moment ago. And I was calling for help downstairs."

"Come in. Eat some goodies. We're having a little soiree. Close friends." She had something green in her hands. "I want Henry to wear this."

"I didn't hear you come up the stairs."

Esme thrust a bundle at her, pressed it towards her, a green sweater carefully folded in white tissue paper. Wool the colour of mown grass, cashmere soft and lovely, which Esme held reverently and lightly brushed against Nora's cheek.

"I'm certain Henry invited you," Esme said. "In fact, I recall he mentioned it." She opened the door of the armoire and reached to the back of the deep shelf. "A few good friends. Some food."

Esme's suit was heather grey, the skirt threaded with strands of lavender.

"Maybe I will come for a drink, but I need help first. I'm locked out of my place. Where's Henry?"

"Scottish wool," Esme said. "The best."

Nora had beautiful clothes when she lived with Carter. She'd had a Chanel suit similar in style to the one Esme wore now, in white. Esme's was heavier, the skirt longer, tailored for her thicker, older physique. Nora had always been thin.

Esme unwrapped another layer of tissue, revealing a blue silk blouse. Nora had her coat on, still damp from the snow, and beneath the coat she wore the dark green store apron stained with coffee that she'd forgotten to leave at work. On her skin, she felt the fabric of the faded black turtleneck and stretched-out nylon leggings she dressed in every day. She was perspiring even though the room was cold. She wanted to take off the wet coat, but she would appear shabby—her once elegant clothes now ruined and worn too often—next to this stylish woman in the elegant wool suit.

"Henry thinks the world of you, dear." Esme lit a red candle and put it on the table by the brown couch. She placed two long red tapers on the dining table, and then she flitted around the living room to dim the lamps. "He thinks you're very special."

There were little bowls of nuts on the side tables. Pecans and cashews. Nora was hungry.

"Goodness," Esme said. "I've forgotten the olives. I must go buy some."

Esme found her fur hat and put it on carefully, positioning it precisely atop her coiled hair. She wound a thick, fringed camel wrap around and over her shoulders, covering the suit. Until she donned the hat she was small, her square face unremarkable. The fur hat transformed Esme; the high honey-toned fur made her taller, regal and elegant.

Nora watched Esme prepare to go out. She wanted so much to put that fur hat on her own head, to pose in a mirror and see if the hat would alter her.

"I'll just pop out to the shop for a second," Esme said. "Make yourself at home."

* * *

Henry's scrapbook lay open on the coffee table, papers and scissors and glassine envelopes next to it. Nora moved the burning candle away from the papers. She ate some cashews out of the small bowl.

His apartment was different from hers, her meagre dark and barren little room, with its small bed and alcove for a kitchen. His was very large, too big for one occupant and crowded, over-stuffed with bulky sofas and mismatched chairs. There were too many rugs and lamps of all styles; and the ugly paintings he'd put up for display.

An open bottle of red wine was on the dining room table, the cork left on a little brass tray beside it. She removed a cut-glass goblet from the cabinet and poured herself several ounces.

Esme had left the armoire open. Inside were locked storage boxes and piles of papers and photographs, a wooden bowl containing screws and nails and keys. Dozens of keys. Nora put her hand in the bowl of keys and let them fall through her fingers.

She found the diary he talked about and was weirdly proud of. The binding almost came apart in her hands, the spine was so thin and brittle. She took the book to the sofa and moved aside some newspapers so she could sit down with it. She opened it and tried to read an entry, but the ink was faint and the handwriting so small and pinched it was difficult to decipher. There were old photos placed between pages, and she looked with interest at some of those. Faces stared out at her. Someone's long-dead relatives. The photos were faded and marked with fingerprints.

She sipped the wine.

He was an odd duck, Henry, collecting such stuff, pasting newspaper articles into scrapbooks. Although, she had to admit, there was something fascinating about the old stories.

Here was something from *The Toronto Star*, dated 1988. A woman named only as L. W. found murdered in her apartment. The killing was described as random and bizarre, the dead woman's battered body placed almost tenderly on the bed, her hair had been brushed, and a blanket was folded neatly over her feet.

Henry was interested in history and, apparently, crime. Well, wasn't everyone?

She was warmed by the wine. She took off her coat.

The details of the murder were peculiar. The woman's potted houseplants had been arranged on top of the bed with her body.

Esme should be back any moment. They'd find Henry and get her key sorted.

The killer had then stolen the woman's car and driven across Ontario for weeks until he was finally caught and brought to trial. The police had searched for the suspect and the car and finally caught him when he stopped at a gas station.

Nora wondered if the poor woman had sensed what was coming for her. Was there any warning or had the killer surprised her while she was in her kitchen, lighting the stove or pulling something out of the fridge, making supper like any other day?

She thought of how a killer might walk up softly behind you.

Nora heard the swish of tires on the wet road outside and inside the rush of water in the pipes coursing through the walls.

She should leave. It was strange being in Henry's place alone.

The newspaper article went on to talk about the trial. The

prosecutor described the killer as a monster. His lawyers hired a prominent psychiatrist who testified that the killer was very ill but treatable. They asked for lenience for such a young man.

How did this woman come to know a killer? Who were they to each other, the victim and her assailant? It was only in the last paragraph that the reporter explained that the killer's name could not be published, his identity was protected because he was only seventeen.

* * *

Nora left Henry's apartment, and she waited on the landing, exhausted and hungry. She sat down on the floor and was so tired that she fell asleep. By the time the staircase groaned with footsteps, she had been asleep for an hour on the floor, curled up outside her door. She opened her eyes and saw heavy beige work boots first, then grease-stained jeans and a thick plaid shirt, frayed at the cuffs.

Henry cleared his throat roughly, and she woke up fully and raised her head to the smell of sweat and metal. He carried his heavy red toolbox, and he put it down by his feet.

"Well, well, well." He pushed blonde hair away from his forehead. "Wasn't expecting you back so early."

"What do you mean?" She smoothed her hair, unconsciously echoing Henry, brushed some dust from her coat.

"I had to change the locks," he said. "Was planning to get you the new key." He knelt down and opened the red toolbox revealing a tray full of hammers. He lifted the insert and fished underneath, poking fingers into the jumbled objects inside. There was a roll of duct tape, pliers. "Some trouble with burglaries."

He handed her a key.

"All in order now. You're perfectly secure."

40

"No," Kyle said, "not again." He looked to the man seated across from him for commiseration. The man stared at the floor. Some of the other subway passengers looked at him as if he were a crazy person speaking to himself. Others nodded in agreement, silently. It *was* an annoyance each time the train paused in the tunnel while men with shovels cleared snow from the outdoor tracks up ahead. The snowstorm raged on and when they reached the station at the end, after a ride that was twice as long as it should have been, he was as surprised as everyone else to have made it there at all.

When Nora greeted him at her door, he handed her two things: a plastic bag from the shopping mall and a white cardboard box tied with string. "For you," he said. "I honestly didn't think it would take this long." She put everything on the kitchen counter, perhaps assuming it was all food. He realized his misstep in not wrapping up the gift, to make it more obvious, more festive. "We could shop together for something special you really want," he said.

Snow piled up in a triangle against her window screen and cool air inched in through the walls. Nora wore a sweater over her long-sleeved top, and her arms were folded around her chest, preserving body heat. He hoped she'd invite him to spend the night so he wouldn't have to go back out in such weather.

"What a great night to stay in," he said. "It's really blowing."

But she didn't take the hint; she was busy looking inside the plastic bag. Then she held the box and sniffed.

He pulled off his boots, balancing on one foot at a time. She really needed to place a stool or chair by the door. "I got you a phone," he said. He'd looked at phones for an hour at the mall, going from store to store until he found one he wanted. Nora drew it out of the bag.

The silver phone was packaged in hard clear plastic that was impossible to open without scissors or a knife. He saw her appraise the phone, an economical thing sold at a kiosk, the kind of simple, throw-away phone drug dealers and old people preferred. To his relief, she smiled.

"This one smells better," she said, holding out the pastry box. "Like cumin and honey."

"Pork buns," he said. "From my favourite place on Baldwin. But they must be cold by now."

He pulled off his ski jacket, damp from walking against the pummelling snow, and folded it neatly, laying it on the floor, remembering she didn't like him to hang things in her closet. He moved towards her and brought into her room the smoky smell of the cold and of the dark winter street.

"I'm so happy to see you," he said, hugging her. His face scraped against her cheek. He'd meant to kiss her on the mouth; it was Nora who turned away as he bent his head down to hers, causing him to scratch her face inadvertently with his poorly shaved chin.

She turned her face away; he wasn't always sure what she wanted. Other women, other girlfriends, had been more direct with him, some boldly asserting how they wanted the relationship, or the sex, to go. He found Nora's reticence strange, but he accepted it.

"I'm sorry," he said, as she put a hand to her cheek. "I had the radio on while I shaved. The news distracted me, and I think I forgot to shave parts of my jaw."

She took her hand off her face. "What was on the news?"

A faint red line appeared on her cheek where his whiskers had marked her.

He kept up with current affairs and enjoyed the all-news stations as much as the ones that played classic rock. He'd been paying attention to local news especially, ever since the Santa Claus Parade, when Nora had returned to the store, upset over some violence she'd seen, her face ashen. He'd expected to hear about it, but nothing was ever reported. The local news was dominated by stories of crowded hospitals. It was a segment about the current flu season that grabbed his attention. Public Health warned people to take precautions against it.

"You'll think I'm a hypochondriac." He sat down on the teak chair. "They said the flu was terrible this year. So, I literally put down my razor to do a search on the phone for the nearest walk-in clinic." He laughed at himself.

"Why? Are you sick?" She perched on the bed looking towards him, her back against the yellow rails.

Was he wrong, or did she actually look worried that he was about to infect her? She slid to the furthest end of the bed, and curled her legs up on the mattress.

"No. I'm fine. And want to stay that way. I went to get a flu shot."

The clinic had been busy with waiting patients, and when he was done he hurried out to buy Nora the phone. The mall was chaotic with boxing week bargain hunters and long line-ups at the cash registers. He wasted time at RadioShack browsing among radios and headphones, wondering if he should buy her something more. Then after the mall he walked to the Chinese bakery, which was out of the way, but worth it because he wanted to bring Nora some of the delectable buns.

"I thought of how sick you were before Christmas. You should get a flu shot too."

She looked at him blankly.

He changed the topic.

"I thought a pink phone was too juvenile. I hope silver is okay," Kyle said. "Can I come sit with you? We can both put our feet up."

She patted the bed beside her.

"Let me explain about this phone," he said.

"So nice of you."

How to say it, when she was sensitive about money and might take offence, that he knew she couldn't afford a fancy cellphone, but that everyone should have one? He'd approach it like a caring boyfriend, which he hoped she'd realize he was.

"It's only a burner," he said, holding the phone. "All you can do is make calls, no Wi-Fi. You don't need to buy a phone plan, and you can use it to call me with the pre-paid minutes." He put his arm around her. "Or call 9-1-1. If you ever needed."

She leaned into him, and he was conscious of his yielding body, his biceps under the thin T-shirt not as hard as he'd like, but he was fit enough and, he hoped, solid and reassuring. She put her hand on his upper arm, and he flexed the muscle.

"If you run out of phone minutes we can—"

"You're bleeding."

There was a round stain on the sleeve of his shirt. "Must be from the needle," he said. "I rushed out of the clinic and didn't pay any attention to it."

The medical clinic, next to a supermarket, had been packed with people. Office workers standing impatiently in stylish suits, seniors huddled in old wool coats, parents tending to babies squirming in strollers. Lots of people coughing and sneezing.

The blood stain had dried. "You should have seen all the kids," he said. He had a vague sense that she liked children. But also a sense that the topic was delicate. That something about the husband, the awful husband, had meant they never had kids.

Kyle thought he should really shut up but something about the way Nora sat silently on the bed staring at the tiny red mark on his shirt, compelled him to keep talking. He liked kids. He wouldn't mind a kid of his own someday. Teach them to play the guitar. "There was this one boy," he said. "This one kid, he was kicking his boots against the back of a chair—"

"A flu shot," Nora said. She looked far away as if she wasn't listening to him.

"Yeah."

She held the new phone in her palm and turned it over.

"Carter didn't believe in them," she said.

Before he could respond she got up abruptly and went to the kitchen. Kyle was sympathetic, but he was pretty sure he didn't want to hear about the husband. She should talk to Izzy. A woman friend would be better able to handle the emotion.

The kitchen cupboard banged shut.

"The hinge is broken," she said.

He put his head around the corner of the alcove wall. "I could fix it with a screwdriver."

Kyle had set something off in Nora that he didn't understand. Her mood had shifted. He watched her fill the kettle and put it on the stove. They waited while it boiled and whistled.

"What do you have with caffeine?" he said. "Is that herbal tea?" He took a jar of finely ground green powder and unscrewed the lid to smell it. The odour was disgusting. He didn't want tea made from whatever this was.

"Seriously," he said. "I could fix this hinge for you."

"Please put that away," she said, taking the jar out of his hand. "I don't even know why I put the kettle on."

"Let's eat the buns. Then we can order in more food."

"The super can fix it," she said. "Which reminds me."

She looked out at the fire escape where snow had collected in deep drifts on the slats.

"We're invited next door," she said. "For drinks."

"Where?"

"The super, the landlord. I never remember which he prefers. Henry."

She must know he didn't like Henry.

"He's having people over."

"I don't want to go there." He saw other jars of powder on the shelf of the opened cupboard. He thought Henry was arrogant and a bore, but saying so would sound petulant. "Let's order pizza and then go to a neighbourhood bar instead."

She put her arms around him. She kissed him. Was she back to herself, in a lighter mood now?

"There's a storm outside! Just one drink. I have to stay friendly with the guy who runs the building." She pushed the palms of her hands into his chest. "It'll be fun."

41

It was because of Henry that Kyle felt agitated. The guy riled him up, made him nervous in front of Nora, as if there was a competition for her attention. Henry had left the door ajar, and there was music playing, so Kyle and Nora simply entered without knocking.

Henry's expression when he turned and saw Nora with Kyle was that of a man who'd been spit on. Anger tinged with disappointment that she hadn't come alone.

Kyle knew that Henry didn't want him in his place any more than Kyle wanted to be there.

Nora sank immediately into the brown leather sofa and poured herself a glass of wine, leaving Kyle standing awkwardly in front of Henry.

"How's it going dude?" Henry had dressed for the occasion in dark skinny jeans and a green cashmere sweater. Sure, Henry was handsome in a way Kyle feared he was not. But the man reeked of cologne or aftershave. It made him want to retch. And should a guy in his late forties really be calling people 'dude'?

The lights were dimmed, shadows flickered, a few pieces of tinsel dangled limply from the chandelier.

"Thanks for inviting us," he said.

Henry said nothing, merely cocked his head like an animal trying to understand. The corners of his mouth went up in a false and condescending smile.

Kyle recognized the music playing, trumpet notes flowed from speakers placed on shelves and against a wall was an actual stereo console, the turntable revolving. The vintage stereo piqued Kyle's interest. He had to give Henry points for having some musical gravitas. He thought the stereo cabinet was from the 1960s. That, at least, was something interesting to talk about.

"Miles Davis at Newport," he said.

Henry was unimpressed by his knowledge and leaned over Nora to top up her glass, leaning in too close, Kyle thought. They'd just arrived, she didn't need more wine yet. The guy was so arrogant. Was that a smirk?

Henry put the wine on the table and sat down next to Nora.

Kyle took a seat across from them on a ratty blue sofa. He had to shove aside masses of books and newspapers to make a spot for himself. A bottle of red wine was on the coffee table, poured out into two wine glasses. Nora reached for one of them to continue drinking from it.

"Where is everyone?" Nora said, looking around the room.

She ate a few cashews from a ceramic bowl. Henry lifted the other wine glass to his mouth.

"Canceled," Henry said. "No one wants to come out in a snowstorm." He winked at Kyle.

Kyle sat stiffly, hands on knees and nowhere to look but four feet away at his girlfriend and Henry sitting together on the couch, like a bad movie he didn't want to see. He hadn't been offered any wine.

"They say twenty centimetres coming tonight," Henry said, crossing his legs and dropping an olive into his mouth. "Surprised you made it here dude."

Kyle heard the hard icy snow blowing against the window-panes. Every few seconds during a break in the howling wind a slash of black winter sky shot through the driving snow.

And at once, like a sickening punch to the gut, Kyle realized that Henry had not invited other guests to a party, that he certainly had not invited Kyle. What Henry had planned for tonight was much smaller, more intimate.

Two wine glasses on the table.

* * *

They'd been there long enough. They'd sipped wine and nibbled on nuts, engaged in boring chit-chat with Henry for an hour. Kyle shifted his position on the hard, high-backed sofa and tried to catch Nora's eye. Surely, she wouldn't find it impolite to leave now.

But she didn't look up from the handful of photographs Henry was showing her, passing them to her one by one while he described them.

"I mean, think about the history," Henry said. "The generations."

He sat very close to her, their shoulders touching. She seemed enthralled, looking intently at each photo, holding each carefully by the edges as Henry handed it to her. Her face was flushed from the wine, and the top button of her blouse had come loose.

"It's getting late, I guess," Kyle said, half rising from the sofa. "Nora?"

She looked up, and her eyes widened as if newly waking and

becoming aware that he was in the room.

"Are you tired man?" Henry said. "You look about to drift off from boredom." He checked his watch. "You can still catch the last train if you leave now."

Henry's thigh was right up against Nora's. Her lipstick had rubbed away entirely, staining her empty wineglass with the waxy impression of her lower lip.

"Kyle's not interested in the building history like we are," she said.

"It's not that," he said, flustered, excluded from their cozy duo. What did she see in this guy?

"I might be a bit groggy from the flu shot I had today." Maybe she'd take the hint and get them both a ticket out of there.

The remark seemed to set off a spark of energy in Henry. He jumped up from the couch and opened a large wooden cabinet, returning with a book, a journal with a pink ribbon hanging from the binding. He put it in Nora's lap.

"I've shown you this before, I think," he said. "She lived here during the 1918 flu pandemic. It's fascinating."

A flicker of recognition came to Nora, and she opened the book. She flipped over the pages.

"I can't read the handwriting at all," she said.

Kyle tried to mouth the words to her. *Let's go.* She nodded and held up a finger as if to say, one minute. Then she gave the book back to Henry.

"Tell us what she wrote," Nora said.

Henry opened the book. He looked triumphant. He began to read aloud.

December 10, 1918

It is no use, they will all die from this terrible

influenza. There are so many cots crowded together and as soon as one patient is gone, another takes his place.

We have used the last of the cough syrup and our other treatments are ineffective. The nurses agree with me the cinnamon and milk does not reduce fever. We coax the poor men to drink it but it is vomited up again.

My patients are so weak, so tired. And the virus is vicious and quick. Men who sit up to drink tea and smile in the morning develop a spiking fever at noon and are dead by supper.

I don't know how to tolerate much more. Thinking of these brave young soldiers surviving battles in Europe only to return home and succumb to this. It breaks my heart.

A man I have tended for a week died this morning. Albert, only twenty. Cheerful until the end, insisting that he would go home and marry his sweetheart in Oshawa.

The body lies still and silent in the cot with the blanket up to his chin.

The man next to him refuses to be moved away to another corner. He wants to keep his comrade company until the car from the morgue arrives later this evening. That's the kind of men they are. There will be more bodies by tonight.

Henry paused. He said, "What a catastrophe." He passed the olives to Nora, who declined.

"And she lived here?" Nora asked. "Doris Carr lived in this building?"

"Yup. 502. With her daughter, Alice."

"We should get going," Kyle said. He wondered if he should leave alone, get going to the subway if Nora was going to be obstinate, but it was so late now, the subway would shut soon, and he'd never get a cab in this weather. He'd have to spend the night at Nora's.

"Read another page," she said. "Read something about Alice."

> *I am not worried about myself. I never get sick. But I fret about Alice. She is small for her age and eats like a bird. I have kept her safe indoors, away from crowds on the street. She is an angel, contenting herself with her dolls and toys. She is four years old.*

> *When I am at work she is all alone in the apartment.*

> *I would not be in this predicament, having to earn a wage and leave Alice alone if I hadn't been so foolish to believe T when he said he would marry me.*

> *I asked my neighbour Mrs. Robertson to look in on Alice and see that she eats supper and gets to bed. I had rather hoped she would take pity on us and bring my child home with her so she would not be unattended. But she did not do so. I suppose she*

is busy with her own family and has no time for my little Alice.

I think also that Mrs. R does not believe I lost my husband in the war. She suspects the truth and thinks we are undeserving of her charity.

I am quite afraid because several of the other nurses have fallen sick and now I must work over-night. Leaving Alice alone all night is difficult. What if she becomes ill and I am not there?

"Did she really leave her daughter all night? Nora asked.

"Finish your drink Nora," Henry said. "I'll open another bottle and read more."

But Kyle couldn't stand one more minute of it and was desperate to leave. The diary sounded made up, the handwriting was indecipherable, yet as Henry unwound the words Nora was more enthralled.

"We should be going," he said. "Henry, how about letting her borrow that to—"

Henry grimaced. Even with eyes downcast to his lap where the diary lay, the look of disgust was evident to Kyle. Nora saw only the book; she followed the brittle pages as Henry carefully turned them over.

"I'll find the part where she meets my great uncle," Henry said. "Allowing the tenants—"

Nora jerked her head as if she'd startled awake. She took the diary roughly from Henry and closed it. She stood up and said she had to go. Then she said the strangest thing.

"Don't you see?" she said. "The little one is all alone. I have to find Dylan and help her."

42

Henry knew when Kyle spent the night with Nora. The odious man, he had no right to her. Henry made a point of listening for the galumphing footsteps on the stairs, the voices through the wall. As if the sounds would reveal some truth he had missed. He listened and planned.

Several times, he'd followed them out of the building. Usually, he stopped after a block or so. He kept back discreetly at a distance as they walked past Lucky Convenience. He told himself he didn't care where they went or what they did. But he saw how Nora leaned into Kyle and tilted her face to his, heard her laughter and saw her breath suspended in the cold air like chimney smoke, and he suffered. It was an affront to witness her evident delight in the other man. When she should be his.

The most recent foray drew him farther out of the neighbourhood. He didn't want to stop following until he had answers, until he understood. He hung back a few paces and merged with other pedestrians and kept his eyes on her.

They turned onto a busy street, and he lost sight momentarily because of all the people on the sidewalk, but then he spied them about to descend the steps into the subway. At the top of the stairs leading into the bowels of the station, Kyle stopped and pulled Nora against his chest and leaned over her. They took their time kissing, forcing other people to jostle around them, and it was maddening how she inclined her head just so. Dangerous to dwell on a kiss and be so oblivious at the very top of a long, steep stairway where it was easy to fall.

He could push someone into Kyle.

He kept back and slunk into the station behind them and observed them pay the fare and pass through the turnstiles. They walked toward the passage for the southbound train. Henry went the same way, easing onto the platform. He mingled with the noisy crowd, and he waited for the train to come, never taking his eyes off the pair.

Kyle had hockey skates slung over his shoulder. The skates were tied together by the laces, and the black leather was scuffed from wear. One arm dangled loosely across Nora's shoulder, claiming the same casual ownership of her and the skates. He seemed very pleased with himself.

Henry would not be so cavalier with Nora.

He watched them stand and wait for the train. They were close to the edge, foolishly perched on the raised yellow caution strip. Someone could rush at Kyle and push him over the edge into the path of the speeding train.

There were perhaps too many witnesses to get away with it. Too many security cameras in the station.

The train screeched into the station and all the doors opened simultaneously. Henry boarded several doors away from them. He could walk from car to car on the train if he needed to be closer. It was easy for someone fit and able, to balance and walk as the train snaked through the dark tunnel. He was careful to stay mixed in with the crowd. It wasn't difficult because there was so much animated talking and movement among the packed-in passengers. He leaned against a pole in the last car and kept his eyes peeled on them as the train barrelled its way downtown.

He had expected her to come alone for drinks the other night. He leaned into the pole as the train shuddered and felt the metal absorb his anger. He had wanted her all to himself, just as he had since the first night when she moved in. He had managed to control his rage when she'd shown up for drinks with Kyle, and he was proud of that.

They got off at Queen holding hands in a sickening display of puppy love. They headed to the outdoor skating rink at City Hall. He watched Kyle help her lace the skates and kiss her again. He wasn't attractive, wasn't even fit. A beer gut protruded from an unzipped parka, yet Kyle had the audacity to make a claim on Nora while he, Henry, kept himself lean and strong. And was rejected.

He would do something about the situation.

He watched them from the shadows between buildings where he had a clear view of the rink. They were joined by the little pixie, the short-haired friend, the one who looked like she was twelve, a kid. The kid wore white and pink, dressed like a piece of peppermint candy, and as he tried to get closer, to hear what they said to each other, the kid looked his way. Not a kid, a young woman with a penetrating gaze.

43

The plan was for Izzy to spend an hour ice skating with Kyle and Nora. It was Kyle's suggestion that they meet up at the rink. He told Izzy on the phone that he was worried about Nora, she seemed stressed and preoccupied and unable to sleep. Izzy heard stress in his voice too.

She asked Kyle what was bothering Nora. He hesitated. There was silence on the phone. Then he cleared his throat.

"That time after the parade," he said. "When she came into the store crying?"

"I didn't see her crying," she said. She'd left the parade early because her ears were cold.

"Nora said the clowns are– in her dreams or something."

"Wait," Izzy said. "I don't remember clowns in the parade." She tried to recall that day. Marching bands, kids in funny hats. "I told Nora I had a phobia and that I hoped no clowns showed up. I mean clowns are horrible, right? She's probably thinking of that."

"Yeah," he said. "She has bad dreams, wakes up and tells

me about them." He went silent again. Then he said, "She talks about her past almost like it's a dream too. Mentions people." He coughed. "There may be a kid somewhere. It's sad. That's all I know."

Izzy was shocked. Nora had never mentioned a child. Didn't say much about herself at all. "Was there a guy, a husband maybe? If I knew more, I could be a better friend, help her."

"Look Izzy, I feel funny talking details, even if I had them."

"I get it." She switched the phone to her other ear, where it wouldn't press against a stud. "You're being a good boyfriend, you keep secrets."

"No," he said. "I don't have anything to tell."

Izzy said she had an idea. "Let's all go skating. Take Nora's mind off whatever is bothering her. Get out and do something fun together."

* * *

Kyle was already on the ice when Izzy got there. She found Nora sitting on a bench facing the rink. Quite a competent skater, Kyle went two laps around the perimeter before he waived to her and Nora on the bench. Izzy laced up, then helped Nora adjust her own skates.

"He put them on, but they were too tight," Nora said. She waived at Kyle. "I don't know how to do this."

Izzy was excited to get on the ice. She could skate as fast as Kyle. "It'll come back to you. Like riding a bike." She tugged Nora up from the bench until she wobbled and sat back down.

"I've never done it," Nora said.

"Have you really never ice-skated before?" Izzy said. "I thought you were from a small town." If they went around the rink, Nora would loosen up, tell Izzy what was on her mind. Then she could help her sort it out. She was good at giving advice

250

to friends, everyone said so.

The outdoor rink at Nathan Phillips Square was one of the city's major tourist attractions. It covered most of the square in front of the modernist concrete City Hall. There were massive sculptures and a peace garden. Concrete parabolas rose high over the rink and that night they were festooned with red and green Christmas lights. When she looked up, the sparkles reflected on Nora's face. Music played from overhead speakers and children chased and shouted to each other over the melodies. Yet, when she tried to coax Nora off the bench, she only shook her head. How could anyone be unhappy here?

"I don't know about you, but in high school skating was our main winter activity. That and drinking beer at keg parties."

"Oh, I've watched people," Nora said. "I took Dylan to the rink in the park. But only to look. She was too young."

Exactly what Kyle had hinted at. Who was Dylan and would it upset Nora to ask?

"Do you want to talk about it?" She said it gently. Kyle glided around the curve and skated by without stopping. "Tell me about Dylan."

"My daughter. I held her hands once and we walked in our boots on the ice," she said. "She loved it."

Izzy was on the cusp of probing further. Nora seemed willing to talk more about her child, but Kyle appeared, sliding to a stop in front of them, his skate blades cutting the ice. "Makes me want to play hockey again," he said. "Let's get out there."

It was as if Nora suddenly remembered where she was. "I'm not an athlete," she said, "and I broke my wrist once, in a fall."

Here was another detail, a broken wrist. Could it be something? Izzy tried to look at Kyle, but he ignored the remark, was focused on skating.

"You two ready to take a spin?" Kyle asked

"Go ahead," Nora said, "Go with Izzy, without me."

Izzy was having none of that. "No way," she said. She pushed off, "I'm too swift for you." She swirled, skated backwards and saw Kyle carefully guide Nora slowly by the elbow. Izzy turned again and flew through the crowd. She skated with strength, with grace, arcing around shuffling couples and a slow old man. She smiled as she passed the senior. She glided on one foot and plotted a way to get the rest of Nora's story. She executed a perfect figure eight in the centre of the rink. She would help Nora fix the sad situation she was in. She skated for a few minutes, losing herself in the sheer joy of it.

She took a lap around the rink, thrilled to feel her muscles move in the cool dark night, and she thought of Nora's little girl, and her husband, and wondered about them. She skated for a long time, passing her friends over and over– her shins were stinging now – and from the corner of her eye she caught something moving towards her, some dark moving thing, and she was momentarily uncomfortable. She looked for her friends.

She found them at the far end, near the skate rental shack, Nora a little breathless with cheeks glowing, as Kyle skated backwards so he could hold both her hands. Nora inched forward tentatively while Kyle steadied her. Such a sweet guy.

"You're still on the ice," Izzy said. "Try to push and glide. You won't fall with Kyle right there."

Kyle said they'd only just come back on the ice. They'd stopped to rest and watch Izzy go round and round. It was late now and she hadn't realized. Kyle took Nora for a last crawl along the edge, and Izzy waited on the bench. The crowd thinned out as skaters moved off the ice. The music slowed down, classic rock became waltz tunes to quiet the crowd and let people know it was near closing time.

Izzy saw people walk away from the square in twos and threes, tired skaters headed back to the subway. She was too cold now that she was still, her hat and sweater damp from the exertion. She would suggest they go for hot chocolate when Kyle and Nora came off the ice.

Teenage girls near Izzy laughed at something one of them said and then moved away. She was alone on the bench.

A man walked in front of the concrete wall by City Hall. She noticed because the red glow of his cigarette was distinct against the dark shadows. He crossed in front of the crowd of people leaving the rink and he stood still, a solitary figure milling about while the park emptied. The man moved out of the shadows and came closer.

The man seemed familiar, a tall blond guy, hatless despite the biting cold.

The music ended, and an announcement said the rink was now closed. A guard in a yellow, fluorescent vest and Kyle and Nora were the last off the ice. Izzy saw the blond man turn abruptly and walk quickly into the darkness. He disappeared behind the food trucks, which had earlier sold French fries and hot-dogs, and now were also closed and driving away for the night.

"That was actually fun," Nora said.

Izzy had the uncomfortable realization that she knew who the blond man was. She wondered if she should say something to her friends.

"And you said you were too clumsy to learn," Kyle said.

The man had been watching them.

"It's easy, just like Izzy promised," Nora said.

They took off their skates and Kyle rushed to return Nora's

rentals before the shutters were pulled closed. Izzy rubbed her sore shins and felt Nora's hand on her shoulder. Nora patted her back and said, "You and Kyle. I'm so happy to have you guys."

Izzy agreed. She liked her friends. She hadn't managed to get Nora talking, hadn't learned about her troubles. But at least Nora was happy now. Talking could wait.

"How about hot chocolate?" Izzy said, when Kyle was back.

Kyle grinned. Everybody was happy.

Izzy did not want to ruin the good mood. So what if the man was looking at them before? He probably wasn't lurking; he was probably just having a night out like everyone else. She would not mention that she'd seen the weird janitor from Nora's building.

44

Later when he was home he heard them come in, heard them moving in her apartment. The old joists and thin plaster couldn't hide much: the kettle whistling, the toilet flushing through cranky pipes. He pictured Kyle on the furniture. The one chair, the bed. He couldn't bear to think what he did to her on that ridiculously small bed. Kyle's low voice and Nora – he imagined Nora whispering, the way women did. It kept him awake. He lay in his own wide bed until the sounds grew dim in the walls and he fell asleep.

In the morning he woke too early with the taste of bile rising from his stomach. He put the radio on and tried to drink coffee. The brew was strong and sent more acid through his roiling gut. He had slept fitfully, his body was heavy and tired. Next door at Nora's, all was silent.

He listened in his kitchen. Not a murmur. Had he slept through Nora getting up and leaving the building? Was Kyle alone, lazily occupying the bed? He could use his master key to find out. He put the coffee mug in the sink.

It was a cold, clear day. The temperature would fall later, and the walkway would freeze. He would wait to look in at Nora's later, after he took care of things. He put on his coat and went outside to the courtyard. As he threw de-icing crystals over the concrete on the front stoop, he felt an ache in his shoulders and back. It was all wrong that Nora should be upstairs in bed with another man.

He took off his gloves and lit a cigarette and used the heel of his boot to break up a chunk of ice on the bottom step. The air was cold on his ungloved hands, so he smoked quickly, drag after drag.

Two men came up the walkway. Both of them were solid and tall, broad-shouldered in dark heavy overcoats, close-cropped hair and no hats. He knew immediately they were police.

He was surprised. No one had come here to monitor him in years, no unannounced spot-checks, even though he was technically still on parole. He stubbed out the cigarette. He didn't want to leave it there on the front stoop, but he wasn't going to pick it up now, while they watched him.

The two men wore long coats, boxy, not well cut or remarkable in any way. Coats men purchased in mid-priced stores downtown. Lowly police constables dressed in uniforms. In his experience, the coats meant they were detectives, of higher rank. They wore their own clothes, cheap and ill-designed though they were, because they were important.

He went on chipping at the ice. The men stopped on the path, flanked Henry on both sides. He wanted to put his gloves back on his cold hands but knew enough not to dig in his pockets to get them. A hand going into a pocket could mean he was reaching for a weapon. And if they were police, plain clothes or not, they carried guns. He made himself motionless. He wasn't going to make these men nervous.

"Good morning," the shorter one said. The man reached under his coat and pulled out a palm-sized something. He waived it in Henry's direction. A Toronto Police badge in an open leather folder, flashed it at Henry long enough to see it but not read it. Back under the coat it went.

Henry knew the rules of his parole, could recite all the conditions from memory. Not to consume alcohol. Not to leave the province without prior written permission. To notify the parole officer if he became romantically involved with a woman.

He knew the rules. He didn't necessarily follow them.

The second man, the taller, broader one, did not show him his badge.

"Morning," Henry said. "Mind if I smoke?"

He offered the pack to both men, who declined. They watched while he put it back in his pocket. He was too agitated to smoke; there was something off about the encounter. Last time, the parole officer had called, and asked him to drop by for a chat. That was years ago.

He waited for the questions and mentally prepared his rote responses. He'd smoke later.

"Where's the manager?"

He picked up the bag of salt crystals, rolled the top closed, before replying. They acted like they didn't know who he was. What was their game?

"That's me," he said.

The taller detective stepped up to the list of tenants on the wall by the front door. He read through the names and then took a photo of the list with his phone camera.

The other man held out his phone to Henry. There was a photo on the screen. Henry glanced at it. "Do you know this person?"

It was not him they were here to check up on.

She looked pretty in the photo. The hair was different, shorter and lighter, the skin slightly freckled from the sun. But it was clearly her.

"How can I help?" he said.

"I asked if you recognize this person?"

He'd never added her name to the list of tenants on the outside wall. They could read the list but they would not find her name.

If he lied, would they know he was lying? Would they revoke his parole?

"Doesn't look familiar," he said. "What did she do?"

They wouldn't tell him anything. They asked questions, said they needed to speak to her and if she lived here they would find out.

"Do you have a different photo," he said. He would buy time, send them away.

They could tell he was lying. Police know the answers before they ask questions. He held the bag of crystals against his hip. The knowledge of his deception burned on their expressionless faces. He was shown a second photo, black and white, a passport or licence photo of a face staring head-on at the camera, flat and inhuman. It could have been taken yesterday or a century ago.

Nora looked like most people do in document photos: lifeless, unknowable.

"Oh, her," he said. "Skipped out weeks ago without notice. Owes me a bunch of rent. I'd like to find the bitch too."

45

Henry thought about the photo. Her smile and freckled skin.

The police were looking for Nora.

He kept many photos of tenants, things he found lying around over the years.

Too bad the police didn't give him a copy.

No matter; he had the real Nora. They wouldn't find her. He told them it was the kind of building people moved in and out of often. They seemed to buy it. He said he'd keep an eye out.

He was excited after they left. He had a new sense of urgency.

He would make Nora tell him what she had done.

He would make her see she needed him. If she needed to be hidden from the police, he could do that for her.

But when he knocked on her door, eager to talk right away and explain how he could hide and protect her, she was not alone. Kyle answered his urgent knock, his eyes groggy with sleep and his hair dishevelled. He wouldn't open the door more than a few inches, keeping his foot wedged and blocking Henry's view of the room.

Nora spoke from inside. Her voice sounded dry, like the first words of the morning, and she asked Kyle who was at the door.

"The super," Kyle said. He opened the door wider and stepped out to the landing and closed the door behind him. Henry saw a glimpse of Nora in the bed.

"I want to talk to Nora," Henry said. He perspired in his jacket and flannel shirt after hurrying upstairs. But what could he say in front of Kyle?

"Look, we had a late night. We're tired. Is there some emergency?" Kyle held the door handle.

Nora's voice from inside. "Tell him to leave us alone."

Henry remained on the landing a moment after the door was closed to him, feeling the humiliation of her words, her rebuff. In his kitchen, he pushed the cat roughly off the counter. He opened the fire escape and then pulled it hard so it would bang shut.

He would make Nora need him. First though, he would read to calm himself.

December 14, 1918

> *Today I will work at the infirmary even though I woke up with a sore throat and aching body. I'd like to stay home in bed. I have a fever and cannot stop shaking. But two other nurses are already sick with flu. There is no one to care for patients overnight. I must report for duty.*

> *Alice is still in bed. She does not look sick.*

> *I cannot fall victim to this flu. What will happen to Alice if I am sick in bed and cannot get up to cook her meals or bathe her? I have no one to*

help me. It is unfair that a child born out of wedlock is shunned by society. Mrs. R is the only neighbour who has been the least bit friendly. The others act as if Alice does not exist.

There was a young nurse who died of flu at the infirmary last week. I will never let that happen to me. I will come home in the evening between shifts to check on Alice. I will ask Mrs. R to look in, if she has time.

46

Nora thought the cell phone was an annoyance. It rang too often with calls from Izzy. And though Nora adored her friend, she simply did not have the same level of enthusiasm for conversation. Izzy called her to talk about some boy she'd met. She said it would be more fun if Nora could text; she'd be able to let Nora know in real time what was happening and no one would overhear. But Nora's phone had one function only: talking.

Izzy called when she was waiting in a long line to have brunch at Barb's Kitchen, a popular restaurant. Nora was at home reading a magazine she'd found in the unclaimed mail downstairs. She nursed a cold—another one—lounging on the bed and consuming cups of tea. Skating had worsened a sore ankle, and her mood from all this was sullen. She'd refused Kyle when he offered to come and keep her company.

Izzy said she'd met the boy on Tinder, a phone app Nora would know about if she had a proper phone. The boy, Sandeep, was parking his car and had let Izzy out to reserve a spot in the line-up. There was an hour wait to get inside the restaurant. Izzy took the opportunity to call Nora.

"What kind of food is worth waiting for in the freezing cold?" Nora said. She flipped the magazine pages.

"City's best blueberry pancakes. And scones."

Izzy said she had to go; Sandeep was back.

Nora's tea had gone tepid. In the kitchen she ran the tap to fill the kettle. Cloudy warm water streamed from the faucet. There was rust on the handles of the taps and circling the drain.

The phone rang again and she picked it up from the floor by the bed where it had fallen.

Izzy said she was sitting at a table now and Sandeep had gone to speak to someone he knew who worked in the kitchen. The restaurant was very crowded, and she was going to order waffles and bacon, she said.

"He's so cute," Izzy said of Sandeep. "He's a bit older than me. An electrician."

Nora said she had to hang up to call Kyle. It wasn't true. He had left her apartment that morning after spending the night, saying he was going to help his mother with some things in her home. Kyle was devoted to his elderly mother, which was admirable.

He was different that way from Carter, who had tired of caring for his aging parents. Tired of the work and responsibility even though she had been the one cooking and cleaning and looking after everyone. Without consulting her, without even asking Ray or Joyce what they wanted, Carter put both of them into a nursing home. Where they'd died within months of each other.

Kyle brought groceries to his mom; took her to medical appointments. He never said a harsh thing about her. If anything, he was a bit too devoted to people in his life. She wasn't sorry to see him leave this morning. It was a chance to have a bit of time to herself. They'd woken late after a night that had been restless for her while Kyle slept deeply in the little bed. He'd learned to lie on his side, feet jammed against the footboard. He tried to make her comfortable, but sleep in the yellow bed with Kyle was a struggle for her.

Asleep, he breathed loudly, heavily, his body too warm, like a pile of burning coal. She wondered why Kyle was not more self-conscious about his weight. He was oblivious to it, pleased with himself and comfortable with his size. He was certain that his body was useful to him and enjoyable to her, and deserving of affection. He enjoyed her body equally and was affectionate. He seemed not to notice things that bothered her, limp hair or thin arms or a nagging sense she was losing her looks. She viewed her own body as a constant threat to her equilibrium, its care and desires an unwanted obligation. Every pang of hunger was a reproach, each sensation of pain a punishment.

She felt this way because she hadn't been a good mother. She'd failed Dylan. Now her own body carried everything that had happened, manifested all that she had done wrong. Felt it always, in her body. And it was making her thin, and sick.

She thought she'd be happier by now, when everything bad was behind her.

Nora made a cup of tea and took it with her downstairs. She went to the first-floor vestibule to see if the mail had been delivered. The carpet on the seventh-floor landing was damp. Trying to avoid the wet patch, she lifted her foot too high and her ankle hurt when the foot came down. The old injury flaring up; still there as a reminder of her husband and as an exclamation point on her imperfect body.

She rubbed the ankle a moment and looked out to the street

through the thick wavy glass and saw cars drive by. A man walking a beagle on a leash, the dog in a red coat and tiny dog booties. There was nothing in her mailbox.

On the way back up she noticed flaking green paint on the third-floor walls. She picked off a dime-sized layer using her fingernails. Old paint was made from lead. Kids used to eat it because it tasted sweet, and it poisoned them, damaged their brains. She let the green chip fall onto the brown carpet.

She'd been so careful to keep Dylan safe. Her home was not decorated with poisonous paint. There were no suffocating bumpers in the crib. She never left her baby alone, of course not. And yet she hadn't been careful enough. There were so many hidden dangers.

She walked up another flight of stairs. Here the banister was so worn, the dark wood stain faded to bone white.

Dylan was gone.

She stopped, running her hand over a smooth curved rail. Sunlight hit the floor on the next landing. A bright winter morning.

Her baby had died. Nora hadn't taken proper care of Dylan when it was crucial, when medical attention might have saved her. She blamed Carter initially. The neighbours were all so sad for her. If only she'd been at the hospital sooner, some said, as if her failure was a mere matter of timing. Everyone was so sorry.

She stood on the landing and looked at a black squirrel in the lane. She listened as the neighbours said she'd done everything she could. And maybe she believed them, once.

Nora felt the sun come through the window on the seventh-floor landing. The truth was that she didn't do what had to be done. She was a bad mother.

Last night while Kyle was asleep and she lay awake trying not to think, she heard sounds. A gurgle like someone swallowing, a human sigh as the wind blew between slats. A noise like murmuring in the gypsum boards. A current of susurrating air in the wall.

She had tried to be happy. She had tried to forget the past and be happy with Kyle. And she had Izzy, new friend Izzy.

But she couldn't forget anything, not really. At night there was no sleep because the little voice called to her.

I'm hungry Mama.

She'd blamed Carter, but she was the one. The mother who'd let the fear of her husband harm her sweet child.

I'm lonely Mama.

She hurried to the eighth floor, to her home. Her small apartment with the small metal bed and the tiny lamp and in the walls, the sweet, small voice calling at night.

The little voice that was only meant for her.

47

Nora left the phone in odd places, under the bedcovers or in a drawer. She did it without thinking and then panicked when she heard the muffled ringtone and couldn't find it. It rang for some time until she found it fallen behind the stove. She picked up the call, certain she was too late, and the caller would be gone, but heard Kyle's voice, loud, friendly.

"He sounds nice," Kyle said, when she described Izzy's date. "She deserves someone special."

He was walking in Parkdale under a railway bridge, for exercise, he said. Trucks rumbled along the road beside him splashing brown water from melting snow. There were loud reverberations, echoes in the tunnel. He sounded like he was underwater. "I can't hear too well," he said. "I'm going down to King Street and the Exhibition grounds. Then the lake." A car horn seared the connection, breaking up his voice. "Wish you could enjoy the walk with me."

"What does the fair look like in winter?" she said, envisioning the barren roller coaster and Ferris wheel coated in ice. But he didn't hear the question.

"Hope you feel better. Talk later." He was gone.

She did not find this city beautiful the way Kyle did. It was austere and dreary, and poorly planned. It sprawled on the shore of one of the biggest lakes on earth, but access to the cold great body of water was barricaded by a crumbling expressway, and the skyline was slashed by rows of bank towers.

She turned off the phone and put it under the mattress.

* * *

Once, Carter had broken her wrist. She didn't recall why he'd done it, what had set him off that time. He'd grabbed her and pushed her to the ground. Instinctively, she'd put her hands out and the right wrist snapped. He said, no point in going for an x-ray. Do the housework with your other hand.

Nora had carried baby Dylan with the one good arm. It was her park friend Bila who gave her a tensor bandage to wrap around the wrist. Bila, who tolerated casual violence from her own spouse but said Carter had crossed a line and she should call the cops, or leave her husband.

But she didn't leave. It wasn't that easy. With no job. And a baby.

More injuries followed. A swing of his fist shattered her orbital bone.

She'd wanted to go to the emergency room that time, worried about her eye, her face. There was a hospital in the next town.

Carter said he was sorry. Begged forgiveness. He said he didn't mean to, but it was her fault, she provoked him. He said if she went to a doctor he and Dylan would be gone when she returned. Later he bought her gold earrings.

* * *

She stayed inside the apartment on Farmdale and told her friends

270

she needed to rest. To be alone for a day or two. Kyle called frequently to check in with her. She felt lonely hearing his disembodied voice, only half listening to anecdotes about the coffee shop. She said no, when he offered to visit.

Izzy called. Said she was in love with the boy Sandeep. She said, I know you think it's too soon Nora, right? They planned a trip to Florida. Did Kyle and Nora want to go too? Nora told Izzy it was good to be young and in love, to enjoy herself.

Nora sat on the bed, looking out to the back laneway. She was far away from Izzy and Kyle and her job as a barista. None of it felt real. She buried the phone under the towels so she wouldn't hear it ring.

She kneeled on the bed and opened the window. She thought of Izzy and of Kyle, and she wondered if she could ever be as happy as they seemed to be.

She could see straight down to the laneway where Henry sometimes leaned against the wall smoking. He was down there now, alone. He seemed like a lonely person. Smoke from his cigarette curled towards the sky in a small trail, just like the longer plumes from the house chimneys beyond the lane. As he hunched in the cold he exhaled, and then he glanced up towards her window.

When her phone rang again the sound was distant and muffled, but persistent; it drew her away from the window.

Izzy asked, "Are you okay? Why don't you come to Florida? It will be a fun break."

She had no money to go on a trip with Izzy to Florida or anywhere else. Her plan for a new life full of happiness was not working as she'd hoped.

She'd been living in the apartment for almost two months.

* * *

She lay on the bed and paid no attention to time. She slept if she could, whether it was night or day. She wrapped herself in the duvet. The window stuck open a crack because the wood casement was warped. The heat, if it came on at all, did so only intermittently.

She drank tea with Esme's green powder stirred into it and she forgot to eat. She was feverish. Someone coughed outside her door and in her delirium she feared that it was Carter coming home.

She stood up quickly, blood rushed from her head, and she became dizzy. Her knees buckled as she fell into the coffee table. She landed on the floor between the bed and the table and raised her head, eye level with a little glass candy dish. A little glass bowl, chipped at the rim in several spots, a broken flea-market trinket. No bigger than a child's fist.

Candied ginger filled the dish, circular amber chunks of translucent ginger, dusted lightly with icing sugar. Nora didn't put the candy there, or even purchase it. Esme may have left it for her when she replenished the tea. Nora put a piece in her mouth and sucked it. The icing sugar was so sweet, the ginger sharp and fragrant.

When did she last eat? She liked the candy in her mouth. It was soft and chewy, spicy, with lots of sugar melting on her tongue. She ate another piece, then all of it, every piece in the dish, chewing slowly, savouring it.

She sat on the floor at the coffee table, and a beautiful child walked towards her.

The child said, *do you like candy?* Her arms outstretched, both fists balled tight.

I have more in my other hand. Just for you.

A little girl in a white nightgown, the collar and hem trimmed with lace. Little white pearl buttons ran down the front placket. The hem of the gown brushed sharp little knees. Bare feet on the hardwood floor.

"Who are you?" Nora said.

Alice.

Too bad, I can't have any candy. Mama said not to eat it until she comes home. Mama put macaroni in the ice-box for my supper.

Buttons on the nightgown all the way down the front. One of them hanging, about to fall off.

"How did you get in here?" Nora said.

A strip of torn white cloth wound up a ringlet in the girl's hair. The cloth had come loose, and Nora reached to touch it. The hair was light and silky and curled softly to the shoulders.

That tickles, the child said. A sweet small voice, hot breath in Nora's ear.

Tickle, tickle. Nora's neck itched from the soft hot breath.

Outside, a dog barked in a yard behind the laneway. It barked again, and a male voice yelled at the dog.

Nora moved to close the window, and managed to push it down an inch.

"Alice, are you cold? Don't be frightened."

Floorboards creaked on the landing, and Nora heard Henry call out for his cat.

Henry's door closed and rattled.

The little girl crawled under the yellow bed and curled herself up.

She whispered, *Mama gave me a rocking horse for Christmas.*

Cold air whistled under the window.

When is Mama coming home?

She pulled the blanket from the bed to wrap the child and warm her. She would *take* her home.

DWELLING

"What floor do you live on?"

The white nightgown fluttered. Soft hot breath in Nora's ear.

I'm hiding like Mama told me. Hiding from the bad man.

48

Nora thought about Carter's mother, Joyce.

A smell in the air conjured her image. A scent of ancient perfume, the kind of old-lady toiletry that wasn't sold anymore; it smelled of lilacs and hollyhocks. Joyce used it, dabbing it on her neck and wrists even while she spent her days bedridden. Nora rarely thought of Joyce and pushed aside her memories and recollections like unwanted junk stuffed in a closet.

It was Esme, not Joyce, standing silently by the teak chair in Nora's apartment. Nora was crouched on the floor, looking under the bed for Alice. The scent from Esme's shoulders was of powder and roses.

"Hello, dear. Feel all better? And the sore foot?"

Lamplight caught strands of hair dangling from Esme's tortoiseshell clip and twinkled on a brooch at her chest. She was dressed in her tweed suit, with a longer skirt, and black patent high heels. When she walked on the bare floor, her heels clicked, and Nora marvelled that she had not heard Esme come in.

Esme offered her hand, and Nora took it and rose to stand,

entwining her unmanicured hands in Esme's, which were polished in blood-red. Nora was conscious of how unkempt she'd become. She couldn't remember the last time she'd brushed her hair or worn deodorant.

"Where is she?" Nora said.

The duvet was on the floor, and Nora prodded it gently with her toe. Dust rose into the air and hovered in a wan stream of light.

Esme clucked in disapproval at the pile of dirty laundry on the teak chair, and Nora shamefully acknowledged that she was letting things slide. She put the clothing on the floor and fought the urge to fold it.

Esme adjusted her hair. She sat down on the chair and crossed her legs perfectly. Nora felt dirty; she wanted to bathe and change her clothes. Her hair was oily and lank, and her skin was dry, flaking off when she scratched.

"If you leave the door unlocked," Esme said. "People will come in."

The unicorn lamp lay overturned on the table. The child must have knocked it down playing by the bed, or running out to go home when Esme arrived.

"Where is your little friend," Esme said. "The white-haired one. That is the question of the hour." She was in the kitchen now, looking in the fridge. "She's carrying on with your boyfriend, you know."

Nora was confused. How could Esme say such a thing about a little girl?

Esme clicked her heels on the kitchen floor. "The fridge has nothing fresh inside to eat," she said. "You and your little friend Izzy are both too thin."

Esme was talking nonsense about Izzy.

276

"You don't know what you're saying."

"Boyfriends get restless when you don't pay attention."

Esme handed her the box of matches from the drawer. A paper box of wooden matches with red sulphur tips. Nora struck a match and lit the stove. A ring of blue flame shot up in a whoosh. What was she about to cook?

Nora returned the matches to the cache of spatulas and knives. There were mice droppings in a crack in the wood and more tiny black pellets in the hollow of a spoon. She jiggled the warped drawer until it shut.

A strand of Esme's hair fell onto the burner and singed, sending up an acrid stink. Nora worried that mice hid in the stove itself, scrambling for crumbs. Waiting to emerge when the apartment was quiet and empty.

Esme said, "Your husband was unfaithful."

Carter had cheated many times, doing little to hide it from her. He found easy targets among desperate female clients or manipulated lonely women in bars with his rhetoric. Nora tolerated it, tried not to know too much. Content with her beautiful house. Her baby.

Esme said, "And do you not deserve some happiness now?"

*   *   *

It was a summer night when Carter was supposedly in Toronto on business. A muggy, hot night and she was still grieving Dylan, dead only a few months from meningitis. She'd begged him to stay home, not to leave her alone in her anguish. Carter insisted the business in Toronto was too important to postpone.

She drove her car to get out of the empty house, drove aimlessly around town that hot evening and by chance she passed Pete's Tavern, a bar near the bottling plant. Carter's Audi was in the parking lot, shiny and incongruous among the dented pick-up trucks.

Confusion pulled her into the lot, gripping the steering wheel, and there she saw Carter burst out of the bar, face flushed, his arm around the waist of a blousy, stumbling woman, both of them drunk.

The woman well known to Nora, a neighbour and a friend.

* * *

"Esme," she said. "Why do you make me think about Carter? He's dead." She waited to see if there was any reaction. When there wasn't, she said, "Let's go to Lucky Convenience."

They walked to the store to buy ingredients for a meal. Esme said hearty soup would be just the thing, and an invigorating walk there in the cold. Farmdale Lane was only partially cleared of snow and slick with ice at each corner. Nora lagged because of the injured ankle. It stubbornly failed to heal.

She shielded her eyes with a hand to the forehead from the glare of bright sun on snow. The plows had left great piles of it by the side of the road. She was cold in her thin coat as the air crawled in at her collar and under her cuffs. She didn't understand how Esme braved the snow and ice in the patent leather heels, but she managed deftly, hardly glancing down at her feet as they went.

And Esme was snug in her fur hat, the fur undulating slightly in the wind, while Nora's ears stung in the cold. Just once, she would like to try on that hat.

"Winter is fine if you dress for it," Esme said.

The slab of pavement in front of the store was a mess, as if a giant box had been dumped out, disgorged over the sidewalk. Broken store fixtures were in a tangled mound, and an old cash register lay sideways on the heap. Withered, dry, unsold Christmas trees were thrown to the curb beside oversized plastic bags stuffed with garbage. In the window, a crudely hand-lettered sign said "For Lease" in black marker.

Esme went in, and Nora followed, stomping her boots on the rubber mat like she always did. The door chimes had been taken down, the bulbs removed from most of the overhead fixtures and the shelves largely empty. Cardboard packing boxes, most already filled, were everywhere.

The owner was alone inside. Nora had never learned his name.

"Hello," he said. "Afraid you're too late. I've sold off most of it." He munched from a bag of roasted nuts.

The family photos were gone. Missing were the pyramids of turnips, onions and carrots, replaced with puddles. The tray of hopeful lottery tickets had vanished.

"You're closing the store?" Nora said, though it was obvious.

"Inevitable," he said, and offered her the nuts, shaking the cellophane bag to show that some were left. She let him pour a few peanuts into her palm.

"I'm going to make pea soup," Nora said, "We need chives." She looked to Esme for affirmation. The fur hat appeared dry and dull in the dark store.

"No one to take over and run a grocery here," he said. Then he laughed, a deep, sardonic laugh. "Hunters wins."

"The store will be gone?" Nora said.

He pulled some dented cans of corn from a shelf, put them into a box, tossed in some bruised apples and cabbage.

"Today is the last," he said. "But I'm relieved. Too old for this." He pointed to the box. "For the homeless shelter."

"What happened?" Nora said.

"They raised the rent. I stuck it out as long as I could." He wiped his hands on his pants and crumpled the empty nut bag.

"Then they sold the whole block to a developer."

He ducked behind the counter, rummaged around, threw a stack of paper bags to the floor.

"What will you do?" Nora said. He had let her run a tab, and she owed him money for her shopping. She waited for him to remember and ask for payment.

"It doesn't matter. My son has a place for me in Calgary." He closed up the box of cans. "Here," he said, handing Nora a bouquet of dried flowers tied with twine. They were faded red and purple roses, the colours of a bruise. "I saved these for you."

She brought them to her nose, leaves as dry as old paper and petals like sloughed-off skin. A faint whiff of decay. She turned to Esme to see if she also noticed the smell, but Esme wasn't there.

"I know," he said, "They stink a little bit. That's the magic. The bad smell means you'll have good luck."

Nora looked for Esme outside among the piles of garbage. She peered out the window with the store owner. He put his hands on his hips, surveyed his dying empire, and sighed.

* * *

Esme caught up with her at the corner. She said Nora should go on to the grocery store, only a few more blocks, but Nora knew she would have trouble with her ankle walking to Hunters. Esme suggested the streetcar, but when they arrived at the stop, a 'not in service' notice was taped to the pole. Someone had scrawled over the notice, 'shit.'

"The city is going to wrack and ruin," Esme said. Then she said they should take a cab.

"Cab?" Nora said. The word felt foreign, wrong. Why was she out in the cold looking for a place to shop? She could not afford to pay for a taxi. She'd lost at least two days of wages while she was at home moping around the apartment, feeling sorry for herself.

"No. I need to go back," Nora said. "I want to make sure Alice is safe."

Esme talked incessantly as they walked and Nora tried to ignore her, to think. The child was hungry; she was going home to make soup for her daughter.

Esme recited a list: split peas, potatoes, salt.

Nora said, "I don't think kids like pea soup." She saw herself in her old kitchen, windows with yellow curtains and French doors open to the patio facing south, warm and bright all year. Dylan in the highchair, swinging her legs, slapping her hands on the tray.

Esme said, "It will be quicker to cut through the back, behind the building."

The laneway at the rear of Farmdale Court was narrow and unplowed, the snow tramped down, by passing traffic into two parallel trails of melting slush. Nora walked unsteadily and tried not to slip. She usually avoided the lane and didn't like using the back entrance of the building. The back door was where Henry smoked and where the garbage was collected. The door led into the basement.

The bare branches of the maple trees in the lane exposed clumps of ragged twigs abandoned by birds, hollow grey wasp hives and black raccoon nests. She hated trees in winter. No cars came by, and they were alone. A squirrel on a hydro pole scolded as she passed. The building cast a deep shadow over the lane.

Esme talked and talked. Nora couldn't think. She was trying to recall Dylan's first word. It was an animal name, she thought.

And then behind her in the lane the grumbling sound of a hulking garbage truck so wide and tall it swayed, scraping the yellow bricks of the building. It honked, and she pinned herself against the fence on the other side. The truck narrowly missed her and passed, belching black smoke in its wake.

It stopped abruptly several yards in front of her, reversed while the warning signal beeped, and pushed into the truck bay beside the back entrance.

Henry was there waiting for the truck. He opened the loading bay door so it could back in and get close to the big metal refuse tip. He waited against the brick, as she'd seen him do from her window many times, as he always did on garbage removal day, standing idle for long intervals, smoking cigarettes, looking out at the lowering sky.

She came up near the back entrance. The truck driver opened his door, jumped out of his seat and yelled hello to Henry. The two men surveyed the positioning of the truck, made certain it was in line with the bin, and then the driver started the mechanical raising and emptying of the load of garbage.

She approached the back door, which was propped open, the basement hallway dark beyond. She didn't acknowledge the men, looked away and down at the slush.

She could almost hear Dylan's babbling, see the little hand reach for the sippy cup.

The garbage stank like rotting meat and urine.

Henry and the driver stood against the brick. She knew they saw her and she didn't like the way they watched her. Like she was there for their amusement. Henry offered the packet of cigarettes to the man, and they both lit up, leaning in together on one match before turning to watch Nora enter the building.

49

TORONTO EVENING TELEGRAM

January 30, 1919

Police Court Blotter, City Hall

Reported in Magistrates Court:

A shocking discovery of a small body today, in a rented room at Farm-dale Court Apartments. The tenant Doris Carr, described by neighbours as often absent. It was assumed the child had gone to relatives during the Flu Epidemic. Faint noises heard a week ago were thought to be a cat.

Crown Counsel has the matter under investigation. The Magistrate ordered a final report by week's end and remarked it was a sorry state of affairs when a child is abandoned and left for dead.

50

Kyle waited in the check-out lane at the Metro Market on Gerrard Street. The line moved slowly, and he vaguely resented the shoppers waiting ahead of him, hunched over large carts overflowing with frozen fish sticks, potato chips and toilet paper. He had one item to pay for. He fiddled with a song lyric stuck in his head, and he tried to work it into something fresh. A new song for his band.

I'll get close to you if I ramble.

He was eager to get up to Nora's place. The lyric wasn't compelling. *If I wander to you.* To alleviate his impatience, he imagined occupations for the other shoppers. The man pushing the cart in front of him in the shabby overcoat was a gold-mining baron, and the wiry anxious teenager now paying for an energy drink was a flamed-out violin prodigy.

Kyle had spent a good part of his day searching store to store for a suitable gift for Nora, sensing that the bargain cellphone had not been very romantic. He wanted to signal to her that he was serious, that he wanted to get closer. He would give her flowers.

His initial impulse was that Nora would appreciate something beautiful, maybe roses, but they were difficult to find during the holidays. Guess everyone had the same idea.

He drifted into the Metro where flowers were bunched in plastic pails and looked artificial, daisies and chrysanthemums in gaudy hues of red, blue and orange. It was a far cry from delicate blooms and impossible to find a nice arrangement. He watched with dismay as other men plucked out dripping bouquets without a second thought.

He settled on a box of chocolates.

He hoped she'd be over her latest illness, whatever it was, and happy to see him when he got there. He could simply tell her that he cared about her. Maybe his feelings didn't yet go beyond that, but it could happen.

Pop songs said it right. *Be my baby. I think I love you.* He chuckled out loud, and the gold-mining magnate paying for ice cream turned back to catch the joke.

* * *

He rounded the corner to the Farmdale Court. Someone had propped a rusty old bike against the sign, not even bothering to lock it up. The back tire was flat.

He walked up the path under the arch of oak trees beneath branches tangled together for bonded strength like kids playing red-rover. Intermittently, withered tree limbs had been hacked off and patched with black tar. He was the only person in the courtyard.

He put the box of chocolates under his arm and dug into his jacket pocket for his iPhone. It was mildly annoying that he couldn't simply text Nora to say he was here, but after all, he was the one too cheap to get her a proper phone. She picked up after one ring.

"I'm here," he said.

"Can't wait," she said, "I—take—so—"

"What? You're cutting out. Are you moving around?"

"When, are—there?"

He stood on the concrete stoop, the cold metal phone like a freezer pack in his palm and against his ear and was about to tell her to buzz him in, but before he could, the big entrance door swung open in his face. Henry stepped out and startled him. The box of chocolates fell to the ground.

Henry was in a sheepskin coat, and a hat with the ear flaps pulled low. He sneered at Kyle and appraised the fallen box. He made no move to pick it up. Kyle bent to do so and felt himself bumped and shoved sideways on the stoop.

"Hey," he said, certain Henry had purposely nudged him off balance.

"Mind the ice," Henry said. "Going to Home Depot for rock salt now."

Kyle brushed dirt off the box—the bump was probably accidental—no one was that callous. He pressed at a dent in the corner of the cardboard.

He should have wrapped it, or put a bow on it.

Henry said, "She's got lots of chocolate. I wouldn't worry about it."

* * *

The stairway was gloomy. The building was inhospitable, that was for sure. The windows on the landings were smudged with dirt and blocked any natural light fighting to get through. Long windowless hallways—what he could see of them as he went up the stairs—seemed melancholy and silent, as if in mourning for past inhabitants.

Hey, that was a good lyric. Maybe too dark though.

The band was going to play a few sets at the Moonstone tonight. A lively bar on the Danforth and one of his favourite places. They were lucky to get the gig. He didn't mind it was unpaid. He couldn't wait to get there. He would convince Nora to come.

Only the sixth floor, and he was a bit winded. All the walking around the city wasn't doing much. He should start going to the gym again. He paused to catch his breath and looked down the hall. No Christmas decorations on the doors. Not everyone celebrated the holiday, he knew that, lots of different people in the big city. But still. What a dump.

He hoped Nora wanted to come out tonight, hear them play. The bar was in his neighbourhood, on a block with an all-night roti shop, a French bakery and a marijuana dispensary. An eclectic area he wanted to show off to Nora. She was missing out on what the city offered, living here in the middle of nowhere in this ugly building. He wished she didn't have to hide from her husband this way.

Nora was out on her landing, looking down over the railing.

"C'mon runner, climb those stairs."

He regretted bragging to her of his high school glory days, when he was on both the track and hockey teams, but made an effort to run up the final steps, nearly tripping in his galoshes. He was embarrassed by his clumsiness, and weakly laughed along with Nora as they embraced on the landing. His arms felt too long holding her, unwieldy, like the tentacles of an octopus. She was less substantial, had become much thinner, her body in his arms floating like seaweed.

"I'm so happy to see you."

She was more alert, energetic. A good sign, he thought.

She pulled him inside with a hand around his waist, kissed

him, her mouth dry and metallic tasting. Her feet were bare, and she raised them up and down on her toes as he came into the room. She seemed nervous.

"For you." He gave her the box of chocolate.

Her mouth twitched in a smile, uncertain. He thought he should explain more, it's a present, a gift because I like you. But she took it into the kitchen and placed it in the cupboard as the moment passed; his feelings unexpressed, the chocolates reduced to groceries, stored away.

He could have ordered flowers online. White roses. He hadn't thought of it. They'd be blooming in a vase on her coffee table, and she'd know how he felt.

"It looks different in here," he said. The furniture looked smaller, dustier.

"Probably just too dark," she said. She pointed to the unicorn lamp. "It needs a new bulb. That one's burnt out."

Her voice was raspy. She went up and down on the balls of her feet again, jittery, something on her mind. He opened the closet to hang his coat and scarf and hunted in vain for an empty hanger in the mess and jumble before he remembered he wasn't supposed to use it. He left his things in a neat pile at the door.

"Izzy has a new guy," he said.

"She called me."

"Oh, so you know already." Of course, she must talk to friends on the phone, not only him. "You didn't get to see the red and green dyed hair though. She's back to white now."

Nora sat on the bed, twirling a strand of her hair in her fingers.

"You should come back to work and see her. Before she goes to Florida or wherever."

"Come sit for a minute." Her lips and mouth sounded sticky.

"Should we make some coffee?"

She shook her head, and he sat down close to her on the bed. She played with her hair, combing her fingers through it.

"I need to tell you something."

She wore a thin white cardigan over a T-shirt and jeans. Something about her twitchiness, the tone of voice, told him that she was going to break up with him. He didn't want her to do that. He kissed her and started to unbutton her sweater, to stop her from saying it.

She let him fiddle with the buttons and kiss her without reciprocating. It unnerved him more, and it felt wrong, if she wasn't into it. She didn't move as he pulled at the final button and cupped her breasts over the shirt. He dropped his hands.

"Sorry," he said.

She patted his knee and got up.

"It's not you."

He came all this way to listen to clichés.

"What are you saying?" he said. "Be straight with me."

She paced between the door and the kitchen.

"I had a lot of time to think. And I need you to hear something." She stopped and stood in the light from the kitchen. "I was married."

"I know." He sat back against the end of the bed, stared out the window at a snow-covered yard, an old washing machine dumped by a fence. "You mentioned it before." He knew there was unhappiness in her past. She never talked about it. But so what. She was in her thirties, and of course things happen to people.

"Look," he said, "All the old Christmas trees out for the garbage. Some still have ornaments on."

She looked where he looked, out beyond the lane and the

rooftops. Christmas trees thrown to the curb in front of a row of houses. She took his hand.

"And my little girl," she said. "I lost my little girl."

51

He listened and held back his questions though they stuck in his throat like a half-chewed wad of meat. She said she was telling him so he'd forgive her.

* * *

Carter kept it hidden in the shed. The shed was at the bottom of the garden where they stored the hose and some tools. She rarely opened the shed because Carter took care of the lawn, but once when she wanted to find a pail for Dylan to play with, she dug around in there. Behind the rake was Carter's red toolbox. She opened the box, and there it was. A gun.

* * *

"Wait. Are you saying?" Kyle found her story difficult to follow. It was too horrible, and he hesitated to ask. Did the kid find the gun?

"Let me finish," she said. She paced in her bare feet.

"You can tell me," he said, though he wasn't sure he wanted to hear.

"Dylan got sick. She was the sweetest most good-natured

child. She was only a baby when Carter devised his crazy rules. He refused vaccines, and he didn't believe in doctors."

"I don't understand," Kyle said. "Wasn't he a lawyer? Educated? And did you have the same views?"

She took off her sweater. There were wet patches of perspiration on her white T-shirt.

* * *

Dylan was sick. At first, it was only a fever, toddlers get them all the time, and Nora thought Carter knew what was best. Then the fever wouldn't break, and Dylan's neck was stiff, and she didn't move, and her skin was a strange colour.

* * *

"Why didn't you take her to the hospital?" Kyle was incredulous.

* * *

Carter told her the illness would resolve on its own, that she was over-protective, but she had to do something, she could see the child was struggling to breathe. And when he left the house, when he went to see one of his women, the blousy drunk who wore a wig, she seized her chance. And brought Dylan to the hospital.

* * *

"It was meningitis," she said.

Kyle hugged her, drew her close, didn't know what to say, what to ask. She pulled away.

"Did she recover?" he said. "What happened?"

"What do you think happened?" She was crying now.

He was confused, afraid to upset her even more than she already was.

"Did she get better?"

"No, you idiot." Her eyes were wild with anger, pupils huge and black. "It was too late."

He tried guiding her to the bed. He wanted to calm her

down, wished he could call Izzy and get her to come over to help him.

"He treated me like shit."

"Lie down," he said. "Tell me the rest later."

"I was a terrible mother. My little girl, Dylan."

*   *   *

Kyle sat on the end of the bed and watched her. A question in his head festered like an open sore, but he wouldn't ask it, not now that she was lying quietly on the bed.

What did the gun have to do with it?

He thought back to her first day at work, lots of paperwork to fill out, employee records and income tax forms, so much information to get from anyone new. He was the manager, he asked for her social insurance number for Revenue Canada. She couldn't remember it, too many digits, she'd have to look it up. Nothing unusual there, not everyone memorized it, didn't mean they were hiding something. And a piece of identification, like a driver's licence, that she was going to produce but never did. He'd asked once more a few weeks later, been rebuffed again and then forgotten it.

"I need to tell you," she said.

*   *   *

She'd laughed when Carter threatened to kill her. So, do it then, she said, you coward. She had nothing to live for with Dylan gone. She knew he kept the gun in the shed. She took it out of the toolbox and brought it into the house and hid the gun in the front hall closet, deep in the back, behind rows of shoes, boxes of sports equipment, inside one of her tall rain boots.

*   *   *

Kyle said he was sorry to hear all this and that it must be upsetting to talk about it. She was clearly in distress. He offered to make tea.

"There is some green tea in the cupboard," Nora said. "The tea Esme gave me."

"Who's Esme?"

"You know, Henry's friend. She was at the party."

"I'll call Izzy to come over," he said.

"Why?"

He thought Nora was muddled. Who wouldn't be, recalling such a horrible story of loss? But he knew he'd never met anyone named Esme.

He rubbed her shoulder, which irritated, rather than soothed her. She wrenched herself free from his hand and sat up, agitated. She shoved him aside and got off the bed.

He said, "You should take a shower." He meant it as a way to calm down. "Or a bath." She had been home alone, become disorganized, neglected to care for herself. He felt helpless, unsure how to respond to her distress. He wasn't a therapist.

"You treat me like shit," she said. She grabbed the lamp from the floor and threw it at him, alarmingly. It was light enough to have no velocity and he reacted quickly to protect his head with a forearm. But he was shaken.

"Carter, you pig. Don't tell me what to do." She flailed at him with her fists, pounded his chest, used her slight weight to push him.

He gripped her arms, easily held her still. He wished he'd called Izzy earlier. Things were getting out of control. He only wanted to calm her.

"It's me, Kyle. I'm not Carter."

She was breathing rapidly. He let go of her to a renewed volley of blows. She kept hitting him. He didn't retaliate. He backed slowly away from her, thinking absurdly of his response to a bear he'd once encountered on a hiking trail. Back away slowly.

296

She stopped flailing. "I'm sorry," she said.

Relief was so sweet. Kyle took a deep breath. Maybe everything would be fine, after all.

"Let's go for a walk," he said. "Fresh air, clear our heads." He thought of getting out of the apartment, getting himself away to the bar downtown, joining up with his bandmates, far from this craziness. But he didn't want to leave her alone, not in this state.

She looked at him strangely, as if meeting him after a long absence, and only now recognizing him. She smiled. He dropped his shoulders, released a breath. Was it over?

She spoke softly. "All you want is sex."

"You're acting crazy," he said.

She spit in his face.

He didn't feel sorry for her now. He couldn't deal with this mental breakdown or whatever it was. He'd wanted to be a good boyfriend, but this was too much. He was done.

He moved away and kept his eyes locked on her. She looked like she wanted to spit again and he wasn't going to give her the chance. He plucked up his boots and jacket and opened the door without putting them on. She lunged at him, scratching his neck.

"I'm not crazy." She gave him a final push through the doorway. "Get out!"

He didn't look back. She yelled incoherently at him as he hurried down the steps, trying not to slip in his socks. She yelled continuously and then she slammed her door shut. Slammed it so hard the glass shattered.

He made his way downstairs and didn't pause until the final landing, where he yanked on his boots. He flew out past Henry, who was mopping the vestibule.

52

Henry gave Nora a new front door. She stood by drinking tea as he installed it. He asked her if she was interested in architecture.

"I bet you appreciate the finer things." He took the old, panelled door off the hinges and set it aside, careful not to cut himself on the jagged edges. He swept up broken shards of glass from the floor with a hand broom and dustpan, slid them onto a sheaf of newspaper. "It's a shame you broke it," he said. "You can't buy this kind of leaded glass anymore."

She sipped the tea. "I suppose this new door is more secure."

The door was solid wood. The building code mandated steel, but this was a heritage property. He was allowed to use wood.

"You can never be too careful," he said. "I mean, that guy wanted you to think he was decent. But obviously, he wasn't."

"There's no way to see who's knocking though. Without any glass in the door," Nora said.

Henry heard the yelling, all her screaming, the door slamming and shattering. He considered asking what exactly Kyle had done that made her so mad, but didn't want her to start regretting that the man was gone. Henry deserved her attention now.

"I can do a peep-hole, if you want." The door was old; he'd found it in the basement where it had been in storage for years. It was heavy and slightly warped, and would probably swell in the summer humidity, but it would function for now.

She wandered off into her kitchen. "You're well rid of that guy," he said. She returned holding a glass of water and offered it to him. She bent to rub her ankle.

"Old injury," she said.

So considerate, he hadn't asked why she was rubbing her ankle. He hadn't asked for the drink of water. Was this what it was like to have a woman anticipate your needs? To have a woman explain her actions simply because you have a right to know?

"You like antiques?" he said. She pressed down on her good foot, circled the sore ankle. Must hurt climbing all the stairs.

"Sure. I had a few good pieces at my house."

He would get her to say more later about where she'd lived. "This is a better lock too," he said. It was a good strong Mortice lock, expensive, that required a key on both the inside and outside to lock and unlock. Not strictly necessary on a solid door, the inside key was usually a precaution where glass panes were easy for burglars to smash and reach the handle. And it might be a bit more inconvenient for her to use.

"I won't charge you for the damage," he said. "I want you to be safe." *I will keep you safe.*

* * *

He came back later to give her the keys and tighten the hinges. She watched him working again and he saw that she had nothing else to do.

"So, you don't have a job now," he said. "I mean, how could you go back?" He screwed a hinge. Black grease oozed out of it.

She looked puzzled, like she hadn't thought of it.

"He was your boss, right? I mean you don't need to be humiliated at work." She looked worried, frowning. "You know what," he said. "I can hold off on January's rent." He fished in the toolbox for the Robertson screwdriver and then remembered he'd taken it out with a bunch of other rarely used tools.

He'd made room in the toolbox for duct tape and plastic zip ties.

"That would be great," she said. "I guess I could transfer to another Lakeview Coffee." She looked at the red toolbox open at his feet, a sheathed utility knife in the tray. "I should apologize to him, I think."

He closed the lid. She was going to get back with the guy. He couldn't let it happen.

He'd never told her about the visit from the police.

"You like decorating right?"

"Interior design? Sure. I like it." She looked at her scavenged furniture and thin curtains. "I could look for work doing that."

She was going off on a tangent. He didn't want her to find another job. Another boyfriend. He was going to have his turn.

"What I meant. If you want. You could help renovate this building." The idea came to him for the first time. He almost grabbed her shoulders in excitement, but he held back. "You could pick new wallpaper, carpet. I'd pay you."

Her nose wrinkled. She stepped back from him. "Maybe."

He would convince her. "Let me show you. Come with me. Just for a minute. There's one unit. Incredible period details, cornice mouldings." He was very excited. He picked up the toolbox. "Just for a minute."

* * *

"I imagine your old house was exquisite," he said. He wasn't sure what would happen when he got her downstairs, hadn't made up his mind. He'd decide when he got her there.

He took her to the fifth floor. She walked beside him in her bare feet on the patterned carpet. He wore his work boots, noticed a splotch of black oil had stained the left one. The carpet was dirty, dirt ground deeply into the fibres. He would know, because he hadn't cleaned it in ages. He wouldn't walk here in bare feet, himself.

"Did I tell you about the house?" she said. She stopped walking. "You know. I need to go back upstairs. To make a call."

The carpet must feel rough on her skin because the weave was old and stiff and matted in worn patches. He pointed out the wall sconces adjacent to each apartment door, tulip-shaped wrought iron filigree, a single candelabra bulb in each, shadows on the wall below the fixtures thin and spidery. He couldn't let her go now. They were almost there.

"You'll love this apartment," he said. Maybe it was the gloomy hallway she didn't like. "I need to replace the bulbs with brighter ones," he said. "You can choose a new paint colour for the walls."

She followed him. He could get her to do anything.

He took her to 502.

53

Henry opened the door with his skeleton key and he went in. She waited in the hallway. He put the toolbox on the floor and still she hesitated outside. He turned around in a half circle and spread his arms wide, as if revealing something magnificent.

"This is it," he said, his voice echoing off the walls.

The apartment was empty of furniture and accoutrements. There were no rugs, no curtains except in the kitchen. A thin beam of sunlight fought to enter through a grimy window. The window looked out onto the street.

He knew they'd rented it out after Lucinda. The family would do anything to make a buck. But when he came back to the building after his time away he put a stop to that. He kept this unit empty. It was the least he could do for his cousin. An homage.

It hurt him that they'd removed Lucinda's things. When he became the landlord, he'd rooted through everything that remained in storage. There was one thing he'd found in the basement. The last remnant of Lucinda's eclectic possessions. It was still there in storage, her collection of antique toys. He took the painted wooden box and brought it back upstairs to 502 and put it in the closet.

* * *

Nora didn't want to come in for some reason. She lingered in the hall.

"Don't be shy," he said. "It's vacant."

"What is this?" she said.

Lucinda had a bohemian style. When she lived here the place was wonderful. She'd hung macrame plant holders from the ceiling and strings of beaded curtains in the doorways. Billowing white cotton on the windows and houseplants everywhere. Lucinda was really into plants. He saw it all clearly in his mind even after all these years.

"I thought you'd be interested." he said.

She was in the dining room now, looking at the carved fireplace mantel.

"This is so different from my place," she said. "Nicer than the eighth floor."

He could put her in here. He wanted to touch her hair.

"The bedroom," he said. "Where it all happened."

"I don't understand," she said. "Where what happened?"

She came out of the dining room back to the entrance, but he took her hand, pulled gently. He wanted her to see more than an empty, unfurnished space, to know his vision for the apartment. His vision for her.

He came here a few times a week. Sat on the floor in the bedroom and played it all out in his imagination. Lucinda hadn't understood him. But Nora would.

She would be fine here. He could bring her whatever she needed.

At his trial the prosecutor called it the murder apartment. Which had enraged him.

Nora pulled her hand away. Was he gripping too tightly?

"I have to go," she said. "I have things to do."

He could make it happen right now. His toolbox was by the door. No one would ever know.

"I'm trying to show you," he said. He'd miscalculated somehow. She was backing away.

"I'll think about it. The decorating. I could use the income."

He would not lose her. Not when he had his chance to have someone forever and always. In the special place.

She was in the hall, she had her back to him. He must stay calm.

"Let's talk about it over wine," he said. He would be patient. He was good at this, was he not? He already had her in the building. She said, maybe. Maybe later. And was out the door and down the hall.

"Wait," he said. He took Lucinda's painted box from the closet and grabbed his tools and followed Nora upstairs.

54

It said 'Toys' in painted primary colours, the paint chipped and faded on the top of the white pine box. It was not much bigger than a box for a doll. The lid opened on brass hinges. Stamped in black ink on the back 'T. Eaton Co. Toronto.'

Nora hated the box and didn't want a gift from Henry. It reminded her of a child's coffin, so small, so terrible. But he brought it up from the fifth floor, jogging to catch up with her, and she accepted it in part to be polite but mostly to make him go away.

He had made her uncomfortable when they were in the empty apartment. She hadn't understood until now why Kyle didn't like Henry or why Izzy called him weird. She thought he was just a lonely man, but today she'd been afraid of him.

He insisted she take the box, walking right into her place and leaving it on the floor. She said okay, I'll keep it until you want it returned. Then he'd left her alone.

There were old toys nestled inside. Tin soldiers and a folded checkers board. A pop gun and a miniature dish cupboard with a tiny china cup inside it.

She'd laughed it off so many times when Izzy said Henry was creepy.

She picked up a little doll, about four inches long. Delicate bisque head with blue painted eyes and pink mouth. Hair that felt almost real. A soft muslin body stuffed with sawdust and sewn by hand. The clothes were missing. She cradled the doll in the palm of her hand and felt a hole open in her heart.

* * *

The child hopped on one foot.

"Alice, have you come back?"

Do you know this game? Alice held the checkers in her small hands. She hopped on bare chubby feet.

Nora smoothed the messy curls falling over the child's eyes. "Try to stand still, don't teeter."

If I fall down the bad man will come.

Nora said, "No sweetie. There is no bad man. That's just a silly fairy tale."

The girl skipped to Nora, the white night gown like swan feathers.

Nora opened the box of toys and took out a red orb with a pointed end. Yellow stripes around the middle. A spinning top.

Mama how does it work?

The child put the wooden toy in Nora's hand, a piece of string dangled from it.

Wide pretty eyes under overgrown curls. Nora tried to brush the hair away from the little face but the girl squirmed out of reach.

The child cried. Looked helplessly at the toy. The string fell off.

I can't make it spin.

* * *

Nora heard the radio come on in Henry's kitchen. He turned the volume too loud and she thought he did it purposefully, irritated by the noise she made playing with Alice.

It was a newscast, an urgent male voice speaking quickly.

The little girl plopped down on her bottom with the toy, tried to make it spin by rubbing it between her hands. Then threw it against the wall.

Loud knocking on the wall. Someone disturbed by the child's noise.

She scooped the child up in her arms.

Knocking. But not on the wall. On the new solid wood door.

"Who is it?" Nora said. Henry had not installed a peephole, as he promised.

"It's me, Izzy."

She turned the handle and remembered she needed a key to open it from the inside.

"Hold on," she said, and ran to the kitchen. The keys were on a hook by the stove under the bouquet of dried flowers from Lucky Convenience. She'd put the flowers there to hide the ugly peg. And to remind her where the keys were.

She unlocked the door and opened it and fell into Izzy's arms. She surprised herself by crying.

"I know," Izzy said. "Kyle told me everything about the fight. He feels terrible. I took a chance and came over. I tried to call you a few times but you never answered."

"I don't know where I put the stupid phone."

"I wanted to make sure you were okay," Izzy said.

"I don't know how it happened." She ushered her friend inside and closed the door. "I never meant to break up with him. I was trying to tell him something and he didn't want to hear it."

Izzy said, "You can talk to me. You know I'm a good listener."

She took off her coat and unwound a scarf from her neck, bright pink with a pattern of black skulls. "I couldn't resist buying it," she said, in response to Nora's expression.

*　*　*

They lazed on the bed and talked. Every so often one of them got up to make tea or stretch and carry on talking. Meandering thoughts, memories, tales of childhood. Izzy told her about growing up north of Sudbury where everyone's father worked for the mines. And lots of the mothers too. Or they worked at K-mart and Canadian Tire as cashiers. And all the kids had the same clothing, plaid shirts and Levi's blue jeans, and Kodiak boots all year long—even the summer felt like a time for boots, the ground wet and muddy.

That's why she came to the city, Izzy said. To get away from all the sameness.

"Hence the hair," she said, laughing. It was bright white, a thin green streak on one side.

Nora told Izzy about life in a town where her family had lived for generations. How she was rootless and lost after her mother died of cancer until she found her first boyfriend at sixteen. She said, every girl at high school had to have a boyfriend to fit in. Our boyfriends were like your plaid shirts, she said. The high-school boys were meant to be practice runs.

"But I was dumb enough to marry Carter," she said.

Izzy told Nora her relationship with Sandeep was going well. She thought they might have a future. She pulled out her phone to show his photo: dark hair and a huge grin. They were going to get matching tattoos. He was game and tomorrow they would go to Parkdale; she knew the best tattoo place in the area. They'd show off on the beach in Florida.

She showed Nora a photo of the tattoo design. A vine with one leaf.

"Every time we have a significant event we'll get another leaf," Izzy said.

* * *

They grew tired of talking. The teacups were upended in the sink and they moved on to wine. They shared the duvet round their shoulders as the room grew colder. Eventually they fell asleep.

Nora woke up first and nudged Izzy.

"We fell asleep?" Izzy rubbed her neck. Mascara was smudged under both eyes. "What time is it?"

The room was hazy with grey light and the air stale and cold. Nora went to the kitchen to check the stove clock. A stack of dirty dishes lined the counter and unwashed cups sat in the half-filled sink. A fast-food wrapper had fallen into the basin and covered the drain like a capsized paper boat. She pulled the plug and ran the tap to fill it. No hot water.

"I need to get going," Izzy said. "I have a date later." She came into the kitchen, the duvet wound around her like a chrysalis. "Your place is freezing."

The radiator in the kitchen was stone cold when Nora touched it. She turned the knob until it fell off. "Nothing works right."

"I had a dream," Izzy said. "And now I'm awake it makes perfect sense." She folded the duvet and left it on the bed. She put on her jacket and scarf. "In the dream you lived with me."

Nora dried her hands on a tea towel. "I wish you didn't have to go," she said. "It was nice hanging out with you."

She felt so close to Izzy, so grateful for her company. The time together had made her feel better and she saw now that she needed to get her life in order. She would start by tidying up. In addition to the dishes in the sink, there was laundry. Even her own body required cleaning. She felt her lank hair.

"There's no hot water," she told Izzy.

"That's the thing," Izzy said. "No offence, but this apartment is a dump. I want you to come live at my place."

"Don't be silly."

"No. Hear me out. It makes sense. You should live with me. Walk with me to the subway and we'll talk about it," Izzy said.

She knew Izzy wanted to be helpful. Izzy had grown up fast. She'd told Nora about the countless times with her father when he was swearing himself off booze. So many mornings, she'd swept out the trailer, pulled her dad off the sofa, told him what to do. Get dressed, clean up the place. Get outside. Izzy was a born caretaker.

"I can't walk you to the subway right now. I should straighten up."

"You would love my building. Everything modern and clean. The view from the twenty-first floor is amazing. The only thing is you'd have to wait till I get back from Florida. But it's only four days."

"I'm fine, really." She watched Izzy put on her black Chelsea boots. "You're so sweet to offer. I'll think about it."

"My condo has a gym and a pool. Not to mention all the bars down the street."

She took her key off the hook in the kitchen. A few petals fell off the dried flowers and landed on the stove. She unlocked the door and opened it. She hugged Izzy.

"You don't know what you're missing," Izzy said. "I'll see you in four days." Izzy picked up a bag of garbage by the front door.

Nora wanted to say, be careful of the sun in Florida with your pale skin, but she stopped herself, not wanting to sound too motherly.

She let Izzy out to the landing, where the cat lay sleeping on the floor. It opened one eye warily as Izzy stepped carefully over it. On the threshold a piece of white paper fluttered as she closed the door and Nora picked it up. A notice of rent increase, effective immediately. It was signed by Henry.

55

Nora rapped on Henry's door, angry and confused. He had some nerve raising the rent. He'd even implied she could live in the larger unit downstairs and he'd pay her to fix it up. She knocked again until her knuckles hurt.

If Henry was going to be so unpredictable, moving in with Izzy definitely made sense. He knew she was between jobs and couldn't possibly come up with more money quickly. And why should it be more expensive to live here when the building fell deeper into disrepair every day?

She would move to Izzy's the moment her friend returned from Florida. She pictured herself with Izzy and her roommates, having beers and nachos in a trendy bar downtown while Kyle's band played covers of rock songs.

Henry was not coming to open his door.

Nora had not understood until now that living alone was so depressing. She had been cruel to Kyle and she wanted him back. She knocked once more on the door, the rent notice crumpled in her hand, ready to throw it in Henry's face and confront him with his deceit.

When there was no answer she tried the knob. She turned it and pushed the door and the door opened.

"Henry?" she called. "Are you in?"

His radio played instrumental jazz, a hazy oboe and waves of piano and she listened for a moment, trying to discern any sign of Henry over the music. Then the announcer came on and gave the weather forecast, which was for light snow. The living room glowed under the soft light of lamps standing in the corners. A teal blue mohair blanket was folded neatly across the back of the brown leather couch. The usual stacks of newspapers and books had been cleared away.

She'd never before seen his place so tidy and welcoming.

Henry wasn't there.

* * *

The telephone was on the sideboard in the dining room, plugged into the wall jack. She'd used Henry's phone before she had her own and she thought of calling Kyle. Her cellphone was misplaced somewhere in her apartment. She didn't know where she'd left it or if it had any calling minutes remaining even if she could find it.

She strained to listen above the soft drone of the radio, listening for Henry returning. He could be on any floor fixing a leak, repairing a crack. She could make a quick call to Kyle and apologize.

There were three bottles of wine in a metal rack beside the phone. There was a thin layer of dust on one of them and she drew a line in the dust with her finger.

She would hear Henry if he came up the stairs in his work boots. He was likely working far away in the basement. He'd mentioned the furnace kept going out.

It didn't cost Henry anything if she used his landline and anyway it was just for a second.

She held the receiver and pushed the number buttons. The mouthpiece smelled like human breath. She waited for Kyle to answer and the thought came to her that Esme might be here in the apartment, resting in one of the bedrooms down the hall. She could take a look but she'd never been in that part of the apartment. It would be intrusive to go there now, without invitation.

Pick up Kyle, please. It rang and rang.

Esme was understanding, she wouldn't mind Nora being here, using the phone. Another woman would see that she had made a mistake with Kyle.

She would tell Kyle she was sorry; she would ask him to get together to talk.

She wondered if Kyle was looking at the screen of his phone right now to see who was calling. She imagined him holding his phone while it rang, maybe standing behind the counter at Lakeview Coffee and checking the caller ID before answering.

She would be kinder to him and treat him with care. She would do better if he gave her a second chance.

A creaking noise in the kitchen and a momentary flickering of the lamps.

She pictured Kyle holding his phone, deciding whether or not to take the call. Did the caller ID reveal a strange number Kyle didn't recognize or did it say the call came from Henry Weston, a guy he didn't like?

It rang and rang. And then it stopped.

*   *   *

She opened the large armoire in Henry's living room. Inside were his treasures, the photos and scrapbooks that obsessed him. She saw the illegible diary he loved so much atop a pile of newspaper clippings, cleanly cut and bound together with a bulldog clip. She looked for his rental book, to see if all the rents were going up, or only hers.

Beneath a sheaf of papers she unearthed a red Grand and Toy accounting ledger. On the first page the building's address was neatly inscribed and below that a notation that it was volume 24. Entries were organized by floor and unit with columns for each year.

She had every right to see how her rent compared to other units. She'd left Henry's door open slightly and she looked now to see if he was coming. Light from the landing made a stripe across the floor.

She flipped through the pages until she found her own unit. She ran her finger along the line of pencilled entries through the years until she saw her own name and the amounts she'd paid for the last two months recorded in ink. She read the listing for Henry's apartment. It was blank. But of course, he didn't pay rent.

She examined the entries floor by floor, viewed the columns filled in various coloured inks. The rental amounts and the dates received.

The most recent payments listed were hers.

An entry was written for a unit on the sixth floor, showing rent last collected there three years ago. After that the lines for that unit were blank. Annotations of collections on the other floors were sporadic and some ended a decade or more ago.

She closed the ledger. You'd think the building had no tenants. Henry was an incompetent record-keeper.

She stashed the book under some others and pulled out the stack of news clippings.

There were articles cut out of various papers about sports or politics that were of no interest to her. Then she·saw a square of newsprint torn ragged along the edges. It was weeks old and was taken from the *Kitchener Record,* a paper from a city near her little town. The headline in black ink said:

Prominent Lawyer Dead. Wife Missing.

And from the hallway, from one of the bedrooms, out of the back of Henry's apartment came Esme. Esme held clothes in her arms. Several wool sweaters she began to smooth and fold.

"My dear," Esme said. "How nice to see you. Can you help me with Henry's—"

Nora shoved the newspaper away and grabbed for others. She worked her hands through the stack, pulled out tear sheets from magazines, photos. Another local paper.

More snippets about Carter's death investigation. Interviews with her neighbours.

But, the neighbours didn't know a thing—not a thing about her, how he beat and hit—

Her neighbours on the quiet leafy street in her town had expressed shock and concern. She'd run next door and asked for help. How awful for you, they murmured, to find your husband like that in the foyer. So soon after your dear sick child who … passed. They called 9-1-1 for her, the same neighbours who had looked away previously at her blackened eyes, her bruises.

"I hand wash Henry's cashmere," Esme said.

A detective had opened a murder investigation. He was looking for her.

Here was a photo. An old passport shot she hardly remembered, taken years ago, before she'd re-styled her hair.

"Why does he have these," she said. "Esme, why is he collecting—"

Esme put the pile of beautiful sweaters down on the brown

sofa. The cat, Toffee jumped on top of the pile and then ran off when Nora reached out her hand. She touched the one on top, forest green and freshly laundered. She felt the soft wool of the sweater.

Henry usually wore plaid shirts and greasy jeans.

He had read news items about her.

Some of her neighbours were quoted in the articles. She despised the neighbours in her town, their false sympathy, their clucking and cooing over Dylan and then over dead Carter. As if the losses were the same.

"You know," Esme said. "The police are after you."

Henry knew the police were looking for her.

Months earlier the police entered her house and they tramped around and noticed the perfectly decorated rooms. They looked at her perfectly styled hair. They took the gun away along with Carter's body. They didn't question her beyond asking if he was suicidal and so she left. No one suspected her or thought her capable of killing her husband. She took the train to Toronto without telling anyone she was going, free then to begin a better life.

She felt the soft wool of Henry's sweater.

56

Henry had to revise the plan. Some things were unpredictable, but he was flexible. It would still work, come to fruition. The key now was to exercise patience. Not to fly off the handle again like he just had.

He had gone downstairs to the basement to catch his breath after the unfortunate moment on the seventh floor. He was deep in the basement mechanical room working.

And yet. Nora wasn't cooperating.

He wiped his greasy hands on a rag and put down the wrench. He took the detective's card out of his wallet, turned it over in his hand as if reading it again would reveal the truth. It didn't mean they wanted to arrest her. Maybe they wanted to tell her she herself was in danger. Well, he would protect her better than the police could.

Cops were cagey. He knew firsthand from his own miserable experience. How they tricked you to admit to something you never did.

Nora was good at keeping secrets.

He'd tried to make her see she belonged with him.

They hadn't come back for her. Cops were lazy.

The basement was so quiet with the furnace turned off. He could almost discern faint sounds from upstairs.

He considered threatening her, saying he would report her to the police unless she agreed to stay with him, to let him hide her. The detective was only one phone call away.

He had Nora's cellphone in his pocket. He pulled it out and scrolled through the contacts. There were only two names. The name of the last person who called was the one he hated most, and seeing it spelled out instantly roused him to a pinnacle of rage and jealousy. He redialled the number.

Kyle answered immediately, as if he'd been standing by waiting for this very call.

"Hello?" the lout's voice, eager to hear from her. "Nora. I'm so happy you called."

"It's not her. It's me, Henry," he spoke quickly, before Kyle could hang up. "She's with me now. We're together. She doesn't want to hear from you again."

*   *   *

His heart raced and he let it settle, standing still in the windowless basement room until he was calm. He felt his pulse, sensed air in his lungs moving in and out like currents in the walls and pipes, the veins of the building. He was the heart of Farmdale Court.

He would catch her now before she left the building on some errand. He would convince her she was meant to be with him.

He turned up the temperature of the hot water boiler. The taps would run lukewarm for another hour, then there'd be nothing but hot, hot water. It would be her reward for staying with him.

He would go to the barber for a haircut. And pick up champagne. He began to hyperventilate and stopped himself. Keep steady.

He switched the furnace back on. It had been off too long while the temperature outside hovered near freezing. The old pipes wrapped in newspaper when they were installed a hundred years ago would hold without bursting only so long. He'd warm things up and keep an eye on the pipes.

If she was still chilly he would say, sit at my side, we can warm ourselves by the fireplace.

First he had to clean up the mess he'd made.

57

He hadn't expected to run into the girl. He left the toolbox on the third floor because he only needed a hammer. He completed the quick task of hammering down nails in some of the warped floorboards. A small, pleasant job to fix nails that rose up unevenly in the hardwood. It happened every season when the wood on the stairs swelled or contracted. He'd scraped his toes walking in the dark and he worried that Toffee might get hurt. He let the cat run around the building and like all cats she crawled into every space. Best to pound down the sharp nail heads to protect the cat's soft paws.

He finished hitting the nails, a job he could cross off the list. Now he was hungry. He would go upstairs to make something good to eat and then go to Nora.

He left the toolbox on the floor and headed up the stairs holding the hammer. Snow fell gently outside.

***

Henry saw the girl alone on the seventh floor. She was snooping around where she had no business being. He asked her what the hell she was doing.

She looked startled, said she was putting something into the garbage chute. Such a small slip of a girl, couldn't weigh ninety pounds.

She said, "Nora asked me to take the trash on my way out."

She looked absolutely terrified when she turned around and saw him there. Right behind her.

Well of course, he was carrying a hammer, must have been a shock.

They were all alone on the seventh floor.

She was a loudmouth, the girl. She gave Nora ideas, wrong ideas. Called this place a dump. His magnificent building.

"Guests are not permitted to wander the building alone."

She laughed at him. "Are you a security guard and a janitor now?"

He held the hammer by his hip and said, "Get out."

"Nora hates it here, she's leaving. Moving out to live with me." She tried to walk away, inched around his body. "And I saw you," she said. "At the skating rink. What are you, a stalker?"

He grabbed the long pink scarf wound about her neck.

It took only a moment. There was no space in the hall for her to get away. He raised the hammer and cracked her skull with a single blow. She didn't fall. Merely put her hand to her head, gazed up at him with wide puppy eyes, mascara ran with her tears. He pushed her to the floor and she was weightless, a doll made from rags. She fell and he straddled her, pulled the pink scarf tight until there was no breathing.

She never had time to cry out, to raise an alarm.

A trickle of blood spilled on the rust brown carpet as he picked up the limp body. White hair with a green stripe in it, so ridiculous. She was light like carrying air.

He cocked his head, listened for sounds upstairs on the eighth floor.

The door to the garbage closet was ajar where the girl had opened it and inside the closet the metal chute also gaped open. A plastic bag of refuse stuck there, snagged on the metal lip. He pushed the bag into the hole and waited while it thumped dully against the metal walls as it fell.

A piece of the white plastic tore on a sharp corner and remained stuck.

Farmdale, magnificent as it was, had many flaws that modern building codes prohibited. Who knew better than he did? Spaces between walls, man-sized water tanks, garbage contraptions with sharp edges and long slippery chutes.

He could say, if anyone came looking, that the unfortunate girl had a terrible accident. She was careless, clumsy.

She threw a bag of garbage into the hole, it stuck on the corner, she leaned in and pushed too hard.

She lay bleeding, lifeless. He picked her up and fed her body into the chute. First the head, then shoulders. The heel of her boot caught on the edge and he shoved hard on the foot until she plummeted and disappeared into the long tunnel.

*   *   *

He argued with the garbage disposal company on the phone because they wouldn't promise to send the removal truck right away. He called twice demanding the manager speak to him. The guy sounded drunk, hoarse and laconic.

This time of year, the voice said, Farmdale Court wasn't on the schedule, call back next week. He fumed at their reluctance, threatened to sue them.

The man cleared his throat loudly into Henry's ear. Fine, he said. It'll cost you double for a pickup tonight. Henry was enraged. But he had to get it done.

He went to the basement to inspect. The skip was mostly empty. He might have to explain his insistence to the contractor. He peered over the tall edge and eyed the contents. She was right on top, the head twisted at an unnatural angle.

The drivers never looked in the bins, usually stayed in the truck while the skip was mechanically hoisted. Some of the guys knew him and could be distracted with talk or cigarettes. They might send someone new, someone curious. But he couldn't wait. The noise of the compactor would disguise what it was crushing.

Just to be safe, he threw some old packing materials—corrugated cardboard and padded blankets—over the thing. He was breathing hard and sweating. He went out into the laneway to calm himself. He'd been on the way upstairs to eat before encountering the girl.

The outside air was dry, thin. It was colder now the snow had stopped. Stark, leafless maple branches lit by the moonlight wavered against the building. Not a light in any window.

58

She walked out of Henry's apartment and down the stairs and then along the corridor on a lower floor, confused, longing for something without knowing what it was.

She was surprised at the police interest in her whereabouts. According to the newspaper, the coroner had examined the body and reviewed the circumstances of Carter's death. Suicide or accident, the pathology report said. Yet the police were looking for her.

She walked the empty hall, tried to think. She needed to hide. A friend could help her. All she had to do was wait four days and Izzy would be back from Florida and Nora could leave the building with her friend.

The hall was dark and she walked looking down at the shabby carpet. Henry hadn't told her what he knew. And yet, for some unfathomable reason, he collected the news articles about her.

She returned to her apartment. The stove clock had stopped at four o'clock, though the darkness told her it was later. The clock had given up, as if time was meaningless. She stared at the dead stove clock, the stove against the wall that was the only barrier between her apartment and Henry's. He knew too much about her.

She couldn't wait four days. She had to leave now.

The apartment was dark and when she tried the light switch in the kitchen nothing happened. The fridge was silent, not humming and knocking like it usually did, and she realized the power had gone out. She flicked the light switch on and off to no avail and outside the window the sky was dark. But there were spots of light shimmering everywhere.

She saw grey clouds against the black sky, clouds blowing over the moon, and the arc of a streetlight illuminating the lane in back. The houses beyond spilled light from windows out onto snowy yards and far in the distance on a high tower the flash of a red dot.

She stood in her dark kitchen. Not a citywide blackout then, just something amiss within the building.

She took the box of wooden matches from the stove top and put them in the pocket of her jeans. There were candles somewhere in the apartment she could light. She found her laundry bag on the closet floor by feeling her way through the clothes and mess and she dragged it out, intending to stuff clothes into it.

Four days was too long to wait for Izzy to return.

As if agreeing with her, a screech of tires issued from the street and horns blared and then a siren faded away into the night. She tore clothing off hangers and stuffed items into the bag—tights, a sweater, the leggings she'd worn at work. She put the suede booties on her feet and swept the empty hangers aside, looking for her coat. She wanted the coat, the one item of value she retained from her old life.

She couldn't find it in the dark.

*   *   *

"Nora, Nora," said a trembling voice, barely audible.

It came from the landing. Esme's voice, though she could hardly make it out through the solid wood. She left her clothes and the bag and went to the door.

"What do you want?" she said. "I'm in a rush."

"I know. Yes." Esme sounded raspy with age. Outside the incessant noise of a truck backing up in the lane obscured and interrupted her voice.

"Listen, Esme. I don't have time now." She wanted to get out of the building.

"Open up, quickly," Esme said, her voice rising. "I understand. Of course, you must leave. Open the door."

She turned the handle, twisted it and pulled.

"The child," Esme said. "You must take the child."

She jerked the handle hard towards her, confused by Esme's insistence. The door was locked tight.

Esme rapped on the wood and Nora pulled the handle again, gripped it in both hands and tugged until it popped off and she stumbled back awkwardly, going over on her ankle.

"Damn this door," she said, the useless handle still in her hand.

"Hurry," Esme said. "Use the key. It's always there."

But it wasn't. The key to unlock the door from inside was not in the keyhole where she thought she'd left it. She ran to the kitchen, tried to run just the few paces from the door but her twisted ankle shot through with pain.

"I'm serious, it's an emergency," Esme said, her voice disembodied, fading away.

She grabbed at the bouquet of dried flowers on the hook by the stove. She felt for the key that must be hanging there. Prickly twigs and sharp cornered leaves scratched her fingers as the stems disintegrated in her hands. She threw the dead flowers to the floor.

"There's no key," she yelled to Esme. "I'm locked in."

She walked to the door, determined not to panic.

"Go get Henry's master key," Nora said. "I'll wait okay?" Silence from the landing. She waited by the door, listening for Esme to return from Henry's place with a key to let her out.

But someone was crying, she heard weeping from behind the walls. A small soft sound.

"Wait, Esme. Don't go," Nora said quietly through the locked door. But there was no response from the landing. "Esme." She stood listening, and heard only crying.

59

She shouted into the hallway: "Esme, come back. Let me out."

When there was no answer she banged with her fists on the wall in the kitchen and shouted again. She heard nothing, no movement, no voice in Henry's apartment.

She knocked harder until her knuckles stung and she called out. She sought something to bang on the wall with, something harder than her bare hands. The cast iron skillet sat on the burner, and she used it like a cudgel to beat the wall, but it was much too heavy to wield. Her feeble blow with the pan aggravated an old injury, hurt her wrist and left only a dent in the drywall. She shouted. Still, there was no response from Esme.

She had to get out, wanted it desperately now she knew she was locked inside. She whirled in the tiny kitchen, groped in the dark for something that could break down the door.

She jerked open the cutlery drawer, grabbed spoons, a can-opener, all useless. She pulled the drawer out completely and overturned it to the floor. The cacophony of metal on the tile enraged her and made her pulse race.

She hadn't been this angry since Dylan died.

The moon in the night sky outside like a vision of her sweet baby's face shone through the window and calmed her. And she remembered the fire escape.

She turned the casement crank and pushed and pushed against the wood and metal in the exit frame. It stuck and would not open. She stood back and with as much force as she could muster, heaved and shoved herself against it. Cold air rushed in like a slap to the face and she stepped out onto the iron landing.

It was disorienting to be outside in the cold and dark, outside on the highest edge of the building far from the ground without protective walls around her.

The bare maple branches shivered out of reach, as if daring her to leap to them.

The iron railing wasn't even waist high. It would be so easy to fall over it in the dark.

She clung to the bricks behind her back, afraid to take a step out. The slats under her feet were too widely spaced with only cold empty air between them and icicles hung from the steps below.

She would have to climb down.

She would have to climb down in the dark and freezing cold and – and then what? The fire escape ended several stories from the ground.

She would have to jump at the end. Maybe break her legs.

She took a tentative step away from the brick wall and reached her hand out towards the thin rail, the dead frozen poles like skeletal fingers. The railing seemed to move, swaying from her touch. She drew back, afraid.

* * *

Henry's kitchen window also looked out to the platform where she stood. Like the mutual wall in the kitchens, his apartment shared the fire escape landing with hers. His kitchen window was only a few feet away.

She yelled out for Esme.

Nora inched over slowly to Henry's window, keeping her back and her hands against the exterior wall. Her teeth chattered in the cold.

His blinds were closed. She couldn't see inside through the roller shades and there was only darkness; the power was still out and no light shone from the interior.

She banged on his window, and once again she yelled for Esme. Then she yelled for Henry.

And from down below, eight floors down on the ground, he appeared.

He was in the lane. He walked out from the back exit and passed by the hydro pole. She saw him turn his face up to the sky and crane his neck and then he turned to look at her.

She called his name.

He smoked a cigarette. She saw the rush of smoke blow out of his mouth.

She didn't think he could see her pressed flat against the dark building. She stepped forward slowly but was leery of leaning too far over the railing to call down to him.

"I can't get out," she yelled. "Bring the key."

He spoke in response but she couldn't hear, his voice didn't carry all the way up to her.

"I'm going back inside," she said, "until you come."

He waved at her, or seemed to, dancing his hand through the smoke as he took another drag and exhaled.

She pried at her escape door with hands stiff and cold. It was sealed shut and wouldn't budge.

She looked for Henry in the lane, and saw only empty and shadowless ruts of ground below the trees.

She'd stupidly locked herself out. In her panic to flee the apartment, she'd failed to prop the exit open.

She banged on the panes with frozen fists. She screamed for Esme and Henry and rattled the window fiercely. Tears clouded her vision.

He'd seen her. He must be on his way up to let her in. She had to calm down and stop banging the window. The panes would break and slice her wrists on shards of glass.

She could not be calm, could not stop crying.

Under her sobs, a voice beckoned. *Come closer.* A voice, some comfort. Esme had been gone so long, and now she returned— *silly Nora, come in from the cold*—a voice entreated her to come in through Henry's window. *You see*, the voice assured her, *there's another way inside*.

She put her cold fingers on the rotting wood frame. Henry's window was open a tiny crack.

She opened it fully and climbed in and entered Henry's kitchen. She was inside.

There dear, it is all fine now, take the little girl and go.

Henry's kitchen was so dark she couldn't see. She reached her hands in front to feel her way like a person in a cave. She felt the small warm body, the light soft hair.

She heard the lovely soft voice. A small voice.

Play with me Mama. I'm all better now.

She reached in the dark for tiny hands and soft curls.

Tell me a riddle Mama.

She held the little hand, would not let go in the dark, three steps, four, to the door and—The glaring flash of light in her eyes, the searing white light blinding her more than the darkness itself.

A flashlight beam aimed at her face.

Henry loomed in the kitchen. He rushed at her and tried to strike her with the heavy flashlight as she grabbed and kicked. She landed a blow on his shin and tripped him up. He yelled, "Nora, damn you!"

She ran. She ran for the kitchen door. Only two steps more. Kicking him sent a searing pain to her ankle and slowed her down. He caught her arm. She twisted away and grabbed for items on the countertop. Found and hurled the wooden knife block and the toaster, whatever her hands grabbed in the dark.

He staggered and dropped the flashlight and fell against the granite counter. The flashlight rolled on the floor, its beam a crazy lighthouse beacon rolling back and forth.

He hit his head against the sharp corner of the granite. He groaned.

The beam of light arced on his fallen body.

She took the flashlight.

He writhed on the floor and moaned.

She stepped over him and fled the kitchen.

* * *

The little face pressed itself against her thigh and tiny hands groped for hers.

Play with me.

The girl flitted through the living room. She was healthy, sturdy legs and pink apple cheeks.

"Come here right now," Nora said. "Please." She opened the door and held the flashlight to show the landing and stairs.

Tell me a riddle.

"When we're outside I will."

The child scooted to the dining room, a good runner.

"C'mon honey. This is not a game."

He groaned in the kitchen.

I was all alone Mama. I was so hungry.

"We have to go away now. If you come quickly, we'll play hide and seek."

The white nightgown skipped to the blue sofa and climbed up. *I one my mother. I two my mother. I three—*

"I know that one, an old rhyme." She searched her memory for the rest of it. The girl jumped up and down on the sofa, and Nora moved to her.

A sound from the kitchen. He might be getting up from the floor. She put out her hand, but the girl giggled and bolted away to the open door and out to the landing. The little voice trailed as it moved down the stairs. *I six, seven, eight—I ate my mother!*

60

Nora followed the child, hobbled by her sore ankle, slowed by fear of tripping. She went down the stairs and she meant to go with the child straight to the vestibule and out into the night.

On the seventh floor a glimpse of something pink lying on the carpet, a piece of cloth that caught her eye. She would have stopped to investigate, to pick it up, but the child ran fast out of her sight.

She found the girl ahead moving down the steps, surprisingly swift on such little limbs. Nora pointed the beam of the flashlight and called to the girl. At the fifth floor the child twirled and disappeared down the dark corridor.

Nora followed, passed each door, the small shadow bounced ahead against the dull wallpaper.

"Come back," she called, as the child slipped out of sight.

* * *

She found her in 502.

The child was alone in the empty apartment, hunched in a corner playing. Nora came up behind the child and folded her arms around her and turned off the flashlight so it wouldn't give them away. He might be searching.

The girl squirmed in her arms, wanting to be released to play. The child pointed to a dollhouse in the corner. Four lonely square rooms, devoid of dolls or furniture.

She carried the child to the window where they could see who went in or out of the building. The apartment looked out on the front courtyard and the path to the entrance was lit by streetlights. The road was quiet. No cars drove by.

The child's heart beat gently against her own.

I've wanted so much to hold you again.

* * *

She was cold in her T-shirt and jeans, and the girl wore nothing but a cotton nightgown. She longed for a blanket to wrap around the child but there was no point looking for one. She knew apartment 502 was completely empty.

She thought she heard movement in the stillness of the walls. He could be coming.

The girl slept in her arms. She wanted to stay there holding her forever.

"You are my sunshine, my only sunshine," she sang softly.

The building was quiet, so quiet she would hear him if he took a single step. She held her breath and listened carefully until she sensed the building was still. She heard the swish of faraway tires on wet roads. Would anyone help her if she ran out into the night?

It was so lovely to hold her baby, the powdery smell of the little head, the doughy arms.

She sat cross-legged on the floor under the window, eyes on the door.

She couldn't let him hurt her child again.

She carried the girl into the closet and closed the door. She crouched in the back corner, the girl in her arms, and hid there.

Blood throbbed in her temples and she drew the child closer.

She listened for sounds of approach between the child's soft inhalation, exhalation. The air musty, claustrophobic.

Mama, I'm cold.

The building was icy cold. The heat was off.

Mama, is the bad man coming?

* * *

She couldn't stay long in 502. Henry would look for her here. She would warm the child for a few minutes and then run. She had matches in her pocket and she took them into the empty kitchen and lit the large ring on the stove. She struck another match and lit all the burners, turned the knobs until the blue flames shot up high into yellow and red.

The flames singed her eyelashes and lashed the wall behind the stove and she was frightened by what she'd done. She ripped from the kitchen window the half curtain with its hopeful pattern of oranges and lemons. Tore it down and before the fire bit into the cloth, she draped it over the stove to dampen the flames.

* * *

She left 502 and banged on several doors and shouted what warnings she could. She wanted to get the child out of the building and had no time to approach every unit. She held tight to the little hand and was reassured that the fire was not out of control because no alarm sounded. She couldn't know that flames had freely pierced the thin walls and paper insulation. In 506 a discarded green easy chair with a sunken seat began to smoulder and in 512 a soiled mattress burned and stank.

As she fled, the fire creeped over mildewed carpet and melted cracked linoleum, devoured dusty books and faded paintings.

"Hurry, my darling," she said. A stench rose up as walls gathered heat, and the rinds of flowered wallpaper smoked and peeled away.

The old walls burned into nothing.

* * *

She scooped the child into her arms.

She flew down the stairs, in a rush now to get out ahead of the fire.

A bump on the landing above. A thud in a hallway.

The squirming child unbalanced her. She feared falling on the stairs.

She was afraid he would be there, downstairs at the front door.

She almost tripped on the cat when it dashed between her feet.

Put me down Mama. I want the kitty.

She made it to the vestibule as smoke filled the upper floors, and he was not there. Only the cat, waiting to be let out.

Outside under the arch of oak trees she heard windows crack and the snap of wooden beams and struts crashing into floors below as the roof began to fall away.

She was on the sidewalk. The air was bitterly cold and Farmdale Lane was deserted. She walked quickly down the street, urged the child to hurry. The building rumbled as it burned and an angry explosion threw sparks into the trees. Flames jutted menacingly from the upper windows. Plumes of black smoke rose into the sky.

She passed the convenience store, windows boarded up, the brick front slashed with graffiti.

She rounded the corner, the end of the dark narrow road and reached the main street.

* * *

The sidewalk thronged with people. Cars rolled by with windows open despite the chill, and hands waved coloured ribbons. Bright lights blazed everywhere. Under awnings and flashing signs, restaurants and bars disgorged happy patrons into the street. Couples in party hats staggered together, women in sparkly short dresses under unzipped down parkas tottered on high heels. College students blew noisemakers, swigged from bottles of wine and cans of beer.

The streetcar came along the tracks and stopped at the light. She hardly believed her luck that it was back in service. Yet there was something different, changed. It wasn't the long, sleek modern vehicle she expected. This one was curved, small and rickety, old-fashioned: a yellow and red historical trolley, 'Special' written on the transom. It looked like it had come from a museum.

She ran to catch it before the accordion doors closed and it moved away.

"I haven't got any money," she said. She mounted the first step to implore the driver to let her ride.

A crowd of teenagers pressed from behind, clamoured to pass her and find seats. She was jostled aside.

"I can't pay," she said, but the driver didn't hear.

People laughed and shouted, c'mon let's go.

A boy said, "It's free tonight lady. It's New Year's Eve!"

Passengers yelled at the driver to get moving. The driver looked at her with hard, bored eyes.

"Oh, don't go yet," she said, frantic. "My little girl is behind me."

Someone shouted, "Let's go. Close the door."

"Dylan," she called out.

She was waiting, waiting for her child.

I'm here Mama.

She held the small, warm hand in hers.

THE SENTINEL
Police Seek Help Locating Missing Woman

Nora Birmingham, also known as Nora Davis, was last seen boarding a Toronto Transit vehicle late on the night of December 31. She is described as 32, dark hair, wearing a white T-shirt and fur hat. Police are concerned for her well-being.

THE TORONTO STAR
Arson Suspected in Apartment House Fire

The Ontario Fire Marshal and police are investigating a six-alarm blaze that tore through a west-end heritage building last week.

Heavy equipment and cadaver dogs have been employed as the site continues to smoulder and cannot be safely entered. Samples will be analysed for cause and origin of the fire. Though firefighters are dousing the remaining structure with water, there is significant danger of total collapse of the Farmdale Lane building.

City Council hoped to save the historic structure, one of the oldest in that part of Toronto, but an engineer determined the damage to be so significant, it will have to be demolished. Construction workers will begin dismantling the gutted building next week.

The massive blaze broke out just after midnight on New Year's Eve. Over 100 firefighters battled the flames. The fire came little more than a week before the building's owner, The Weston Group, was set to meet with officials after City Council rejected the company's proposal to demolish the building. The building was deemed uninhabitable after the company failed to complete City work orders and address code violations and had been unoccupied for many years. It was in negotiations for sale to a developer who planned to build a condominium tower on the site.

Attempts are underway to locate a caretaker who may have resided illegally in the building. Questions remain about the suspicious nature of the fire.

—

ACKNOWLEDGEMENTS

A first novel is initially a solitary endeavour. Along the way supportive individuals appear from the ether to help give it life, and they deserve my gratitude. Publisher Matt Joudrey; talented editor Kiki Yee; the At Bay Press team. Writers Robert Rotenberg and Nancy Lam, who graciously read early drafts. Friends and family who listened, marveled and supported me wholeheartedly. And most importantly, Jonah, Pietro and Elisa—you are what truly matters.

Photo: Dean Macdonell

LAURIE FREEDMAN studied English literature and graduated from Osgoode Hall Law School. She worked as an assistant crown attorney in the criminal courtrooms of Toronto before writing her debut novel, *Dwelling*. Please visit the author at lauriefreedmanbooks.com

OUR AT BAY PRESS
ARTISTIC COMMUNITY:

Publisher - **Matt Joudrey**
Managing Editor - **Alana Brooker**
Substantive Editor - **Kiki Yee**
Copy Editor - **Priyanka Ketkar**
Proof Editor - **Danni Deguire**
Graphic Designer - **Matt Stevens**
Layout - **Matt Stevens and Matt Joudrey**

Thanks for purchasing this book and for supporting authors and artists. As a token of gratitude, please scan the QR code for exclusive content from this title.